MW01094024

THE SPHINX · BOOK ONE

CURSED
BY THE GODS

RAYE WAGNER

CURSED BY THE GODS

by Raye Wagner

Copyright © 2015 Rachel Wagner

Third Edition © 2016

All rights reserved

ISBN 13 - 978-1546544197

ISBN 10 - 1546544194

This is a work of fiction. Names, characters, organizations, places, events, media, and incidents are either products of the author's imagination, or are used fictitiously.

No part of this book may be reproduced, or stored in a retrieval system, or transmitted in any form or by any means, electronic, mechanical, photocopying, recording, or otherwise, without express written permission of the author.

The following brands are used in this work of fiction: Barbie, BMW, Burberry, Civic, Crock-Pot, FedEx, Goodwill, iPad, iPhone, Mercedes, Microsoft, Monopoly, Porsche, Rice Krispy Treats, Salvation Army, and Tupperware.

Originally published as Curse of the Sphinx in 2016.

Edited by Jen McConnel, Lindsey Alexander, Heidi Johnson, Ashley Bodette, and Krystal Wade

Book Design by Jo Michaels

Cover Design by StudioOpolis

The unauthorized reproduction or distribution of a copyrighted work is illegal. Criminal copyright infringement, including infringement without monetary gain, is investigated by the FBI and is punishable by fines and federal imprisonment.

To Mom and Dad
If I succeed, it is because you first taught me to believe.

APOLLO'S CURSE

On this night, and in this land
Hear the curse, how it will stand.
Your body and your beauty be
Touched and marked eternally of me
And when your family is complete
Then Death will visit on swift feet
And rob you of the joy divine
The joy that should be yours and mine
Until we wed, and love, and more
This shall stand forevermore.

Hope has

a secret…

CURSED BY THE GODS

PROLOGUE

THE DEAD THEY escorted always cried. From the time of death until their delivery to Hades, tears dripped and trickled from their grief-stricken eyes. Clearly, there was *something* they felt a need to mourn. Athan trudged through the musty mists of the Underworld, his thoughts swirling in blackness as gloomy as his surroundings. Surely life wasn't meant to be as barren as the banks of the River Acheron.

"Athan!" Hermes beckoned. "Hurry up, Son."

Focusing on the bright aura surrounding his father, Athan sprinted ahead.

"You're quiet today." Hermes's voice had a rich lilt to it, the accent of the divine. "Did you know this demigod we escorted? Was he a friend?"

The young man they'd delivered to Hades had hung his head as he wept, refusing to even acknowledge his guides.

Athan shook his head. "No."

And *definitely* no. He'd given up on friendships long ago. Getting burned by his best friends, the people he thought he could trust, did that to a person. At least he had his dad. Not that he was always around, but Athan knew he could trust Hermes. And Athan would do just about anything for his father.

They walked through the desolate waste separating the Fields of Asphodel from the River Acheron. Shrieks from Tartarus, what humans called Hell, pushed through the dense fog. Dark mist swirled at their feet, carrying with it the saturated scent of decay. Moans and cries rolled off the river before it came into sight, misery lapping with the waves.

At the dock, Charon's tall figure cut through the fog, his dark robe billowing behind him on the small ferry.

"Hermes." Charon's hollow voice came from deep within his hood.

Athan looked down at the pitch waters where the dead wailed in despair, their tears feeding the river. If he looked closely, he could see the faces of the mortals who'd drowned themselves in their own desolation.

"Charon." Hermes held out his hand and dropped two small coins into the ferryman's emaciated palm. "How are you?"

A ghostly chuckle emerged from within the folds of fabric, and the god stood aside to allow passage onto his vessel.

"Hermes!" A lithe woman with warm russet skin and dark chocolate curls ran out of the mist and onto the dock. She wore a traditional chiton, a dress trimmed in gold, and in her hands

2

she clasped a long rod with ancient Greek markings running the length of it. Across her chest she wore a small, but very modern, messenger bag.

"You must hurry." Her rushed speech also held the musical inflection of divinity. She shoved a piece of paper into his hands. "Messengers from Olympus arrived just after you left. Apollo has summoned Thanatos to kill her."

Athan glanced at his father.

The god's warm hazel eyes were flint, his jaw clenched, and his hands balled into fists.

"You don't think . . ." Hermes looked at his son.

This must be what Hermes and Hades had held their whispered conversation about in the throne room of the Underworld.

"Atropos was commanded to cut her thread," the girl continued, "She will delay as long as she can."

Atropos. One of the three Fates, the goddess responsible for cutting the thread of life. Athan didn't know who *her* was, but for four gods to meddle with her future? Extraordinary.

Hermes ground his teeth. "I brought only enough obols for passage. Not enough to speed the way."

"Charon." The goddess's lilting voice brought the cloaked figure to the edge of his boat, and the god tilted his head at her. "Please take them quickly across and to the portal." She threw a handful of golden coins toward the ferryman. Several clattered on the wooden dock, a few plunked into the river, but the majority of them rattled at the bottom of the skiff. "More awaits when you return."

3

Charon waved his hand and the small coins levitated from the boat's floor and into his palm, the water dripping through his bony fingers. "No need, Lachesis. This is more than sufficient."

Two additional figures emerged from the mist. Both were young women—one tall, dark, and angular with several pairs of shears hanging from her girdle; the other walked with her head down, her loose blond curls obscuring her face. Her hands worked knitting needles in a furious clacking, and pale thread trailed behind her.

"He'll never make it in time, Lachesis." The dark-skinned girl's sharp tone matched her shears.

Athan narrowed his eyes. The pictures in his textbook looked nothing like the beautiful goddesses standing before him. These were the Moirai: the weaver, the measurer, and the cutter of the thread of life.

Anxiety tickled his throat, and he coughed.

The pale girl, Clotho, looked up from her needles, and her hands froze. Her blue eyes locked on him.

"It is fine, Atropos." Her voice was steady, and her gaze stayed fixed. "This is what is necessary." She nodded and then dropped her head. The clacking of the needles started again.

Trepidation fluttered in his chest. The gods didn't notice you, unless . . .

They pulled away from the dock, and the boat rocked on the water. Athan shifted his footing, and when he looked back, the young women had disappeared into the swirling vapor.

"*Skata*!" Hermes's curse broke the heavy silence. "Can you move us any faster?"

The water churned where Charon's pole pushed through the black depth, and they glided noiselessly across the river. Time seemed suspended, and yet each moment felt an eternity.

Hermes released another string of curses, the profanities rolling from his tongue and stagnating in the thick air.

"Dad?" Athan gripped his father's arm. "What's going on?"

Hermes exhaled and ran his hand through his hair. "We must hurry. There is no time for me to take you elsewhere, or I may miss too much."

Athan's mind raced, but he nodded.

"I'll veil us. Just don't *do* anything. I don't want Apollo to know we're there."

All these gods . . . Who were they going to see? Athan was about to ask when a dock swirled and solidified before them.

"Thank you, Charon," Hermes said as he leapt from the boat.

"Anything to vex Thanatos." The ferryman chuckled.

As Athan stepped from the boat, Hermes grabbed his arm, and the two of them lurched ahead.

Athan and his father were standing in the corner of a small living room. In the kitchen, a striking blond woman holding a telephone to her ear crossed the linoleum floor. Tears streaked her haggard face, a sharp contrast to her beautiful white-silk cocktail dress and her careful updo.

Hermes disappeared, and as Athan looked down at his own body, he realized he'd been veiled, too. It was an odd sensation to not see his own body.

Glancing around the apartment, he noted simple furnishings: a couch and loveseat, table and chairs. The walls were empty—no art or family photos. A marble sculpture of Hecate sat on the mantle. The only other decorations were four wooden letters sitting atop the mantle of the fireplace. Clearly painted by a child's hand, they were vibrant green-and-blue and spelled the word *hope*.

"Come quick," she said into the phone. Then, "No, I'll wait here."

A warm breeze tickled the air, bringing with it the smell of honeysuckle and sunshine. A flash of light momentarily blinded him, and when Athan's vision cleared, Apollo stood in the doorway of the kitchen. The blond god of light, prophecy, and medicine arrived barefoot. His skin was sun kissed, and he wore a pale linen skirt trimmed in gold that fell to his knees. A bronze sash hung from his left shoulder to his right hip. Apollo was muscular, and his face was both beautiful and terrifying.

"Foolish girl." His harsh words seemed at odds with his melodic voice.

The woman turned, and the phone slipped from her fingers.

"It is fulfilled." He stepped toward her, his lips flattened in accusation. "You did not even give me a chance. One rash decision and your fate was sealed. There is nothing, absolutely nothing, I can do. Do you understand?" His nostrils flared. "I would have made you happy."

With a moan, she sank to the floor and buried her face in her hands.

A dark mist, similar to the one Athan had seen in the Underworld, spilled from a shadow on the wall. The darkness solidified, and another figure appeared a few feet in front of them. Tall with inky hair, this god, Thanatos, was dressed in the dark colors of the Underworld.

The woman's eyes widened, and her breathing hitched. "Oh, gods! *No!* You can't!" She looked from one god to the other. "What will happen to my daughter?"

She made her way to her feet and stumbled toward Apollo, arms outstretched.

The sun-god withdrew every time she took a step toward him, staying just out of her reach.

She fell to her knees, arms imploring. "I didn't know." She shook her head so hard wisps of golden hair fell loose around her face. "You can't do this. Who will take care of her?"

Apollo glared at her. "*You* did this." His finger punctured the air in front of her. "*You* married him. A stupid mortal, thus fulfilling the curse."

Turning toward the god of death, Apollo waved a hand dismissively. "Take her." Apollo's skin began to glow brighter and brighter until the light engulfed his entire figure.

The woman closed her eyes and pulled away from the heat.

Athan felt a sudden coldness hit his core, but he shook off the chill. If he took even one step forward, he would break contact with his father. One step forward and he would be exposed. This wasn't his affair.

Thanatos glided to the crumpled figure and placed an ashen hand on hers.

She snatched her hand away. "Don't touch me! I know who you are."

His delicate features twisted into a grim smile. "You cannot cheat death, Sphinx—or a curse."

The Sphinx? A curse?

"But you don't understand." She tilted her tear-streaked face up, and her golden eyes locked on his midnight ones. "I have a daughter. She needs me." Her hands fluttered uselessly in her lap.

Hermes cleared his throat.

Athan looked toward the sound and saw his dad. They were visible!

The ashen god turned, and his posture stiffened.

"Hermes." Thanatos's eyes narrowed.

The woman turned to them. "Please help me. My daughter . . ."

Hermes looked at Athan, lips pursed, look calculating. The god turned back to the woman. "I can send my son—"

"*No!*"

The woman's scream became a roar of protest, and Athan watched in horror as Thanatos pulled her soul from her body.

"Thanatos!" Hermes lunged across the room.

But it was too late. The woman's body and soul were separate, no longer the same. The form now crumpled on the floor was still human from the waist up, but large feathered wings lay folded behind the feline haunches that had appeared in place of her legs. This was the Sphinx!

"You can't bargain with them, Hermes. They have nothing to offer except their pain."

The woman's soul turned to Thanatos and fixed him with a glare. Her mouth opened, but nothing came out.

"She cannot speak?" Athan looked from his father to Thanatos. In all the years Athan had been travelling with his dad, he'd never even tried to talk to one of the deceased.

Thanatos laughed. "The dead cannot speak in the realm of the living." He shifted and then amended, "Not before judgment. I'm surprised you did not know this, son of Hermes."

"It's Athan," he said, tilting his chin up and extending his hand.

Thanatos chuckled but did not take Athan's outstretched hand.

Hermes pushed his son's arm down. "Don't shake hands with Death, unless you're done living." He pushed the other god away. "You've done what you need to do here. I'll do the rest."

The spirit of the woman watched her eyes wide. She flailed her arms, moving her mouth in a desperate attempt at communication, but the silent outpouring was useless.

CURSED BY THE GODS

Thanatos's smile became a thin line, and he reached for her. "She is strong, that one. She did not want to come."

She turned away from the god and looked down at the crumpled form.

An unfamiliar heaviness filled Athan's chest.

Hermes took her hand. "You are the Sphinx?"

She nodded.

"But you are not the first one?"

A shake of her head.

"And you have a daughter?" When she again nodded, he continued, "Is she a Sphinx?"

Another nod.

"*Skata!*" The curse rang, an exclamation of impossibility. "How old?"

She flashed ten fingers and then another six.

"Sixteen?" Hermes looked at his son, then back to the Sphinx again.

There was another Sphinx? How was that even possible?

She nodded, her eyes wide, and pointed at Athan.

Hermes looked at his son. "Well? What do you think?"

What was he asking? "You want me to go get the Sphinx?"

Hermes shrugged as if he were suggesting a quick trip the grocery store then leaned forward, eyes fixed with intensity.

"Find her and bring her to me." He stepped away and continued. "You saw what happened."

Athan's heart pounded to life, the thrill of the hunt taking over. He could do this. And it would be a nice break from baby-sitting reluctant, ignorant demigods.

"Will she be human?" He pointed at the monster's body on the floor. "Or am I looking for this?"

She pointed at her soul and flashed her fingers, then to the body on the floor, and held up two. Her mouth continued to move, but it was pointless. Whatever detail she meant was lost without her voice. But he gathered the creature would be able to shift; sometimes she'd look human and other times the Sphinx. He had no idea how that could even be; he'd never heard of a monster that could shapeshift. Not that it mattered. A sphinx couldn't be too difficult to find, so he'd just focus on that. "Is she dangerous?"

The woman shook her head.

What was she going to say? His mind went back to the history of the Sphinx and the hundreds of men she'd strangled outside the gates of Thebes. A monster with the power of an immortal—she could kill him if he wasn't careful.

Thanatos laughed. "You're going to hunt the monster?"

"Thanatos." Hermes glared at the other god.

"What?" The god of death sneered.

"If you are not gone in two seconds, I will make it my personal mission to bind you in Tartarus," Hermes threatened.

"I do not answer to you."

"Hades will hear my petition."

Thanatos narrowed his eyes. "You will not be the only one hunting her, Hermes. Just know that others will see her for what she is."

"Is that a threat?" Hermes glared at the dark god. "Get out of here. Now."

The god of death stepped into a shadow and disappeared.

Hermes faced his son. "Find the girl. You have a few months at most if Hades sends his Skia." He paused momentarily, rubbing his hands together while he thought. "Bring her to a temple. And, Athan, I want her alive."

"She's just a monster, Dad," Athan said, with a grimace at the reminder of his past.

Hermes laughed, but it was manic and brash. "But that's not all she is. Besides, are you afraid?"

Even if Athan were, he wouldn't admit it. All these gods interested in this monster, she must have power. He'd make sure his father was the one to wield it. "It won't be easy to get her to a temple."

"Just find her. I'm going to take this Sphinx's soul to the Underworld. Perhaps I can talk Hades out of getting further involved. I don't know what he would hope to gain." The last bit was mumbled, a question for the universe.

"I thought Oedipus killed the Sphinx in Thebes," Athan said.

Hermes raised his eyebrows. "So we were told, and therein lies the riddle."

"Why do *you* care, Dad?"

"I hate Apollo." The venom in his answer singed the air. "He's an arrogant ass who meddles where he shouldn't."

Since when had the gods cared about mortals, monsters, or even their demigod children, except as their personal playthings? But the animosity between Hermes and Apollo was longstanding.

Hermes took the soul's hand and looked her in the eye. "We'll find your daughter." Then he turned to Athan. "Start a fire. Make it look like a Skia attack. I'll meet you at the portal in two hours."

"Skia?" The shadows of Hades didn't kill monsters, did they?

Hermes pursed his lips. "I want as little attention as possible on the Sphinx until I know what Apollo is up to. If it looks like Skia attacked, everyone will assume it was just another demigod killed."

"But once the mortals find her body . . ." Athan pointed at the creature.

"The body will shift again once her soul leaves this world. Curses from this realm will not hold in death."

Interesting. "If I wait until her daughter comes home—"

Hermes rolled his eyes. "Remember, whoever she was talking to is on their way here." He pointed at the phone on the floor. "And, when they get here . . . it's likely the mortal law enforcement will be called. If you want to wait, at least be smart about it. I'll see you soon."

Hermes turned to the spirit of the Sphinx.

"Wait, Dad! Which portal? Where are we?"

Hermes turned back to his son. "Bellevue, Washington."

With that, Hermes and the womanly apparition teleported from the apartment.

Bellevue. A suburb of Seattle, not too far from the conservatory downtown. Athan took a deep breath and turned to his task: a fire.

By the time he got outside, he could see the flames licking the windows.

As he reached the parking lot, a gray sedan pulled up. A dark-haired woman flung open the door and ran toward the building, nearly colliding with him.

"Best be careful," he warned, pulling her to a stop.

Her body went rigid with the contact.

Acrid smoke filled the air. It would be only seconds before—the window exploded. The woman wrenched free from his grasp and ran.

Flames greedily lapped at the sides of the building, and, in the distance, Athan heard the sirens wail.

ONE

"HOPE, ARE YOU awake?" Leto's voice was just above a whisper, just louder than the hum of the engine of their car as they made their way out of the city.

Hope shifted in the bucket leather seat but didn't look at her mother. "Yes."

The early morning hours were dim and quiet as they drove up Highway 18 toward I-90. Hope rested her head against the window of the car, letting the cold seep from the glass into her skin. Strands of her honey-blond hair fell from her messy ponytail, and she tucked them behind her ear. With a heavy exhale, she left a foggy patch on the glass and then dragged her finger through it.

They passed a temple for Demeter, goddess of agriculture, and Hope stared at the bright lights meant to be a beacon to parishioners, until they disappeared into the gray pre-dawn. She'd always wondered what happened in the temples, but of course they'd never go. Gods, demigods, and religious zealots would all be her enemies. Like the boys in her nightmares who chased her and her mother in an attempt to kill them. And somehow they were called monsters? Right. Hope shook her head to clear it of these depressing thoughts.

It would be good to be out of the apartment this time. Last month they couldn't go because the sky decided to unleash unholy amounts of water, and spending two days inside the small space they called home made Hope crazy. Besides, she loved to fly.

Leto pulled off at the top of the pass, drove past the closed ski area, a shrine for Boreas, god of winter, and down an access road until they hit gravel then dirt.

When the sky began to lighten, they both got out of the vehicle and undressed. Hope's teeth chattered as she glanced over at her mom, who was stretching up to the sky. There! The first rays of sunlight spilled over the horizon.

The pressure in Hope's back built until it felt like she was being squeezed into a corset, and then . . . *Whoosh.* Her wings unfurled. Her legs cramped, the muscles seized, and her human legs folded, replaced by lion-like haunches. Her skin tingled. A million fire ants were biting, biting, biting . . . Finally, the pain dissipated, and soft golden fur appeared on her breasts, torso, and lower extremities. The change was over.

Hope pulled her hair up in a messy bun, then glanced over her shoulder at her amber wings; the crimson-tipped feathers looked like they'd been dipped in blood.

"Are you ready to fly?" Her mom came around the car on her paws and hands.

"Are you kidding?" Hope said with a laugh. She loved to fly, loved the freedom of it. Relished it. Even craved it.

A sudden strong breeze almost lifted her off the ground.

"Careful," her mom cautioned.

As Hope pumped her wings, a gust pulled her away from the earth, and she was airborne.

The sky in the east was pale blue with feathers of yellow as the two Sphinxes flew over the mountain range.

"Where to?" Leto's voice carried over the wind and tickled Hope's ears with possibilities.

"Somewhere warm."

Leto's laugh was crisp, like the air. "It's only cold because we're on the top of the pass. South it is, then."

As the sun climbed, the air warmed. The two creatures flew, weaving away from populated areas. They passed the blackened skin of earth where a forest fire had raged and the snowy caps of Mount Rainier, Mount St. Helens, Mount Adams, and then Mount Hood. Her mom pointed each of them out as if giving a geography lesson.

"Getting tired?" Leto dropped lower in anticipation.

"Not yet. Let's go just a little farther."

The air was much warmer at the lower elevation, and rivulets of sweat tickled Hope's skin as they dripped down her neck. She stared ahead at Mount Bachelor, the bright whiteness looming as they drew closer.

"*Hope!*"

Her gaze jumped to where her mother was, just ahead, only to find empty air.

Time seemed to slow. The hum of an engine, way too close. Her mother yelling her name. The sun suddenly too hot, and her skin chilled with panic.

Her mother was above her.

"What in the name of the gods is *that*?"

The voice belonged to a male. And he was likely human.

"Get your phone!"

"Get a picture!"

"Get your gun!"

Oh gods! Hope pulled up, beating her wings as fast as she could.

Bam! A huge branch dropped from the sky, right on the hood of the car. The tires squealed, and curses issued from the windows.

"Hera and Zeus!" her mother cursed, dropping a second branch. "What are you doing?" She motioned for Hope to follow.

Shame burned Hope's cheeks, but her heart continued an erratic rhythm of panic. The two flew over a copse of trees and into the foothills of the Cascades.

"I called your name at least three times. What were you thinking?"

"I didn't hear you," Hope said.

Leto looked around, pointed at a clearing in the trees, and dropped to land.

Hope landed several feet from her mother and braced herself.

"What's the *first* thing I taught you? You've got to be aware of your surroundings. Your vision, your hearing, your reflexes are useless if you aren't paying attention. I won't always be there to rescue you. If we're ever found out, they'll kill us! Zeus Almighty!"

Her mom was right. All of Hope's supernatural powers would be worthless if she wasn't paying attention. And had those men been demigods, they could have killed her; death had been that close.

"I'm sorry."

"Sorry won't keep you safe. In this world, we are the monsters to them. Stay invisible. Always. Stay invisible."

Hope nodded. She'd heard this talk about staying hidden before. In fact, she'd heard it her entire life. The elusive, and much sought after, concept of safety was why they moved so much. Her mother's obsession with not letting anyone close enough to know their secret. Curse creatures were hunted. No one would accept them.

"If you aren't going to pay attention, maybe we should stay inside the apartment when—"

"No! Please. I'll pay attention from now on. I promise."

"We can't afford mistakes." Leto stalked over on her hands and haunches, her feline grace suited to her wooded surroundings. She put her hands on her daughter's shoulders, and their gold eyes met. "Please. Please, be more careful."

They spent an entire two days in the clearing, surrounded by tall pines, moss, and wild grasses. When it was time to fly back to the car, neither said anything, but they flew high, close to the mountains, far away from human eyes. High enough that even the demigods couldn't see them.

The message was clear. Stay hidden to stay safe. Don't let anyone in. Protect the secret of their curse. It was the only way.

"HITLER?" MR. BURTON's gaze swept over his students. "Any guess as to his divine parent?"

"Ares, god of war." A guy with a baritone voice answered the question, then muttered under his breath, "Supposedly."

The teacher ignored the snarky comment and continued with his lecture. He paced the front of the classroom, glancing down at his notes. "And Marie Curie?"

"Athena." Another student shouted the answer, and several other students cheered.

Hope put her head down on her desk, wishing for what she knew she couldn't have. It would be nice to be a part of their laughter. It would be nice to be included.

"Good. Very good. You should all do very well on your quiz tomorrow. Now, shifting gears. How many of you know the story of the Sphinx?"

Hope sat up but refused to raise her hand. If she'd known class was going to be about *her,* she would've slept in.

Mythology, like English and math, was required all four years of high school. And if she lived in the same blissful denial as the rest of the students, it might have been fun to learn about *mythology.*

Hope glanced at her classmates.

Most of them would live their entire lives believing the gods had withdrawn from humanity, with the exception of the occasional demigod offspring. Most would never be bothered by a deity. Never have to worry about immortal hunters. Never feel the curse of the gods. She sighed.

As it stood, her sophomore mythology class, Of Men and Monsters, was turning out to be thoroughly depressing. Even so, she was getting a solid *A.*

She drew a daisy and then connected it with the other ten already on the margin of her paper. She shaded in the leaves, waiting for Mr. Burton to continue.

"Hey. Hope."

Warm fingers wrapped around her wrist, and she glanced over into the eager face of Caidyn Brown.

"Do you have a pencil I can borrow?" His dark skin contrasted with his bright smile.

The corner of her lip responded. "Sure. Just a sec."

She reached into her bag, pushing aside keys and paper. She grasped two thin cylinders and held out his options. One was pink and glittery, a gift from her mother, the other a standard yellow number two bought in bulk at the beginning of the year.

"Pink and sparkles?" He took the proffered pencil. "It must be my lucky day."

She snorted. Because what man didn't like pink? "If you like it that much, keep it."

"Eyes up here, people," Mr. Burton interrupted.

She turned to face the board where Mr. Burton wrote *Sphinx* in red.

"All right. How many of you have heard of the Sphinx?" He turned back to the class.

A few hands went up.

"What is it?"

Hope shifted in her seat.

"A monster."

"A cursed person."

"A figment of your imagination."

The last commenter got raised eyebrows.

"The Sphinx was a monster." Mr. Burton threw a miniature candy bar at the student who'd given the correct answer. "And a monster, in mythology, is . . ."

Several hands went up.

"Yes, Gage."

"A monster is a mixed breed created by a god. Usually cursed for some offense."

Candy flew through the air.

"And what was the Sphinx?" His gaze roamed the room. "Alani."

"Lion and eagle."

He tilted his head and pursed his lips. "What else?"

The room was silent.

"Human." Hope said it. She didn't even know why. She'd gone the entire semester without saying much of anything. And she didn't even like chocolate.

Mr. Burton nodded his approval and tossed another silver wrapper.

Hope caught the candy and set it on the desk, wishing she could retract her answer. She was supposed to stay invisible. In plain sight.

"You going to eat that?" Caidyn whispered.

She held the candy out, and he took it. "Thanks."

Their eyes locked, and she had the distinct feeling that precipitated the change into her other form. Excitement. Trepidation. Shuddering, she forced her attention back on her instructor.

"There is significant debate regarding the Sphinx," Mr. Burton continued. "Some say she was born of monsters: Orthrus, Chimera, Typhon, or Echidna." He wrote the names on the board.

Her heart beat faster, and her palms began to tingle with the desire to hit something. "Maybe the Sphinx was human," she blurted. "Maybe she was cursed."

It was like she had no control over her mouth today. She pressed her lips together until the pressure turned to pain. She needed to shut up.

"Maybe." Mr. Burton tossed more candy at her, but she slumped back into her seat and made no move to catch the treats. "There is no question the monster was feared because of her murderous instincts."

As Mr. Burton's Q&A continued, Hope forced herself to tune out. She knew her history. How her grandmother sat outside of Thebes, questioning every man who wanted to enter the city. She asked the same riddle to each, and when they couldn't answer, she strangled them.

What the myth lost through time was how her grandmother, who was actually the granddaughter of Hera, was hiding in Thebes from a son of Apollo who was determined to kill her. While she was there, she fell in love. But her lover was killed as she tried to defend the city. Mad with grief, and attempting to protect Thebes, she wouldn't let strangers into the city. The myth told nothing of her pain. Murderous instincts? Right.

And Oedipus? Sure, he came to free the city from the monster, but the myth was wrong, like so many others. The very morning he showed up, Phaidra had killed the demigod who'd been after her. She wasn't interested in fighting Oedipus. Instead of solving the riddle, he struck a deal with her. She fled, and he got all the glory.

TWO

"HOPE?"

Her name brought her back to Mr. Burton's class, and the now almost-empty classroom. She focused on the glittery pencil drumming on the edge of her desk.

"Hey. Did you want your pencil back?" Caidyn held it out.

She shrugged. "If you want it, you can have it."

"You sure?" He waved it in front of her as if it were a prize.

She relented with a smile. "Uh-huh. You can keep it."

It was the longest conversation she could remember having since her arrival at Kentwood.

When her year started, Hope had been the new pretty girl in school. New and pretty sparked curiosity. But her lack of social skills, and her mom's insistence that Hope keep to herself, were a block of concrete in the ocean of interest. Within a few weeks, she was invisible. Again. Exactly how it was supposed to be.

But she hated it.

And then two weeks ago, Caidyn moved from Atlanta. Attractive, athletic, and friendly, he persisted in talking to her, even when she put her foot in her mouth.

They walked out of the classroom together and toward her locker.

"So, I was just thinking," he started.

Her cheeks tinged with warmth, as they always did with his attention. She was one measure hopeful, one measure dreadful as she anticipated his words. Students parted as Hope and Caidyn walked down the hall. She wasn't naïve enough to think the deference was for her. Caidyn drew attention everywhere he went.

He leaned toward her and bumped her shoulder. "You're pretty smart, and I'm pretty smart. Maybe we could get together and study sometime?"

The elation at being invited was almost immediately replaced with despair. "Um, I'm not allowed to have study groups." The warmth in her cheeks turned to fire, even as she pulled away. "I mean, I'm not allowed to go to study groups."

His smile didn't falter as he considered her. "Why not? Is your mom the Wicked Witch or something?"

"No." Maybe.

"Whatever. Tell her it's a class assignment. I'll be on my bestest behavior, a real prince." He waggled his brows.

She blushed and stuttered. "I . . . I don't think that would help any."

He stepped closer and whispered, "What if you told her you were studying with a demigod? We could sort through the monsters and devise the best way to destroy each one."

Her heart stopped. A lump of terror exploded in her chest.

"Are you . . . are you kidding me?" The words tripped out of her mouth.

"Will it convince your mom to let us hang out?" He smiled, and a glint of amusement shone from his dark eyes. "If I told you my dad was Hedylogos, would it make any difference?"

Zeus Almighty!

"Is he really your dad?" Her voice dropped to a whisper.

Caidyn shrugged. "Would it matter?" He leaned toward her. "You know who Hedylogos is?"

"God of flattery." Of course she knew. She knew them all.

Caidyn brushed hair away from her face with his fingertips and whispered, "I can tell you're immortal. Just like me."

She flinched as if he'd struck her, and her heart beat a rhythm of fear. He could tell? How could he tell? Her gaze darted around for an exit, but she was snared by the intensity in his eyes.

His gaze dropped to her lips. "And the god of sweet talk." He straightened back up. "Maybe you shouldn't tell her that part, though." He took a step back. "I can come over to your house; that way your mom can supervise. Do you think that will work?"

She shook her head. She needed to get out of there. She mumbled something she hoped sounded like she would need to check with her mother first. Hope's cold, clammy hands were shaking. She gripped her backpack to make them stop.

The bell rang.

He was looking at her funny. Like maybe she'd said something wrong? She swallowed the lump in her throat and pushed out, "I'll . . . I'll let you know tomorrow."

Caidyn winked at her. "Perfect. Hey, why don't you come eat lunch with me today?"

He started walking backward.

She shrugged. She wasn't going to eat lunch with him. She'd probably never see him again.

"I'll find you!" Caidyn waved, then he turned and sprinted down the hall.

She stood alone, panic racing through her veins. A demigod? Could that even be? Here in Kent? Gods! She needed to tell her mom. She needed to tell her mom right now.

"I'M HOME!" HOPE dropped her bag on the linoleum floor just inside the door.

The two-bedroom apartment in Bellevue was far enough away from anywhere they'd lived in the last several years that no one should recognize them. It was close to major freeways and only thirty minutes from the airport. They were on the second floor of an old complex, the last remaining complex in Bellevue with only two floors. The older buildings had been torn down in the last few years, rebuilt more in sync with the very modern, high-rise city. For whatever reason, this one had been spared. It meant cheaper rent but transient occupants. Which was perfect. Except old apartments always stunk of fresh paint.

The bland beige carpet was met with bland beige walls of a slightly lighter shade. True to every move Hope could remember, the walls were bare and the furniture cheap and functional. A statue of Hecate sat on the mantel, the shrine an alleged protection from the Skia of the Underworld.

"Oh good." Leto's voice floated down the short hall of the apartment. "How was school?"

Hope shrugged. It was late July, and she was taking two classes at the community college out of desperation. Because of their recent arrival, she had two weeks' worth of work to catch up on. It was a relief to have something to do before her junior year started.

The trust fund from Hope's grandparents was substantial, but her mom kept them in quiet obscurity, just one more attempt to keep them from drawing attention.

Her mom poked her head around the corner of a small bedroom. "I said how was school?"

"Fine." It was always fine. Fine. Fine. Fine.

"Good." Leto came out of her bedroom. "Can I get you a snack?"

Hope rolled her eyes. "I'm not five. I can get my own snack."

She stepped around a box, into the barren kitchen, and opened the fridge. They needed to go grocery shopping still. The few snacks of string cheese and dried meat were scattered on the top shelf of the otherwise empty refrigerator. Hope slammed the door shut.

A muscle in her mom's jaw clenched, but she didn't take the bait. "Priska said she's coming by tonight."

Priska, her aunt, always heralded their comings and goings. But Hope was so sick of moving. So sick of running and hiding from the figments of her mother's imagination. Maybe Skia really did exist, and maybe they were bad. But Hope didn't think they'd ever actually seen one. Except for the picture Priska had shown of a man with black eyes and pale skin, which incidentally, had only been a Photoshop rendition. Not that Hope didn't hear about Skia All. The. Time.

Hope dreamed that if they could just stay in one place, maybe she could someday make a friend. Maybe she could have a sliver of a normal life. But probably not. "Does this mean we're going to move again?"

The moving boxes were still stacked in the bedrooms of the apartment. It would be another day before Leto had everything unpacked. Knowing her mother's tendency toward the compulsive, it might even be two.

"Ha, ha!" Leto went back into her room. "Go get your homework done. Maybe we can talk Priska into staying for games."

At least that was something.

Over the last year they had moved seven times. Seven. They hadn't stayed in Vancouver much longer than they'd stayed in Mount Vernon or Kent. Same for Pasco, Bellingham, and Aberdeen. And now they were in Bellevue—but for how long?

Hope picked up the gray backpack and headed to her room. Her bed was pushed up against the wall, and the cream comforter promised to make everything better. She pushed the empty boxes to the side and fell onto her bed.

The edge of something heavy dug into her ribs, and she rolled to the side and grasped a thick book. She tugged the leather-bound volume out and let it drop to the floor with a thud. Hope lifted her head just enough to verify that it was the *Book of the Fates*. Her mom had given it to her the day before, and she'd thumbed through the story of her grandmother, Phaidra, but slammed it shut after only minutes of reading. Hope didn't want to know any more of her depressing history, even if it was the only accurate record. She buried her face into the soft bedding.

"I put away most of your clothes, but you'll need to finish your toiletries." Leto said from the doorway.

"Mfft."

"Are the kids at school nice? How are your teachers?"

Hope rolled over. "They're fine."

"I'm so glad. I think we're going to like it here."

"I'm sure we will. For at least a week."

Leto said nothing.

Bellevue was just across the lake from Seattle and boasted a large mall, several movie theaters, and restaurants on almost every corner. It was a nondenominational city, one with temples for most of the Olympians and several Titans. Not that any of this mattered. She would be going exactly nowhere without her mom or, if she was lucky, Priska.

"Priska will be here in an hour."

Hope rolled onto her back and stared up at the ceiling. "Okey-dokey."

She heard her mom's forced exhalation, followed by her retreat down the hall.

When Priska came, Hope vented to her for what felt like hours, until Leto finally tapped on the door. "Sorry to interrupt, but it's time for bed."

Priska stood up. "Sorry you're having a rough go, sweet girl. I'm sure it will get better." She stooped and retrieved the leather-bound book on the floor. "Have you started reading this?"

"Not yet." Guilt nagged at Hope's conscience, but she pushed it down.

"Hmm. Maybe you should."

The door closed but didn't latch. Hope could hear them speaking in the hall. She slid from the bed and crept across the floor, then she eased the door open.

"I think this is important for her." Her aunt made the statement as if it were fact. "She's never had any friends—"

There was a snort.

"All I'm saying is I think it's important for her to have friends, and that's impossible if you move every two months and keep her under lockdown."

Leto sighed. "You know it is only for her safety."

"Hey," Priska placated. "I'm on your side. On all of this, okay? I'm all about keeping you safe. I just think maybe it's time to do something different. For her."

THREE

"**Do you want to** go into Seattle for the day?" Leto stood just outside Hope's room, hand hovering at the door.

Hope's plans to spend the day in bed came to a screeching halt. Her book slipped from her fingers, and she turned to her mom with disbelief. "What?"

"I thought it would be nice to go to Pike Place Market, and then maybe walk down to the aquarium."

"Sure." Hope threw off the covers and climbed out of bed.

"Great. Priska has work this morning, but said she could meet us for lunch."

Hope froze, her mouth agape.

"This is me trying to do something a little different," Leto said with a small smile, her eyes filled with hope.

A *little* different? This was a lot different. A spark of something warm and exciting tingled as it spread through Hope's chest. A quick dance through her closet found clean jeans and a T-shirt. She brushed her teeth and pulled her hair back, worried that her mother would change her mind.

Leto chatted aimlessly about books and movies as they drove across the 520 Bridge, but Hope sat dumbfounded, barely listening. Finally, the suspense made the words explode out of her.

"Why are we doing this?"

Stillness settled between the two of them.

Leto sighed. "I don't want you to turn out weird. I mean . . . any weirder."

Weird? Hope laughed. "So, does this mean we're going to start doing *normal* things?"

"I . . . I think we should try it. See how it goes. Maybe turn over a new leaf."

"You mean I can make friends, have study groups . . . go on dates?" Un—freaking—believable. She didn't even know what it would mean, but possibilities suddenly stretched in front of her.

"Don't push it. Let's start small and see how things go."

They parked on the street just south of the market and followed the scent of donuts to a tented stall. Armed with a paper bag full of hot cinnamon-sugar sweets, mother and daughter walked down to watch the mongers throw seafood.

The pungent smell of fish permeated the air. Two men in orange rubber overalls and boots talked with shoppers; another one was filling outstretched hands with samples of salmon jerky.

"*Two red snapper!*" One of the men yelled an order, and then—

"*Watch your head!*"

"*Red snapper!*" A large fish flew through the air.

Hope cringed and ducked.

"*Snapper one!*" A man behind the counter caught the fish and ripped a large piece of brown butcher paper. The monger deftly wrapped the large fish, his fingers reaching for a roll of tape.

"*Red snapper two!*"

She turned in time to see another fish soar overhead.

Somehow, the monger caught the fish midair.

"*Snapper two!*" He turned back and tore another piece of butcher paper.

Her gaze wandered the crowd. At least fifty people were gathered on the sidewalk, watching the show. A little girl screamed and pointed at an ice display with a large fish whose jaws were moving up and down. A man bobbed up from behind the counter, and the crowd laughed.

A cloud passed over the struggling summer sun, and a chill blew through the air. Two kids climbed on a large brass pig, and one shouted for her picture to be taken.

Out of the shadows of the stairwell, a man seemed to materialize. Dressed in black, his pallid skin looked almost ashy. With no shirt but a tank top, he should have been cold in the morning air, but he moved through the crowd, as if unaware of the temperature. And no one moved out of his way. He bumped through the throng, not stopping to apologize, and it was almost like the people couldn't—no, that couldn't be. It was like they couldn't see him.

The man looked up at her, and her breath caught. His eyes!

"Mom!" She tugged at Leto's coat.

Leto, laughing at the fish show, turned to her daughter. "What's the matter?"

She pointed to the crowd where the apparition had been. Except . . . he was gone. Disappeared. She scanned the surrounding crowd, looking for the otherworldly creature. He'd evaporated.

Hope swallowed. If she told her mom what she'd seen, would they ever go out again? "Nothing. I thought I saw something, but . . . it was nothing."

"By the gods, don't scare me like that." Leto's hand relaxed and came out of her purse empty but shaking.

Hope hung her head, but her heart was still pumping. "Sorry."

"No worries." Leto pulled her phone from her purse and tapped at the screen. "I'm just telling Priska where we are so she can meet us for lunch. She said she'd be caught up in a couple hours." She put the phone back and glanced around the square before her eyes settled on Hope. "Let's go see what else is here."

"Okay." Her gaze flitted over the throng, but there was no sign of the dark figure.

They went through countless artisan's stands and then into the open-air stalls where piles of produce, herbs, and vegetation surrounded them. The temperature had risen with the climbing sun, and Hope asked when Priska would be there so they could get lunch.

"At least another hour. Oh, let's get some flowers for her." Leto surveyed the premade arrangements wrapped in white paper. "You know how she loves Gerbera daisies." She pointed at a bunch with red and orange blooms.

Hope looked up from the bouquets to see the shadows at the back of the stall shift. A short man dressed in black advanced, his step both graceful and predatory.

This was not the same man she'd seen by the Fish Market earlier, and yet his movements were eerily similar, as were his pale skin and dark eyes.

Her heart rate doubled, and she instinctively stepped back. Her conversation with Priska came crashing back. Hope knew what this monster was.

"Leto! Hope!" Priska pushed through the crowd toward them. Time seemed to slow.

Leto took the change from the vendor and turned toward her best friend, expression morphing from excitement to terror. The paper-wrapped bouquet slipped to the ground.

Hope looked from her mother to her aunt, and her muscles tensed even as her vision tunneled. Out of the corner of her eye, she could see the dark figure coming straight for them. She suppressed the cry bubbling up her throat.

Priska crashed into them, grabbing them with shaky limbs. She jerked her head side to side, her eyes bulging. "Holy Hades! *What in the name of All. The. Gods. are you doing here?*"

Hope's gaze swung back to the stall. Unable to look away, she watched as the man melted back into the shadows. The vendors were oblivious to him, even after he overturned a bucket of lilies and one of the workers jumped to save the blossoms from being trampled. No one, not one single person, turned to look at him.

"This place is crawling with Skia!" Priska scolded them. "If I'd known you were coming here . . . I would've never agreed—"

Leto shook her head. "I had no idea. I figured with all the people we'd be safe. I even brought the blades. I'm sorry. I'm so sorry."

Skia! Hope's heart tripped over and over again.

The immortal knives had been passed down by her grandmother and were Leto's, and subsequently Hope's, only protection from immortal beings. Her mom must have them in her purse.

"Of all the places you could've picked." Priska looked back and forth between the two of them. "You haven't seen any?"

Leto shook her head.

"By the gods, you have incredible luck." She let out an exhale that sounded like a million worries. "Let's get out of here."

They started to the car, walking close together. Hope watched the two vigilant women, then glanced around as if she would see something they missed.

An Asian couple hurried past, the woman speaking in her native tongue. A kid on a scooter, followed by his harried father. A jogging stroller pushed by a woman with neon-orange shoes.

They walked past a bank, and a young man stepped out from the doorway and bumped into her.

"Pardon."

It took a moment before she realized he'd apologized. When she turned to acknowledge him, he grabbed the brim of his baseball cap and tilted his head at her, effectively blocking most of his face from her view, with the exception of his smile, and . . . a dimple? He was fair, but not in a pasty way. He wore short sleeves, and dark tattoos banded his arms. She couldn't help but stare. He was definitely alive, and definitely not Skia.

Nevertheless, she had the distinct impression he was watching them all the same.

"Hope!" Her mom's voice broke her focus, and Hope turned to see the two women standing at her mom's blue sedan at least a hundred feet up the street. "For the love of Artemis, please stay with us!"

Hope hurried toward the car but glanced back. The young man was gone.

"Sorry, Mom." She turned and offered a half smile.

Leto shook her head and pushed the button to unlock the doors.

"Did you see something?" Priska pierced Hope with her gaze.

She ducked into the car, thinking about her answer. If she told the truth, her newfound freedom would disappear. If she had to pick, death sounded better than isolation.

"She was staring at that boy." Leto shook her head.

Afraid her voice wouldn't convey the conviction, and embarrassed that she had been caught by her mother, Hope deflected, "How did you know there were Skia there?"

"Are you kidding me?" Priska's brows raised. "There are always Skia, but this area is close to a conservatory for demigods. The more immortals there are around, the more Skia." She turned back to the front, but her voice was strong, almost angry as she continued, "If they find you, they'll kill you. In the future, probably best to stay out of downtown."

"Does this mean we have to go home?" The expectations of a day out began crumbling around Hope.

"No." Leto looked at Priska. "No. We're doing something different. We can go to the mall . . . in Bellevue. And we'll have lunch on the Eastside, too. There are lots of great restaurants there."

"Then why didn't you just stay in Bellevue?" Priska's muttering carried to the back. "It's quieter there. Safer."

Leto pinched the bridge of her nose. "We'll stay on the Eastside from now on. Trust me, all I want is to keep us safe."

FOUR

"IF YOUR MOM marries my dad, then you guys will stop moving, right?" Sarra brushed her raven-colored hair over her shoulder. Her dark curls fell forward, a stark contrast to her pale skin, as she leaned into the aisle to talk with Hope. "Then you can stay until we go to college."

Hope wasn't going to correct her. There was no way her mom was going to marry Paul. There was no way they would stay in Bellevue. The fact that they'd been there almost six months puzzled Hope, but for the first time in her life she had a real friend. Or at least the closest thing to it. She wasn't about to tell her mom that Ms. Chandler had brought up her regular absences just that morning.

Hope stared at the clock, waiting for the bell that would announce class and stop Sarra from chatting about the impossible.

Sure, it was nice to have Sarra and her father, Paul, around. It had been four months of tentative steps toward normalcy. For some reason, Leto had decided Sarra and her father, new move-ins to the apartment complex shortly after the Nicholas's arrival, would be safe as friends. And, slowly, her mom had let her guard down.

But the curse made it very clear, every single month, that Hope and her mom were not normal. They were monsters, and if Paul and Sarra knew . . . Hope wanted to believe that their friendship would withstand that information. That the dinners, the sleepovers, and more recently the weekend trips would continue regardless. But a lifetime of reminders couldn't be erased over a few months.

And something told her there was a ticking time bomb hiding beneath all this normalcy, something ominous just on the horizon. She hadn't seen Skia again since the trip to Seattle, all those months ago. But if Skia found Hope and her mom . . . The creatures from the Underworld were no longer a nebulous figment of her mom's imagination. Nor were the demigods.

Maybe Hope should say something to her mom tonight.

"Anyway, it would be awesome to be sisters. We could share a room and stay up late sharing secrets—"

Hope snorted.

"What?" Sarra asked, just as the bell rang.

Ms. Chandler called the class to order.

Hope steeled herself for another worthless mythology lesson. Her gaze flitted over the pictures of the gods and heroes hung around the room, exaggerated caricatures with something that was supposed to relate to their prominent powers. Her gaze landed on Apollo, the sun rising behind him while he cured the sick and music notes floated in the air. As if.

Ms. Chandler said something about immortal weapons, and Hope turned her attention to her instructor. Maybe she would learn something new after all.

"Hephaestus forged weapons for each of the gods, two daggers each. Most of the gods gave the daggers to their demigod children as a means of defense. The knives were eternal, could not be destroyed, and they gave the demigods power to slay other immortal beings. Like the monsters." Ms. Chandler glanced over her class. "Yes, Teresa?"

"Why would the demigods kill all the monsters? I mean, it's not like they were all scary, right? I mean, nymphs?"

"The nymphs, like other monsters, were mixed breeds—part divine, part mortal—and their power certainly made them a force to reckon with," Ms. Chandler replied. "If you had done your homework, you would know that they could cause dumbness, blindness, and even madness."

The class fell silent with the reprimand.

"Not all monsters were what you would consider scary looking. Many looked human, or partially so," Ms. Chandler continued. "In fact, the sirens were beautiful. Their beauty was the lure that made them so deadly. And think about the Minotaur. King Minos put him in an underground maze to try to protect his people. Even then humans had no defense over the divine. The immortal weapons gave the demigods an advantage."

"But that was forever ago. Some say it didn't even happen," Teresa said. "That it's just myth."

Ms. Chandler inclined her head, as if in agreement. "I can understand some disbelief. How many of you have met a monster?" When no one raised their hand, she continued, "What about a demigod?"

Still no one indicated in the affirmative.

Almost as if Hope's knowledge would jump out of her mouth, she bit her lips closed. How could people not know?

"Really? That's interesting." Ms. Chandler frowned. "Well, there is some suspicion about possible dwindling numbers of demigods. However, others believe their *psachno* group is doing a better job of getting demigods to conservatories at a younger age."

Hope sat up.

"What's a *psachno*?"

Hope was saved from asking by another student.

"Excellent question. *Psachno* is Greek for seeker, or one who seeks. It is believed that within their conservatory communities, each demigod has an appointed role. *Psachno* find other demigods and bring them to the safety of conservatories which are divinely protected from Skia and monsters," said Ms. Chandler. "At one time, there was a group of demigods dedicated to the eradication of monsters. *Fonias*, I believe they were called."

Ms. Chandler thumped her desk, drawing the class's drifting attention. "What would cause an entire race to be killed?"

"They're a threat. To humans and demigods. Monsters have killed millions," said a girl named Jessica.

"So, what happened?" Ms. Chandler asked the rhetorical question, effectively drawing the attention back to the subject.

"The demigods slaughtered them." Jessica announced the annihilation of the mixed breeds in a tone that spoke volumes.

Hope wanted to hit her.

Ms. Chandler nodded. "About a hundred years ago, an enthusiastic son of Ares led the charge. And for the last century it has been believed he's been responsible for the annihilation of almost all the monsters. Some may have escaped, like Scylla, but these exceptions are likely protected by the gods who created them."

The door opened, and a portly woman with bleached-blond hair put her head through the opening.

"Excuse me?" She looked from the classroom of teens up to Ms. Chandler. "I need Hope Nicholas to come with me."

Ms. Chandler looked at Hope with raised brows. "Go ahead. You can get the assignment when you come back."

"She won't be back this period, Ms. Chandler." There was a tightness around the woman's eyes.

Hope and Sarra exchanged a look, and Sarra mouthed that she would call Hope when class was over.

Ms. Chandler waved. "Then she can get it tomorrow."

Hope put her binder and her copy of *Myths and Legends* away and then slung her backpack over her shoulder.

What on earth could she be needed for at the office? She and her mom had shifted three weeks ago, so it was too early to have to do with the curse. Maybe they were going away with Paul and Sarra for the weekend, but then Sarra would be coming too . . .

Hope followed the squat woman down the hall and into the office, the awkward silence ballooning into a presence between them.

Finally, Hope couldn't take it anymore. "Um, why am I here?"

The watery-blue eyes that met Hope's were drawn as if trying to hold back overwhelming emotion, and the woman's bright-pink lips pulled down into a sympathetic smile.

"Oh, baby. Ms. Tessie will be with you in just a second." The woman looked around the empty space and shuffled behind the counter, tossing over her shoulder, "I'm so sorry, sweetie."

Sorry? What was she sorry about? An empty feeling began to crawl up from the depths of Hope's soul.

"Hope Nicholas?" Ms. Tessie stepped out from her office and waved Hope toward her door.

Dread exploded in Hope's chest, its flames licking at her heart.

Ms. Tessie wasn't the principal. She was the school counselor.

"Come on into my office, please." The counselor was still young, her dark hair cropped in a pixie cut. She had a silver stud in her nose but was dressed in a cardigan and pant set that looked like she was trying hard to be older than her actual years.

"What's going on?"

Ms. Tessie said nothing until the door was closed.

In the seconds before she spoke, Hope noticed how Ms. Tessie's hazel eyes had more gold flecks than Priska's.

"I think you'd better sit down." Ms. Tessie pointed to a plush leather chair opposite the dark mahogany desk that took up most of the room.

Hope swallowed. "No, thank you." She swallowed again. "What happened? Where's my mom?"

The young counselor's lips pulled down into the same sympathetic smile. "I'm so sorry to be the one to tell you. There's been an accident, and . . . your . . . Your mother's passed, Hope."

She blinked as if to clear her vision. Over and over again. Passed? Her brain stuttered over the term, rejecting it. This couldn't be happening. It had to be a dream.

"There was a fire . . . at the apartment. Your Aunt Priska is on her way . . ."

Hope's backpack slid to the floor. Someone was pounding on her chest, and she couldn't catch her breath. She felt her heart beat, beat, beat, and then it ripped in two. She couldn't feel her hands, and something wet was dripping onto her shirt.

"Oh, sweet girl."

Foreign arms wrapped her in a smothering embrace, squeezing out the light in her eyes, in her life.

Gone. She was gone. Her mom . . .

"No! No! No!" Hope wrenched from the oppressive vise and backed away. "No. There has to be a mistake. You're wrong." She glared daggers at the counselor, turned, grabbed the handle of the door, and ran.

The tears streaming down Hope's face obscured her vision, and she ran blindly until she couldn't run anymore, and then she walked.

She could smell acrid smoke even before she arrived at the complex, and the flashing lights of police and fire trucks lit the hazy air. The school bus momentarily blocked her view, and then a crowd of kids stood gaping at the scene.

Hope pushed past them and stood at the bottom of the steps that would lead to her apartment. Yellow tape blocked the entrance. Her heart sank deep into her chest, and her legs wouldn't hold her up any longer.

"Hope?" Sarra approached, her violet eyes puffy and rimmed in red.

Hope looked up at her best friend.

"My mom . . ." She couldn't say it. A sob broke, and Hope put her head in her hands, trying to block out the reality swimming in front of her. This couldn't be real.

A warm hand on her shoulder was followed by an arm, and then Sarra sat next to her, scooting close. "I'm so sorry."

Hope couldn't speak. She buried her head in her arms and let the tears fall.

"Do you know what happened?"

Hope waved at the evidence above. It was all she knew for sure. A fire? They couldn't be killed by fire, could they? Skia? Demigods? A god? Something had found her mom.

The shrill blare of a horn blew, and Paul's white car slowed in front of the two girls.

"Sarra, get in." His voice was tinged with panic. He circled the front of the car and opened the passenger door. "Right now."

His eyes stayed focused on his daughter, as if the world might collapse if he let her out of his sight.

Sarra stood slowly. "In the car?" She blinked once. Twice. "Now?"

"Now." He stepped forward, grabbing her arm, and pulled.

Sarra stumbled and looked back at Hope.

Paul pushed Sarra, forcing her through the open door and into the car, avoiding her questions and her pleas. He didn't even look at Hope.

The door closed, and Paul leaned against it, his head in his hands.

"I'm sorry." He mumbled the apology, just barely audible. "You're a . . . monster. A beast. You're not safe, and I need to keep my daughter safe." Without looking at her, Paul got in the car and drove away.

FIVE

HOPE STARED AT her hands as if the answers might appear within her palms, but the only thing she saw were the lines and cracks, a map that went nowhere, that meant nothing.

She was a monster. Of course Sarra wasn't safe. Of course they wouldn't love her. Of course they left when they found out.

Hope's vision blurred, and she bowed her head to the consuming grief.

"You shouldn't be here."

The broken voice was familiar, and she turned to see Priska, her face splotchy with emotion.

"Come on." The older woman extended her hand.

"No." Hope's protest was a weak whisper.

Priska pulled Hope to her feet and put an arm around her waist, as if to hold her up. "It's time to go."

"Where?"

Tears ran down Priska's cheeks. She cleared her throat but still choked on the words. "I'm taking . . . you home with me tonight."

Home with her? But Hope's mom . . . Maybe this was a mistake. Maybe her mom was just injured. Maybe she was at the store. How would Hope know? How would she know what really happened? "Can I see her? Can I see my mom?"

Priska looked horrified. "You don't . . . You don't want that memory."

"Am I going to stay with you?" Hope looked down at her aunt.

Priska wiped at her face and took a deep breath. "You can stay with me as long as you want."

She opened the door to her gray sedan, and Hope collapsed in the passenger seat. The drive to Mercer Island was silent. Did Priska feel the same way? As if the world had tilted and someone just needed to right it. Hope kept hearing the counselor say *she passed*. Passed. Passed where? Passed what? What did that mean?

She walked into Priska's house in a daze, clinging to the warm hand guiding her. Hope spent hours sitting at a window, staring at the sky as it changed from gray to black and back to gray again. The gray lasted so long, so much longer than the black.

HOPE SAT ON an armless chair, staring out the window at the gray drizzle. "Was it Skia?" Her voice cracked as if she were breaking it in. When her words met with silence, she turned to fix her gaze on Priska. "Did Skia get her?"

Her aunt's head dropped. "I'm so, so sorry. I failed her. I failed you."

Hope's heart skidded and tripped at an erratic pace. "What does that mean?"

"I don't know what happened." Priska's eyes were puffy and swollen. "She called me . . . just before . . . She saw Skia when she was out. Said she had something important she needed to tell me. Asked me to come over as fast as I could."

Skia. They should've moved. Hope should've said something sooner. If they'd only moved. Maybe her mom was calling Priska to help her pack . . . Except they almost never packed. That's why all the furniture was cheap. Disposable. No, it wasn't making sense. "And? What happened?"

"I went, but . . . it was too late. I was too late." Her voice cracked.

Too late? A wave of pain crashed in Hope's chest and rolled lower. It was Skia. Oh, gods. The pain receded and an ache followed. Seconds later, the pain was back, and bitterness burned the back of her throat. Hope raced from the room.

She retched into the toilet, the yellow bile making the water bright. Tears left salty streaks on her skin. She pulled tissue from the roll and blew her nose. Her mother's death was her fault. If Hope had said something sooner, they would've left. And they would be safe. Together.

"I'm so sorry," Priska said, and the words fell all over the floor in a mess too big to step around.

A gaping chasm opened between the two of them.

But Hope had told Priska about Leto and Paul. Priska had said she would talk to Leto, and they would move. It was Priska's fault.

"I thought you were supposed to help keep us safe." The words were an accusation, and they found their mark. "I thought Hecate was supposed to keep us safe."

Priska stood in the open doorway, but Hope refused to look at her.

"I know. I know. Hades in hell, I *know*! Don't you think I know? I told her! I told her it was time to move. Told her that whatever she thought she had with that man was nothing. I told her!" Priska was sobbing, her small hands covering her face. "I don't know what happened . . ."

Hope sat dumbfounded while the older woman wept.

Priska sagged to the floor. "I don't know what to do anymore. Do you know what it's like to be an epic failure?"

Hope didn't know what to say. She'd never seen her aunt like this. Hope grasped, but words were elusive wisps floating away. Her aunt didn't lose it. Not like this.

"Do you know what it's like to watch time and again as your loved ones die? Over and over and over again? And you can do nothing, absolutely nothing about it? It would be easier to cut out my own heart, and I am so, so, so sick of it." Priska's sobs started again.

Hope's eyes got bigger and bigger until they felt like they were going to pop out of her skull. What was Priska saying? The words made no sense.

A haze of silence descended, filling the space with a throbbing ache. Hope could say nothing to comfort her aunt, and nothing Priska said made her feel better. So, she waited, not knowing what to do, not wanting to do anything. Eventually, her gaze went to the frosted window above the tub, and she watched as the light faded.

"Zeus Almighty."

Hope looked away from the window to Priska standing over her.

"I think we better go to bed." Priska made no movement to help Hope but stepped away, giving ample space to get up.

Hope pulled herself up, feeling pins and needles in her legs from sitting too long on the tile floor.

"Second door on the left, you remember?" Priska walked down the hall without looking back.

Hope remembered the room. It had allegedly been her mother's for a few months before she'd married her father, and then again after he left.

Hope couldn't sleep in there, in a room filled with loss and pain. No. She wouldn't sleep there. Not tonight.

Not ever.

"HOPE." PRISKA SAT on the edge of the overstuffed sofa and tapped her back.

Hope sat up, blankets falling from her shoulders, the *Book of the Fates* thumping to the floor. She'd fallen asleep clinging to the immortal book, one of the few things that had escaped the effects of the fire. The room was dark, but light seeped in from the cracks in the shutters. The smell of peach tea wafted from the mug her aunt was holding.

Hope's restless sleep left her disoriented and confused, but there was something wrong—she just couldn't remember what.

It hit like an anvil to her chest. Two days. It had been two days. In six more days, she would shift and become the Sphinx. For the first time in her life, she would change alone.

Priska pulled Hope into a hug, arms lingering for only a few seconds. "We need to talk about what happened."

She tried to swallow the mass of sorrow lodged in her throat. She wanted to curl into a ball and cry until her feelings fled, until she had no emotion left. This weight was too much.

"I'm going to change without her," she whispered.

Priska's hand was on Hope's knee, and then it was gone. "I think you should stay in the apartment this time, when you change. Just . . . stay. I don't think you should go anywhere right now."

"I don't think I can do this."

Priska's teeth were clenched, her lips pursed. "You've done it a thousand times."

She hadn't done it a thousand times, but Priska was right.

"There's something else, Hope. When I was there, at the apartment, I'm pretty sure I saw a demigod."

"A demigod? I thought you said mom saw Skia? That Skia were hunting us." She thought about how her mom had burned. "And what about the fire?"

Priska pushed against Hope's legs, scooting back further onto the couch. "When I got to the apartment, after your mom called me, I noticed a young man walking away from the building. He looked familiar, but I'm pretty sure . . ." She ran her hand through her dark hair. "He's a demigod."

"A demigod?" Demigods with their immortal weapons. The other reason they ran. Demigods hunted monsters for sport. "Is that what happened?"

"I don't know." Priska's lips pulled into a tight line. "There were Skia close by. She'd seen one a week earlier, when she was grocery shopping."

Hope stared at her aunt, momentarily dumbfounded. It was like they were all closing in on them. Had Leto said something to Paul? That would explain his fear, his panic.

"But none of it makes sense. Demigods don't start fires. That's more of a Skia ploy. And the only god who would care is . . ." She didn't say his name, but they both knew. "And then only if the curse were complete."

"What does that even mean?" The words circled around her head, creating a cyclone of chaos. So many questions. "And why doesn't the *Book of the Fates* say what happened?" She'd spent hours last night staring at the blank pages that should tell her mom's story. "Why is her story not written?"

Priska shook her head. "I don't know. I don't know how soon after death the Fates write the story. I don't know." She sighed. "I think we'd better move. It isn't safe here."

"I need to know what happened," Hope said. "I need to know who killed my mom."

She could stay with Priska and help. They could solve this together, and then Hope could take her revenge.

"Hope." Priska interrupted her musing. "It was probably Skia. The most important thing is still to keep you safe."

"But I want to know. I *need* to know."

Priska sighed and held out her hands as if she were weighing them against each other. "If you want me to find out what happened to your mom, you being with me will not be safe."

"What are you saying?"

Priska put her hand on Hope's shoulder. "You need to stay hidden. If we stay together or not, you'll need to be holed up in some small town where you can become invisible. The last few months were pure foolishness. You should've never stayed there that long."

Hope couldn't argue that, and the familiar guilt gnawed on her soul. More than anything she understood, someone had found them. Someone who knew what they were. Someone who knew how to kill them.

Priska sighed. "If you want me to hunt down your mom's killer, you'll need to be by yourself for a while."

Alone? Hope had never been completely alone. How was she going to do that? The idea of school, on top of trying to keep up a house felt overwhelming. There was no way she could do it. Fear clawed at her stomach and up into her chest. Grasping for something, someone she could stay with she said, "What about Paul and Sarra?"

Even as she said the words, Paul's voice echoed in her mind. He'd called her a monster. She shook her head. "He knows something."

Priska froze, her features hardening with laser focus. "What do you mean?"

"He came just before you did . . . at the apartment. Got Sarra away from me and drove away like demons were chasing him." Something inside Hope didn't want to believe he'd called her a monster, and she refused to admit it.

Priska sank into the cushions of the couch with a sigh. "I don't know what happened there. I guess I can look into that, too."

Hope scrunched her brow with worry. She just wanted to have some connection to someone. "Maybe . . . maybe I could say goodbye to Sarra?"

"Call her," Priska relented with a frown. "But make it fast."

Hope stood and retrieved her phone. With trembling fingers, she dialed the number of the only friend she'd ever had. Sarra picked up on the second ring.

Her voice felt like the last chance for something that had eluded Hope her entire life. The normalcy she craved, the desire for friendships, a symbol of acceptance and love. She wanted some balm to soothe the gaping wound in her heart.

"Sarra? It's Hope." Tears spilled from her eyes.

SIX

THE KINDNESS THAT had defined Sarra, that had made her the ideal friend, disappeared in an instant. Replacing the soft voice of her friend was a razor's edge. "Why are you calling me?"

It was a punch to Hope's raw emotions. "I . . . I thought . . . I thought we were friends."

"You're a monster. A freak." There was a pause before she continued, "You lied to me. Don't call me, Hope. We aren't friends." *Click.*

Hope stood motionless, staring at her phone.

Priska came over and took the small device from her trembling hands.

"There was a reason your mom kept you from the world for so long. Having friends can be wonderful. But humans fear what is different."

Hope could only nod while she swallowed back her hurt, shoving the pain into the dark recesses of her heart. If isolation was so safe, why didn't they just move into the mountains and live in a cabin? Just as fast as the thought came, Hope dismissed it. There was no way she could survive in a cabin in the woods. It was time to grow up. "Where am I going to go?"

Priska pursed her lips and was silent for a moment before answering. "I think you need to find a quiet little town to hide in. Get into a routine, keep your head down. You'll need to be emancipated, and until that happens . . ." She took a deep breath before continuing. "You'll need to go into the foster care system."

Priska outlined her side of the plan. While Hope hid in Eastern Washington, Priska would go to Turkey, where the original temple of Artemis stood. There, she could petition her mother for divine aid. Both of them knew the mortal police wouldn't find anything.

"But we don't need to do this. I can move with you and help keep you hidden until you're old enough to be on your own."

Hope pushed back the frustration caused by her aunt's words. Her decision was made. She needed answers. "No. I'm almost seventeen. I can handle being alone if it means finding out what happened."

Priska nodded. "You understand—"

"I get it, Priska." Hope could hardly breathe. "How soon can we start?"

"The day you shift back to human. I can take you into Children's Services first thing Tuesday."

Hope felt the last sliver of light in her life extinguish, and she bowed her head. "Let's file the paperwork, or whatever we need to get done. I want answers."

THE WARMTH IN the lobby was a stark contrast to the chill in the air outside. Hope stood alone in Mr. Davenport's carefully decorated lobby, her canvas sneakers almost buried in the plush carpet. A fireplace insert gave off little warmth, but the flames danced behind the glass, giving the room a cozy feeling. A loveseat and several chairs were settled at angles encouraging conversation. A marble-topped bar held pastries and muffins, as well as a carafe of coffee and another of orange juice.

Hope stared at red circles and brown squares while Priska and Mr. Davenport argued in his office. Glowering at the abstract art, Hope pretended she couldn't hear them, but every word leaked down the hall.

"But why does it have to be you? Isn't there someone else that can . . . hunt the information down?"

"Charlie." Priska paused. "You already know there is no one else."

"What will you do?" The tremor in his voice was so uncharacteristic of the stalwart attorney.

"I will call the agency today and see if we can find someone suitable to start next week." She ignored his question. "I just need to know if you want me to find a temp, or should I find someone permanent?"

"Themis and Eunomia," he cursed, referencing the goddesses of law. "How long will you be gone?"

"A month, maybe two or three, depending on what I find out in Ephesus." Another pause. "You'll be fine. Now, do you want a temp?"

A long exhale. "Yes. If you hire someone permanent, I'll just have to let them go when you get back. You are coming back, right?"

"Of course I am." Her laugh sounded forced.

Gods, this was so lame. While Priska hunted down Mom's killer, Hope would be *hiding*. Like a coward.

"So, will you get that filed today?" Priska asked.

"Are you sure? If you're not here and I file for emancipation, she'll have to go to foster care until it's done."

"We already talked about it. She knows."

"Why not wait, Priska? Why the rush?"

"Eventually, the news of the Sphinx will spread, then I won't be able to get anything without drawing suspicion my way."

Wait. He *knew*? Priska had told him . . . how much? Hope inched closer to the hall.

"Fine. I'll file today, but it will be close to a month before we can get a hearing. And we have to show that her father is really out of the picture."

"That won't be hard. He left before she was even born."

"She really doesn't have anyone?"

The pity in his voice made Hope's eyes fill, and she blinked away the tears.

"I hope you know what you're doing, Priska."

Hope heard the door handle turn, and she jumped back in front of the geometric canvases.

"All ready to go, Hope?" Priska raised her eyebrows.

Hope nodded.

"I'll be in touch, young lady. We'll need to go to court for the hearing. If your petition is granted, and I suspect it will be, you'll be free in the next month." He held out his hand, then wrapped hers in both of his. "Keep your chin up. It'll be okay."

How could he say that? He didn't know.

He had no idea.

HOPE GRIPPED HER jacket, pulling the thin material tight. It was the end of February, but in Western Washington it didn't matter the month. The cold rain started in September and continued through the end of June. But it wasn't the temperature, or the rain, that bothered her. The wind in North Bend was fierce, and as she hugged her clothes to her body, she wished for her winter coat.

She should've driven to school. She usually did, but she walked out the door of the Smiths' home that morning without her keys, and the constant yelling deterred her from going back in to get them. So she trudged her way back to the house in the cold, wet afternoon, dreading the noise and commotion that would assail her when she entered the door.

Out of habit, she stopped at the mailbox as she did every day since her hearing. They had appeared in court less than a week ago. Less than a week ago, a judge had declared her emancipated, and she was just waiting for the proof in writing. How long could it take to mail a piece of paper? Hope thought it would be a quick process. She'd been wrong.

And while Priska called every night, her time at the temple of Artemis had yet to expose who was behind Leto's death.

Hope pulled the tab down, put her hand into the metal box, and grabbed the stack of mail. After adjusting the strap of her backpack, she thumbed through the envelopes.

There! The crisp white paper had her name, Hope N. Treadwell, typed in the middle, the return address King County District Court. Hope wiped her thumb over her mother's maiden name. Priska had recommended using it. Just as a precaution. Unconsciously, Hope dropped the rest of the mail and tore open her envelope. She was so happy she could sing. There it was in black and white, no longer a ward of the state: she was free.

This would be better. Life would be better. At the very least, she wouldn't have to barricade herself in a bedroom when she shifted into the Sphinx. She'd hid in her room the last month during the change, yelling at anyone and everyone to leave her alone. She'd pushed every piece of furniture against the door to ensure that they did. The counselor explained her anger was part of the grief process. But it wasn't grief; it was fear. Fear that someone would discover she was a monster.

The morphing only lasted two days and one night. The night of a new moon, when Artemis's power was weakest, and Apollo's the strongest.

Now was the time to enact the rest of the plan. She would need to disappear, go into hiding, like she and her mom had done in the past. She needed a place in the middle of nowhere, somewhere the gods, demigods, and Skia would never visit. Somewhere even the humans would leave if they could. There were countless small towns in Eastern Washington. Certainly she could disappear in one.

She walked through the front door, and the crying from Jameson was coupled with Sammi's screaming for her doll. Hope ignored both, going straight to her room and locking the door.

She pulled up a list and skimmed through the names of towns on the eastern side of the state. Easton, Tullahoma. She scrolled down until . . . Goldendale. Goldendale. She liked the sound of that. A no-rain name. She tapped her phone a few more times and saw an abundance of homes for sale or rent. This could be perfect. Maybe today was her lucky day.

The listing agent bubbled her enthusiasm through the phone. "I'm so, so excited. This is the first home I've rented in years. I'm not sure why no one is moving to Goldendale. It is so, so quaint. I'm sure you will just love it."

"Do you live there?"

"What? Oh gods, no. I'm in Redmond, honey. You couldn't pay me to live in a small town. But I hear it is really lovely."

"How big is it?"

"Well, let me see." The clicking of a keyboard kept the silence at bay. "The nearest big city is Portland, but you could get almost anything you need in the Dalles, and that's just a thirty-minute drive. But they have their own school, and two grocery stores."

"Do they get many tourists?"

The agent's laugh was more derision than humor. "Um, no. With the exception of the observatory, there really isn't anything to do in Goldendale. Do you want me to look for something else?"

"No, this sounds perfect."

It took more time to settle into a small community, but maybe Hope would be able to stay longer without risking discovery by another immortal.

She called a moving company and arranged to have them pick up her things from storage in the morning and deliver them to the house on Main Street in Goldendale in the afternoon. After coordinating for an agent to meet them, Hope grabbed her bags from the closet, wrapped the statue of Hecate in soft cotton then packed the rest of her stuff. It only took a few minutes, and she looked around the room with relief.

"Hope Treadwell!" Mrs. Smith's abrasive voice was followed by a pounding on her door. "Get out here right this minute, young lady. I need some help."

This was the only reason Mrs. Smith had taken Hope in. At sixteen, she was perfect for babysitting. It also helped that the Smiths received a healthy stipend for fostering.

She opened the door and glanced down at the mousy woman. Hope waved the envelope at her and then stepped around Mrs. Smith into the hall.

"Oh." Mrs. Smith's shoulders slumped in defeat. She must have already gotten a call from Children's Services.

Hope wondered how long the woman had known and didn't tell. It didn't matter. Hope just needed to get out of there. Without a word, she brushed past the older woman, loaded her car, and drove away.

SEVEN

HOPE ENTERED GOLDENDALE High School, and the residual scent of pine disinfectant wafted through the abandoned halls. She'd intentionally arrived early, anxious to get things in order, eager to be settled.

As she walked into the front office, a bell chimed at her arrival. A well-nourished middle-aged woman glanced up from the computer, her flat brown eyes widening as she noted the new face. Hope glanced down at the nameplate on the desk: Ms. Slate. The silence became increasingly awkward.

"Hi." Hope's voice broke, and she cleared her throat. "I assume this is where I'm to register?"

Ms. Slate didn't even so much as say good morning but turned and began gathering papers.

Hope waited, noting the older woman's over-processed burgundy hair and clothes that were too tight to be called *fitted*.

Ms. Slate whipped back around and handed a packet of papers to Hope. "You'll need to fill that top one out now and wait while I get your classes together."

Hope took the proffered pen and began writing. She stuttered over the last name, crossing out an *N* before writing *Treadwell*.

Feeling the hairs on her neck prickle, Hope looked up to see the plump woman staring at her.

"Here's your schedule and your locker assignment," she said. "Class starts in fifteen minutes. You can bring the rest of the papers back to me at the end of the day." Ms. Slate grabbed the paper marked Registration, put it in a wire basket on the counter, and sat back in front of her computer.

"But you don't even have my name."

"Hope Treadwell." She didn't even look away from her screen as she spoke. "Your attorney called Friday and told us you'd be coming."

Hope nodded. "Of course. Thank you."

The woman continued her furious typing.

Nice and friendly here. With a shrug, Hope left to find her locker.

In the few minutes she'd been in the office, the hallways filled with students. It was no surprise to feel the shift of scrutiny turn on her. The real estate agent said she was the first person in years to move into the small town of Goldendale, and as an emancipated student, she was an anomaly. She tried to ignore the whispers, but with her supernatural hearing, the voices were undeniable.

"Yeah, I heard her parents are dead and she lives by herself."

"Doesn't she have any family?"

"I don't know."

"Maybe she doesn't want to live with them."

"But she can't live by herself, can she?"

"Maybe she's on the run." Coarse laughter.

From a group of cookie-cutter girls: "I don't understand why she would come to Goldendale?"

"Who would want to live here?"

"Look at her clothes. If she has money, why does she dress like that?"

"Well, I don't think Burberry is out with their line of school clothes, yet."

"Maybe she forgot her tiara at home," someone suggested. There was a round of giggles.

And the inevitable group of jocks, who thought they were the gods' gifts to women.

"That's what I'm talkin' about. A girl with her own place."

"Yeah, then your mom won't be walking in with Rice Krispy treats again."

"Shut up. She's smoking hot. I'll bet she's really lonely. I'd better, ya know, go cheer her up."

"Uh, no one is *that* lonely."

She'd heard it all before, and even worse. As she spun the dial on her locker, someone approached.

"Hey there, beautiful. Can I help you find your first class?"

She rolled her eyes before glancing at the chunk of testosterone standing next to her. She almost gagged on his cologne. "No, thanks. I'm sure in a town this small, the school can't be so big I'll get lost." She shoved her backpack into the locker then met the young man's bulging eyes. "Oh. And I don't like Rice Krispy treats."

She snapped her locker shut and turned away, leaving the young man with his mouth unhinged, his pack of friends howling with laughter.

She walked into her first class, mythology, and found an empty seat on the front row. After setting her bag on a desk, she went to have her paperwork signed by the instructor, Mrs. Biggers.

"Good morning. I'm Hope Treadwell." The practiced words were still stiff and uncomfortable, but Hope forced a smile, while waiting for acknowledgement from the drab, middle-aged woman.

Mrs. Biggers looked up. "Good morning."

As the teacher came around to the front of her desk, Hope noticed Mrs. Bigger's bright-red leather clogs, a stark contrast to her sedate appearance.

"I'm Nancy Biggers. I'm excited you'll be joining us. It's always refreshing to have a new perspective." Without waiting for a response, Mrs. Biggers continued, "Well, here's a copy of

Mythology and Men and the reading list for the remainder of the year."

Hope glanced down as she grasped the book. But Mrs. Biggers did not let go.

"What amazing eyes you have. Gold? Is that your natural—"

Taken off guard, there was a moment of hesitation before Hope cut her off. "Contacts."

Mrs. Biggers nodded and released the book.

Hope turned to go back to her desk. Her seat, however, was now occupied by a short girl with long, dark hair and dark eyes. Hope's bag and papers now sat on the desk to the left.

"Hi." The girl leaned forward. "I'm Krista. I hope you don't mind that I moved your stuff."

Hope nodded. "No problem."

"I'm nearsighted," Krista added.

Krista wasn't wearing glasses, but it wasn't worth pointing it out. Hope slid into her seat and focused her attention on Mrs. Biggers's lesson.

"All right class, let's get started. Today we'll be talking about Aphrodite. Does anyone know the myth behind Aphrodite's birth?"

There was laughter from the back.

Mrs. Biggers addressed the cause of the disturbance. "Boys. Something you would like to share? Do you find a lot of humor in mythology or just Aphrodite? Perhaps you would like to do an analysis on the comedy found in Aphrodite's interactions with men?" She left the last question hanging like she meant it.

"No ma'am. Er, no thank you. I'm sorry we disrupted." The dark-haired boy who'd offered to help Hope to class stammered out his apology.

Mrs. Biggers continued, "So you'll have the next four days to write a five-page paper on whether you believe Aphrodite to be a benevolent goddess or not, and you need to cite at least six interactions with mankind supporting your claim. Be sure to address the conflicting view. Remember, this assignment is meant to persuade."

Relief. There were lots of myths about Aphrodite, and this assignment was new to Hope. Now there would be something to consume her evenings. With a mental sigh, she opened up to the index to find the pages dedicated to the goddess of love and desire.

"Hey." Krista was leaning toward her, her whisper too loud for just the two of them. "It was Hope, right?"

She met the gawking girl's stare, nodded once, but said nothing.

"So, uh." The girl paused. "How do you like Goldendale?"

With a cursory glance, Hope noticed more than one interested face looking at her.

"Fine," she replied. With an arch of her eyebrows, she tried to convey her disapproval of the interruption.

But Krista was not easily put off. "I heard that your parents died and you actually *chose* to live here."

When Hope merely nodded in response, Krista continued pressing. "Why?"

At one time Hope might have been offended, but she'd experienced the barrage of curiosity that came with being a new face in a small community. She knew she was hot gossip.

Taking a deep breath, she voiced the practiced lie, "I like small towns. My mom and I moved a lot, and I've always preferred them. When my mom found out she was ill, she helped me pick out a place where I'd be safe. We have no other family, so she helped me do the paperwork to be emancipated. That's all. Look, Krista." She continued before the girl could come up with anything else. "I know you're just trying to be nice, but I'd really like to do my work now. Maybe we can talk later."

She made the suggestion merely as a courtesy. Over the last couple of years, and the many moves, she'd met too many girls like Krista and knew they weren't fishing for friends but gossip. And it wasn't as though Hope was looking for friends. Because, who would want to be friends with a monster?

"Oh, right. Sure," Krista replied, her lips pulling into a saccharine smile.

Hope tried to match the fake smile, but her eyes dropped. She picked up her book, flipped through the pages, and read in silence until the bell rang.

By lunch, she realized her story had already spread. She was glad the school was small and that people talked. Perhaps this time would be easier.

The bell rang, and, as the students herded toward the cafeteria, Hope made her way to the double doors of the library. As she stepped through, she saw at least two dozen computers, several desks tucked around the edges, and, off by a corner window, a wise librarian had placed a few overstuffed chairs.

She dropped her bag by the worn chairs and sank into the soft seat, her body sagging as tension released.

When the bell rang, her muscles stiffened as if anticipating an attack. Pushing down her anxiety, she trudged off to class. Both her diffidence and the gossip helped deter significant interaction with the students, and when the last bell rang, she allowed herself to feel the exhaustion from the day.

Despite her anxiousness to be gone from school, when Hope got into her car, she remembered her empty house, and her heart sank into her stomach. She was suddenly in no hurry to get home. She abruptly took a left turn into a small shopping plaza where a gas station, a mechanic garage, and a Red Apple grocery store were clustered together. She parked in front of the Red Apple.

The store was old; its white tile floor grayed with time, and the fluorescent lights cast unnaturally bright light through all the aisles, emphasizing the worn appearance of the store. But it was clean, she noted, as she walked past the prepackaged foods and headed to the meat counter.

The butcher was busy adding chicken to the display case but stopped when he saw Hope approach.

"Can I help you?" he greeted from behind the counter.

The man was lost somewhere in his fifties. He wore a long blue plastic apron tied around a plump midsection, and his hair—where he still had it—was gray, circling just around the back of his head from ear to ear.

"I would like sixteen ounces of filet mignon." She scanned the case, looking at the beef as a way to celebrate her independence.

The butcher's eyes widened.

"Excuse me," he said with suppressed laughter, "I don't often get requests for that kind of steak." He was smiling, and the smile changed his face, made it less commonplace. It was a smile of great buoyancy. "Let me see what I have in the back," he said, then he disappeared through the double doors behind him. He came back a few minutes later carrying two slabs of meat. "I have twelve ounces of top loin, or sixteen ounces of sirloin. Both are fresh today."

She didn't even think about it. "I'll take both."

He chuckled again and began to wrap the meat.

She looked around the store, reading the signs hanging from the ceiling. Baking supplies, soups, canned vegetables, cereal—

"You like riddles, young lady?"

Taken off guard, she turned to the butcher and nodded.

"Listen to this." He took a deep breath. "You throw away the outside and cook the inside. Then you eat the outside and throw away the inside. What did you eat?" He finished wrapping the second piece and handed her both packages.

She stood silent, staring at him while she contemplated the puzzle. It took only a minute before she broke into a smile and replied, "An ear of corn!"

"Hmm. I guess that could work." He nodded. "But I'm a butcher. You've got to think meat." He pointed at the packages in her hand. "My answer would be a chicken."

He was still smiling, and Hope felt a portion of her gloom lift.

He came around the counter, and as he peeled off a plastic glove, he said, "My name is Peter Stanley." He stuck out his hand. "I'm here during the week, seven to four. Let me know ahead of time, and I'll get you anything you need."

She took the outstretched hand and shook it. "I'm Hope. Thank you, Mr. Stanley, for the meat. And the riddle."

As she drove home, she found herself thinking of Mr. Stanley's riddle and smiled as she mumbled aloud to herself. "Chicken."

But her emotions cooled, and by the time she got home, the doubt and fear had effectively crept in. Stupid. Stupid mistake. She couldn't afford to stand out. She couldn't make friends. She couldn't get close. Not even to the butcher. It wasn't safe.

As Hope started putting away the groceries, she thought back on all the warnings from Priska and her mother over the years. Hope thought of their words, the same warnings that, had they heeded, had they stayed invisible, would've saved her mother's life.

Don't get close. Don't stand out. Don't make friends. Be invisible. Be safe.

She repeated them over and over as she set the food in the fridge, sealing her words with a promise as she closed the door. Isolation meant safety.

As she stacked the cans and boxes in the cabinets, the words played over on continual repeat. And then she sealed the words with a promise as she closed the doors to the cabinets. Secrets stayed hidden. Invisibility meant safety.

She could be lonely. Loneliness didn't kill anyone. She would be strong. She would push everyone away. And when Priska came back, she would find a way to get revenge.

Over and over, as she unpacked, she carved the words into the grooves of her brain, making them a mantra. With every item, she drove the nails into her coffin of isolation.

Because the most important thing was safety.

EIGHT

IT WAS LATE, and books covered the bed. Despite the effort to study, Hope jerked awake from the obnoxious ring tone. She pushed her chemistry homework aside and grabbed her phone.

"Hello?" Her voice was groggy with sleep.

"It's Priska."

Hope rolled onto her back and held the phone to her ear. Who else would it be? Priska had given her the new phone, and Priska's was the only number programmed in it. There was no one else who even had the number besides the school. "Yeah?"

"How's school?"

She snorted her response. "Fine. Suzy Sunshine is in three of my classes, and I think I'll try out for the cheer squad."

Priska's laugh was just a fraction off. Forced. And then she continued, "And did you get settled? Clothes and kitchen unpacked?"

"Yep. It's all good." But not really. Just hearing Priska's voice was causing waves in the pool of Hope's emotions. "How are you? How's Turkey?"

"Unproductive. The priestesses were a nightmare. I finally got through today, but so far no one on Olympus is talking about your mom, or her death. Artemis said she'd keep her ears open, but it sounds like Skia." There was a long sigh. "I'm going to leave tomorrow."

Hope sat up. "Are you coming home?"

"Not yet. I'm going to try and get into a conservatory. I want to see if there is any chatter among the demigods. Sometimes they know even more than their parents."

"A conservatory?" The conservatories were safe from Skia and provided free housing for the offspring of the gods. These homes were also exclusively for demigods, some even requiring the immortal parent to vouch for their children before they would allow entrance. "How much longer will you be?"

The more she listened to Priksa, the more Hope wanted her to come home. But that would mean that they wouldn't know what happened to her mom. And that wasn't acceptable.

Hope let out a slow breath while giving herself a mental pep talk. She wanted this.

"I don't know. A month, maybe two? It depends on how long it takes to get in. This is the only other thing I can think of." Priska paused. "I'll call you every night until I get in."

"And then? What happens when you get in?"

"Not sure. I'll play it by ear. But with all the subterfuge, I may not be able to call."

Hope was silent. The phone calls weren't nearly enough, but she clung to them, her only contact with someone who loved her.

"I promise I'll text you every night, Hope. I'm sorry. I know this isn't easy for you."

But this is what she wanted. "Will you be safe?"

"It's part of why I'm going where I'm going. There's an Athenian shrine close by, and I hope the conservatory has at least one of her daughters. They tend to be resourceful women, not impetuous. I'll be fine. Remember, lie low."

Hope knew. "Okay."

"I'm sorry. I wish there was another way."

Hope nodded at the phone. Her chest squeezed, and the dam was threatening to burst.

"And Hope?"

"Yes?" she hiccupped.

"Stay put until I get back. No friends. Don't stand out. And keep the immortal daggers close by. If you can get away with carrying one, it would probably be wise to have one on you all the time."

The daggers? She swallowed hard. They were two mismatched knives that her grandmother purportedly stole from demigods she'd fought hundreds of years ago. One was about six inches long with a blood-red ruby in its hilt, the other a couple inches longer, bright gold with inscriptions of the sun. They'd probably been packed in one of the boxes of her mother's things. Hope would need to dig them out. But she couldn't do one more thing today. She'd look for them in the morning before school.

"Be careful." Something about the plan made Hope uneasy.

"Don't worry. I'll be fine," Priska said.

But even after they hung up, Hope lay awake. What would she do if something happened to Priska?

THE DAYS AT school bled one into one another. Mrs. Biggers lectured on symbolism used by the gods. In chemistry, they learned about ionic charge. At lunch, she sat in the library. In Spanish, she memorized irregular verbs. When the school bell released her, she went home. Her only relief came in the runs she started taking. With every step, she told herself she was doing what was necessary. That she wasn't running away from anything but racing toward a finish that would bring her answers.

But the words were hollow wishes that disappeared with the sweat from her run. Nevertheless, Hope began to settle into her life in Goldendale.

Gradually, interest in the new girl waned. A few more courageous boys tried to *befriend* her, but curt replies put them off. Most girls, either intimidated or offended, didn't reach out at all.

Overall, she should have been happy with her success. But as the days passed, a cold weight settled in her chest. She was hollow, empty, and very, very alone.

She held out a sliver of hope that Priska would come back soon, because the last thing Hope wanted was to be on her own. But deep down, she wasn't fooling herself. She *was* on her own.

Some people counted sheep to help fall asleep. Others drank warm milk with honey. As Hope lay in bed night after night fighting the sleep that would force her to relive her losses in dreams, she constructed a brick wall. Carefully, she placed brick after brick on wet gray mortar, building an impenetrable fortress around her heart.

SHE'D SPENT A restless night at a hotel in Toppenish and climbed out of bed an hour before dawn. It would be her first flight without her mom, and she hoped the time outside would be liberating. She drove till she found an abandoned barn far outside the small town, a perfect hiding spot for her car.

The sky was hovering between black and gray when she began to undress. As the first rays pierced the sky, her body tingled, and a surge of energy pulsed through her. The morphing took only seconds, and then soft, golden fur covered her breasts, torso, and haunches. The amber feathers of her wings stretched out several feet, and she pulled them close to her body while pulling her long blond hair up into a messy knot. Grabbing her messenger bag, she made her way out of the barn.

She pulled herself into the air, climbing high enough that anyone looking from the ground would be perplexed by the large bird but not be able to distinguish its features. She would be up in the peaks before the sun rose, high enough to be safe.

She spent the day reading, allowing the words of a well-written fantasy novel to distract from her own bleak reality. If she crammed her quiet moments with something, anything, she wouldn't feel the pain.

Not nearly soon enough, the stars lit up the night sky with only a sliver of the new moon.

"Finally!" She exhaled and released her wings, allowing the wind to tickle and tease at her feathers before she beat them up and down. Once airborne, she left the seclusion of the mountains and swept into the valley below.

A sense of freedom played in her heart, and she felt a stirring of hope. She danced in the air and looked to her side, where her mom should be. Unbidden memories overwhelmed her. Their flights together. Her rich laugh. Golden eyes. Her constant worry for Hope. Her love.

It wasn't fair. Gods, it was so unfair!

Tears blurred her vision, and she tumbled from the sky. Branches scratched and clawed as her paws flailed to the ground. She slipped on something hard and round, and, with a thump, she slid into the trunk of a squat apple tree.

Physically bruised and emotionally broken, she roared her frustration and yanked up the offending tree as if pulling up a weed. The cool air was sticky sweet. Angry with the apples on the ground, the trees that scratched her skin, and incensed with the injustice of her life, Hope's pent-up emotion exploded. Screaming and out of control, she marched down row after row of the orchard, wrenching trees up by their trunks, leaving a wake of destruction behind.

As the sky lightened, she was pulled from her rage. She surveyed her surroundings and the ruin she'd caused. Guilt and shame filled her. Unsure of what to do, she took off for the protection of the mountaintops. It would be sundown before her body would change back to human form, hours before she could do anything.

Icy patches of snow still stuck to the moss-covered ground, and rays from the morning light reflected diamonds. The evergreens swayed in the wind, and Hope lay on the ground shivering, her breath like steam from a teapot. The fur that covered her body shielded her from the biting air, but nothing protected her heart, and she sobbed.

Hours later, when the catharsis of tears was over, her mind cleared. She could get through this. She would get back into a routine, just like Priska said. And Hope would run. She wouldn't go flying again; not until she was sure she could control herself, control her emotions. She would still change, there was no way around that, but she would stay in the solitude of her house. No more destruction. No more risks.

The brightness of the sky faded from azure into pinks and lavender on its way to indigo. She stood, and with two powerful beats of her crimson-tipped wings, she lifted into the air.

Remorse pushed her to fly past the farmhouse adjacent to the orchard she'd uprooted. She'd send money. A lot of it. How many years would it take to grow an orchard that size? She shook her head. In the back of her mind, she could hear her mom's voice cautioning against flying low. Hope considered the risk that someone might see her but quickly dismissed it. No human could see this high.

She landed outside the dilapidated building and slipped inside just before the sun dipped below the horizon. She stood up on her haunches, stretching toward the sky, her wings spread wide. As the sun disappeared, she pulled her wings in. They collapsed, folding into her back, and instantly she could feel the pressure of their containment. Cramping in her lower extremities was followed by a searing pain, as the muscles of her haunches extended into human legs. The fur sloughed from her body, dropping like a discarded blanket. Hope thoughtfully brushed her hand over her skin and then dressed.

"**You did what?**" Priska huffed. "*Skata*, how could you be so careless?"

Sitting on her bed, Hope spilled her guilt out over the phone. "It just happened. I . . . I don't even know what started it . . . But I want to make it right. Can I send money? I got the address."

"Call Charlie in the morning. He'll tell you what needs to happen. You'll probably need to sign some paperwork, but he can take care of it." She sighed. "How are you holding up? Besides, the whole—"

Hope wanted to cry. There was a constant ache of loneliness that threatened to swallow her whole. She cleared the emotion from her throat so she could respond. "Fine."

"Obviously not, or you wouldn't have torn up an orchard." Priska laughed. "An apple orchard—that's a new one."

"I'm glad you find it amusing." Hope bit her tongue. Too late.

"Don't get all twitted out. It's not the end of the world. Have Charlie send some coins from your grandmother's treasure chest, and the owner won't ever have to work again."

Hope's grandmother, the first Sphinx, had worked for a pharaoh in ancient Egypt. Her payment in coin and jewels had increased in value over the centuries, not to mention her income as a physician for hundreds of years.

At least they had something to talk about. So many of their calls were just a short check in. Hope missed her aunt. Fiercely.

"Did you locate the conservatory? Have you found any demigods?" What Hope really wanted to ask was how soon Priska was coming home.

"Yes, actually. I'm hoping they'll invite me in soon. Gods, I can't wait to be done."

"But . . ." More than just the ache of loneliness hit Hope with her aunt's words. Was she a burden? "You want to know, too, right?"

"You know I do. That's why we're doing this. I'll call you tomorrow. Stay safe."

"You, too." Hope tapped the End button and then dropped her phone on the down comforter. If Priska turned up nothing in the conservatory, then what?

NINE

MR. BURGESS'S TEDIOUS baritone was droning on about the applicability of balancing chemical equations, and Hope was struggling to stay awake. It wasn't just that she was tired. She was exhausted, like she'd run a marathon instead of her usual three-mile loop. To top it off, it felt as if someone had thrown sand in her eyes. She shouldn't have gone running so late last night, but it was beautiful and cool, and she hadn't been sleeping anyway. She was paying for it now.

In addition to the fatigue, the ever-present pressure in her back throbbed. It was always worse a few days before and after changing, but the ache of sore muscles, like she'd worked out too hard, was always present.

Fighting sleep, she sat up straight and let her focus drift to the conversation behind her.

"Where did he move from?"

Krista. Hope inwardly groaned. She was about to pull her focus back to Mr. Burgess but caught the response.

"Seattle area. His mom died last week in a car accident, I think," Angela whispered, but the excitement in her voice was palpable.

Hope focused in earnest. The pain of losing her mother was suddenly raw and fresh. An ache swelled for this new student and his loss.

"Oh, that's awful." Krista actually sounded sincere. "What about his dad?"

Hope gritted her teeth; she doubted Krista could even be sincere.

"I guess he's not around. Mrs. Stephens is his great aunt. Or something like that."

"Mrs. Stephens?" Krista moved abruptly and dropped her pencil. There was a moment of silence from the two girls. "I don't know which is worse, losing your mom, or having to live with that kind of crazy."

On this point, Krista was probably right. Mrs. Stephens was definitely not all there. Hope had seen the older woman once at the grocery store and watched in pity as she chanted a rhyme about animals seeking night and battling fear. All while staring at the meat case. It didn't seem to bother Mr. Stanley, but the woman was cracked.

"I've never seen him here before, you know, visiting or whatever. I'm sure we would have noticed him."

"No. His mom wasn't close to Mrs. Stephens. It's some weird relationship, like his dad's mother's sister's daughter, or something like that."

That would be his second cousin. Hope rolled her eyes. She remembered that Angela's mother was the school counselor. In listening to how much Angela knew about the newcomer, Hope was grateful she'd declined the school's services. She again felt a pang of sympathy for the boy.

"Athan Michael."

"Ethan?"

"No, Athan, with an *A*," Angela explained. "It's Greek. My mom said—"

"Have you seen him yet?" Krista interrupted.

"No. He just got here yesterday. I guess it will be a couple of days before he—"

Krista cut Angela off with a sharp intake of breath. "He's crazy hot!"

Angela giggled, and Hope lost interest. They rarely said anything of value, and if they did, they didn't mean to. Now, she really did feel sorry for the new boy. Not that she would do anything about it. She just couldn't get involved.

The bell rang, and Hope stood and collected her books. The other students, gathered in groups, ignored her as she walked to her locker. She pulled out her books for math and Spanish and then turned toward the library. That's when he caught her eye.

The only reason she could see him was because of his height. His skin was tanned, with olive undertones, and his tawny hair disheveled in a way that told of too much time in front of the mirror, or no time at all. His features were intense, but his body language said he couldn't have cared less. A large group surrounded him, and rich laughter drifted from that side of the hall.

She stood, momentarily transfixed. He was undoubtedly the most beautiful person she'd ever seen.

He must have felt the weight of her gaze. His jade eyes met her gold ones, drifted over her body, and then came back to her face.

She couldn't help the heat that rushed to her cheeks, but she couldn't look away.

He winked.

She was so startled she actually jumped. Flushing heat blossomed up her neck to her face, and she averted her gaze. Without another thought, she walked as fast as she could, but when she got to the end of the hall, she realized she'd gone the wrong way. With a huff of disgust, she doubled back to the library.

She settled into her favorite corner, her mind spinning. *How could someone be so . . .* She couldn't even think of a word to describe it. He winked at her! He was flirting right after . . . right after his mother died? Shouldn't he be mourning or something? What a *loser*. It was the only word she could come up with. All sympathy for the boy disappeared. She was angry and felt somehow betrayed.

The bell rang, and she grabbed her books and headed off to algebra II. She was usually the first to enter the classroom, so she was surprised to see a small group of students in the back corner talking. She sat down, ignoring the noise, and pulled out her homework.

"So, are you a math prodigy or an all-around nerd?" The voice was soft and deep, his speech highly inflected and full of liquid consonants. English was definitely not his first language.

She glanced up from her paper and followed the hand on her desk up to the face of Athan Michael.

"Uh, excuse me?" She stumbled over the words, her heart skipping and tripping in her chest.

"I was wondering. You have your homework out, and it's done." He pointed at her paper. "Are you always on top of things, or is this your favorite subject?" Intensity flashed in his green eyes, and a slow half-smile pulled at his lips. When she said nothing, he raised his brows expectantly.

"I'm not even sure how to answer that." As soon as the words left her lips she wished she could take them back. It wasn't that she couldn't answer, she internally berated herself, but was he being serious, or was he teasing? And if he was teasing her, to what avail?

"I might need a tutor. Are you game?" He smiled, a full smile all the way to his eyes, and it was as if he was bestowing a grace upon her.

She could see what Krista was talking about earlier. He *was* good-looking, and he knew it. Hope's opinion dropped off a cliff, but her heart hadn't seemed to have gotten the message. It picked up until it was in a race to beat out of her chest. Irritation over her own physical betrayal made her steel herself. She was a rational creature. Not a ball of hormones.

She narrowed her gaze. "It's Athan, right?"

Still smiling, he nodded.

He must think he was reeling her in. Her gaze hardened. "Listen, I don't think you'll have any problem finding a tutor, but I don't think we'd get along."

It was like pulling magnets apart, but she turned back to her homework. Even so, the tension made it impossible to focus, the letters and numbers swimming all over the paper as she waited.

There was no immediate response, but he didn't go away either. After what seemed like an eternity, she glanced up.

He laughed softly. "I think I understand what you're saying."

Moments later, she heard him in the back of the room, relating the story, greatly exaggerated to his own disparagement. She didn't trust herself to turn around.

As soon as the bell rang, she bolted.

She was halfway down the hall when she heard someone call her name. Reflexively, she stopped and looked back. Athan walked toward her, his gaze trained on her.

This was not happening. She turned away repeating her mantra to herself. Invisible. Isolation. Safety.

Safety.

That was all that mattered. How attractive the new boy was irrelevant. Hope needed to stay safe.

"Hope." He caught up with her. With his long stride, he easily kept her pace. "Hey, I wanted to apologize about earlier."

She stopped walking and regarded him. Why was he being so persistent? Couldn't he take a hint?

"I didn't mean to offend you." He rushed through his words, making his lilting accent more pronounced. "I was just hoping—"

"Look"—she held her hand out to stop him—"I'm not trying to be rude, but could you just leave me alone?" Her face pinched, a furrow lining her forehead. He couldn't know how hard it was to be lonely. But it didn't matter. Just like every other person at school, he was a threat to her safety. She needed him to leave her alone.

He took a step back but said nothing.

"I'm not sure what you've heard," she continued, "so let me help you out. I'm not interested." Her emotions ballooned as she spoke. "I'm not looking for friends. I don't want a boyfriend. I don't tutor. I don't need to be tutored." She wanted to hit him, and she stuffed down the flare of anger. "Leave me alone. Got it?"

His eyebrows drew together in a scowl, but then, almost imperceptibly fast, he quickly rearranged his features into something more amiable.

"*Ouai.* You're very . . . direct. I'm sorry to have bothered you." With that, he walked back to a group of boys.

She stood and watched. She saw him shrug when Lee asked what happened. With a shake of her head, she went to collect her homework. If Athan left her alone, it would be fine.

Over the weeks, Hope had made one exception to her rule of isolation. She rationalized that it was a casual acquaintance that would never lead to anything. She was just one of many that shopped at the Red Apple, a nobody that wouldn't be remembered. So when she was feeling out of sorts, she would stop by the Red Apple. If Mr. Stanley just happened to be there, they would share a riddle. Somehow, it made her feel a little less alone.

So it was no surprise that as she drove down Roosevelt, her car, almost on its own, pulled into the parking lot of the grocery store. She went to the back and saw the butcher helping a young mother at the counter. He winked when he saw Hope, and she tried to return the sentiment, but it was halfhearted, at best. While she waited, she leaned against the meat case and tried to clear her head. But the interaction with Athan gnawed at her. She was grateful when Mr. Stanley's voice interrupted her thoughts.

"Have you found a good riddle for me?" His deep voice was warm and friendly.

"Actually, Mr. Stanley, I was hoping that you would have one." The furrow that remained on her brow spoke of her troubled spirits.

As if he could sense her mood, he nodded, and his features pinched in concentration.

"In a marble hall as white as milk, lined with skin as soft as silk, within a fountain crystal clear, a golden apple doth appear. No doors there are to this stronghold, yet thieves break in to steal its gold." Mr. Stanley finished the riddle and regarded her expectantly.

Most of his riddles were food related, usually livestock. She leaned back against the display case and thought of a farm.

Mr. Stanley said nothing as he went back to cleaning up the scale and counter.

"It's an egg, isn't it?" she asked.

Mr. Stanley chuckled and nodded.

"You really should branch out, Mr. Stanley." She smiled, her spirits lifted enough that she would make it through another day. An old riddle she memorized years ago came back just then. "I do have one for you . . . nonfood."

"All right." He stopped cleaning and stood waiting, rag in hand.

"I can be cracked; I can be made. I can be told; I can be played. What am I?" Her breath came out in a brief laugh. The first in several days. "Remember, it's not food. Speaking of which, can I get something good?"

She waited while Mr. Stanley wrapped a flank steak for her.

"Cats and bats, and lots of boys." A singsong chant from an older woman interrupted the momentary silence.

Hope turned and took a step back.

The incongruous form of Mrs. Stephens approached. Her white hair was pulled up into a high bun, little wisps framing her unlined face. Her small body was lithe and graceful, and she moved with the energy of youth. She stepped into Hope's personal space and narrowed her eyes.

"Pussycat, pussycat, where have you been?" Her gaze shifted but never left Hope's.

Hope was speechless.

"Did you hear me, little one?"

Hope could only nod. What could you say to complete nonsense?

"Here you are, Hope." Mr. Stanley held out the white package. "Enjoy your dinner."

With relief, she turned her attention. "Thank you."

She took the small package from him and forced herself to walk away.

As she maneuvered past carts and produce, she could hear Mr. Stanley chatting with the batty old lady. "Mrs. Stephens. Always a pleasure to see you out and about. What can I get for you today?"

How could he talk to her like she was normal? Something about the older woman gave Hope the shudders. She tried to dismiss the odd encounter, but a shiver ran down her spine as she climbed into her car.

TEN

SHE BOUNDED UP the steps to her house, taking two at a time, and noticed a piece of paper tucked into the door. She pulled the scrap from the jamb and read the scrawl: *A joke.* Mr. Stanley must have stopped by on his way into work and left her the answer to her riddle. She wondered if he'd figured it out or if he'd caved and looked it up online.

After unlocking the door, she walked into her small home, reveling in its coziness. Her living area was open—the kitchen, dining area, and living room all connected. A matching couch and loveseat filled the living room, and a TV hung from the opposite wall above the mantle where the statue of Hecate sat. Down a short hall were two bedrooms, and a cramped bathroom squeezed between them. A study sat off the living room. It was everything she needed, and therefore perfect.

Her smile didn't last. After her shower and breakfast, Hope noticed a flashing light on her phone indicating a message. Anxiety gripped her, and she hoped her aunt would have answers.

I'm in. Text only from now on. Wish me luck.

Not answers, but almost as good. Hope's heart pounded, and she tapped out her perfunctory response to Priska.

Good Luck!

Hope took a deep breath in an attempt to release her anxiety. After all, this was what they wanted. With any luck, Priska would find answers soon, and she'd come home.

"**WHO CAN TELL** me about Skia?" Ms. Biggers smiled at the class as if she were discussing divine ambrosia.

Hope had heard of teachers being passionate about their subjects, but this one took it to a whole new level. That being said, Ms. Biggers did seem exceptionally knowledgeable. Hope sat up and flipped her notebook to a clean page.

"Uh, they're mythical," Tristan muttered under his breath.

Ms. Biggers sighed and rolled her eyes. "Anyone else?"

A cute girl with auburn hair raised her hand. Was her name Richelle or Michelle?

"Chelli?"

"They're from the Underworld. Hades created them."

"Very good. Hades, god of the Underworld, created Skia in response to the gods' bastard children. It was a move for balance, a way to keep the demigod population in check."

Balance?

Ms. Biggers continued her lecture. "Just as death is an inevitable part of life for humans, Skia ensure that death will be a part of the demigods' lives. Death isn't evil. It just is."

Hope's hand went up.

"Yes." There was a pause, and then Ms. Biggers waved in Hope's direction. "You have a question?"

Hope blushed. "Uh, yeah. Do Skia kill other things?"

There was a giggle from behind her.

"Other things?" Ms. Biggers frowned. "Like animals or humans? No."

"No, I meant, do they kill monsters?"

Several more chuckles.

"Ah." The frown turned into something that communicated pride. "No, class. This is a very good question."

The room quieted.

Hope scooted forward on her seat.

"Of course, the answer's hypothetical, as monsters are probably extinct. But theoretically, the answer would be no. Skia hunt demigods, the ones that are left, at least. It is believed, with the disappearance of the gods, that the demigods will disappear one day, too. Then the earth will be inhabited entirely by humans." Her gaze grew distant.

"Too bad we can't get some elves to join us from Middle Earth," Krista said under her breath with a heavy dose of snark.

"Or angel-children." Angela sighed.

"Ah, Angela. You're mixing your mythology. Nephilim is the term you're looking for, and they're children of gods and humans, a different way of saying demigods." Ms. Biggers chuckled. "Now, your assignment. Analyze the myths surrounding the death of a demigod. Find one that could be the result of Skia and write a supporting supposition. The point here again is to persuade the reader to your point of view. You can work alone or in pairs. It's due tomorrow. You have the rest of class to work on it."

Could Priska be wrong about Skia? And if it wasn't Skia that killed Mom . . . Had a demigod found them in Bellevue?

Guilt sat heavy in Hope's stomach. If she'd said something to her mom sooner . . . Her own selfishness in wanting to have a normal life had led to this. If they'd only moved . . . they would've been safe. Her mom would still be alive.

A FEW MINUTES before nine, Hope finished her paper. She tilted her head side to side, cracking her neck. By the gods, she was tight. Her muscles were stiff from sitting for so long.

Orpheus was a depressing subject to write about, and while the myth surrounding his journey to and from the Underworld to claim his wife was well known, the story of his death was not.

It was not unreasonable to believe that Hades would look at Orpheus's actions as selfish. When Orpheus appeared in the Underworld and begged to take his wife back to the mortal realm, it was because he loved her too much to live without her. But then he refused Hades's offer to remain in the Underworld with Eurydice which would have kept Orpheus united with his love. Even after the refusal of the offer, Hades still gave Orpheus a chance to get his wife back. But Orpheus was impatient and broke the terms of the contract, thus losing his wife to death. After all this, it was more believable that a "reaper," or Skia, killed the demigod than a bunch of women tore him limb from limb because he wouldn't sleep with them. Not if he truly loved his wife.

She shook her head. A run would help clear the thoughts buzzing inside. She quickly changed and went out into the night.

The crisp air tickled her bare skin. After the first mile, her mind cleared and she was no longer cold. By the second mile, she was lost in the rhythm of her run. As Hope jogged down Main toward Columbus, she noticed another runner. Someone coming toward her.

As soon as she recognized him, she debated turning around. But the idea of Athan being behind her was even less appealing. Stuffing down her apprehension, she fixed a smile in preparation to acknowledge him.

She could tell the second he recognized her. His pace slowed, and his face, previously set in the concentration of running, shifted.

"Hey." She tipped her head toward him.

He nodded and ran on.

She could hear the sound of his retreating steps, and then she turned right on Columbus, and all evidence of him disappeared. If she ran into him again, she'd have to find another route.

As she turned left on Broadway, her thoughts drifted to her assignment and then to the alleged love that drove Orpheus to the Underworld. Love really made people do stupid things. If what happened with her mom and dad was any indication, love was just trouble.

As her mom told it, Leto had made a mistake. She didn't tell her husband about the curse until after they were married. It wasn't just that she turned into a Sphinx at the new moon. No, if she ever had a "complete family," i.e., a husband and child with anyone other than Apollo or his offspring, she would die. While Leto told Hope over and over that love needed to be built on trust, actions spoke louder than her words. When Leto told Hope's dad about the curse, he fled.

Just like Paul and Sarra.

That hurt.

Hope was finishing the loop around Goldendale when she saw Athan again.

She hadn't been friendly with him, even bordering on offensive at times, but she did *not* feel bad about it. It was exactly what was necessary. So, regardless of what his life had been like, regardless of the fact he'd lost his mom, too, she did not feel bad.

Almost as though she'd called his name aloud, Athan jogged toward her, his green eyes fixed on her.

"Hey, Hope," he called as he approached.

Her stomach did a little flip, but she only slightly slowed her pace. It didn't matter that he was good looking. He needed to go away. "I'm not finished with my run. Do you mind?"

To her surprise, he started to jog next to her. "How about if I finish with you?"

Flustered, she opened her mouth to tell him no, but instead she said, "Okay."

Where did that come from? And why did she sound like she was asking a question? She just wouldn't talk to him, and maybe he'd leave her alone.

He said nothing, and their steady footfalls pounded a rhythm. *Thump-thump, thump-thump.*

The oddest sense of security trickled over her, the sensation faintly familiar and not at all unwelcome. How odd . . .

"Do you run at night a lot, Hope?"

The security evaporated, replaced with a desire to shut a door in his face. Sadly, there wasn't a door anywhere nearby. The sooner she got home the sooner she could get rid of him.

"Not usually." She dared a glance from the corner of her eyes. Why was he so good-looking and such an idiot? "Maybe once or twice a week."

He stumbled then surprised Hope with his rejoinder. "Do you think that's safe?"

There was no sense in telling him what was safe, or not, in her life.

"Thanks for the concern. I'll be just fine." She was relieved to see her house on the left, and she slowed her pace. "Here's my stop. I hope the rest of your night is"—she really didn't care how his night was, and she finished lamely—"nice."

She was up on the porch, bending down to get her key, when she realized he'd followed her up the steps. He leaned against the door, effectively blocking her. His gaze intensely pinned her in place.

Uncomfortable with his gaze and his presence, she demanded, "What?"

"Why don't you run during daylight hours?"

She made no move to unlock the door, he was in the way, but flipped the key over and over in her hands, trying to send the message that she needed him to move. She wanted to yell at him to leave, and yet part of her wondered at his interest. "I usually *do*. I just needed to clear my head." She frowned. "I appreciate your concern, but really, we're in Goldendale. I stay on main streets, I'm a black belt in Tae Kwon Do, and I'm stronger than I appear. I really think my safety shouldn't keep you up tonight."

She waited for him to back off the porch. But he didn't.

She huffed, her patience running thin. Why wasn't he leaving? "If you don't mind, I really need to get inside and get ready for bed. It's late. At the risk of sounding parental, you should do the same."

He shifted his weight. "Okay. Just, if you want a running partner, you could always give me a call."

That's what this was about? Ugh. *Never*.

"I'll keep that in mind," she bit out with sharp sarcasm.

The playfulness disappeared. He leaned forward, his gaze steady, intense. "Think about it. I'd like for us to be friends."

He bounded down the steps and was halfway up the block before she could process what he'd said.

Friends?

Over the next few days, she kept wary watch over the stupid mortal boy. It was exhausting. He interacted with everyone. Everyone got a smile, a joke, a touch, a laugh.

He obviously wanted to be friends with *everyone*.

But there was a practiced intensity that made it feel . . . false.

Like watching a movie.

Her worry about being singled out faded then disappeared.

How are things *going? Any news?* Hope typed out the text and waited, as she did each night before bed.

Nothing concrete. More demigods here than expected. Several from Athena, but others, too.

Who else? What did that mean?

Him, among others. Not sure that it means anything, except there are more demigods than I thought.

More demigods? And some from Apollo . . . *Should I be worried?*

No. Just be careful.

I am. Careful. Safety. The familiar mantra pounded with her heartbeat.

I'll check in with you tomorrow.

K. Bye.

Hope set her phone down with a sigh. Years ago, Priska had told her that each god only had one demigod child. Clearly that wasn't the case. What else didn't she know?

Sleep claimed Hope for a few hours, and she was buried in a cocoon of warmth. A buzz from her phone nagged at her senses, and she grabbed the offending device.

One new message at 2:14 a.m.

Hope swiped across the screen and opened the message.

Got it. Unbelievable. Call u in the am.

She sat up, all vestiges of sleep gone. She wanted to call. Her fingers itched to dial Priska's number. But Priska would have called if she could.

Call ASAP. I'm up.

It would have to do.

A minute later, Hope checked her phone to make sure the text went through. Five minutes later, she checked to make sure she didn't miss a response. And again, five minutes after that. And again, and again, and again. But nothing.

Sleep pulled, and Hope fought it, clutching her phone like a lifeline.

When the phone beeped, her alarm going off, Hope wanted to scream. Priska should have called by now. Why hadn't she called by now?

She spent the day on her bed, her phone in her hand, her stomach in knots.

It didn't matter if she missed school. It didn't matter if she didn't eat, or take a shower. It didn't matter. Because nothing was going to make her miss this call.

But it never came.

ELEVEN

THE INTERCOM BUZZED. "Ms. Biggers?"

Hope flinched. The cumulative lack of sleep and panic had settled into hopelessness and dread. Perhaps it was paranoia, but something in her gut told her this was for—

"Please send Hope Treadwell to the office."

She could feel the weight of twenty-two pairs of eyes on her back, and she flushed.

She'd gotten back to Goldendale last night, but without any reassurance about Priska, Hope's anxiety remained high, and she'd hardly slept the last six nights. She reached over and grabbed her backpack.

"Go ahead, Hope. Get your things together," said Ms. Biggers, waving her hands. "You can get the assignment from Krista later."

Hope stopped her hand midair. *Right.* She glanced at Krista just in time to see her turn away with a sneer. At least the feeling was mutual.

Hope stepped out into the hall and trudged to the office.

"Go ahead and sit there, Miss Treadwell." Ms. Slate indicated a row of hard plastic chairs. "Mr. Jeffers will be with you shortly."

Shortly. Was that code for time to stress you out more?

Hope tapped her foot; the anxiety demanded some form of release. The trip last week to Seattle had been completely unfruitful. After waiting three days at Priska's apartment, she went to see Mr. Davenport. Priska had been in contact with him the entire time she'd been gone, too. But all communication from her had stopped for both of them. Her last text to Mr. Davenport was about a minute after the one Hope got, promising to call in the morning with travel arrangements. Then, nothing.

Mr. Davenport had tried to locate her through tracking her phone, but the last known location of her phone was Atlanta. He'd filed a missing persons report with the police. He'd even hired a private investigator to look for her.

On the sixth day, Mr. Davenport pushed Hope to go back to school and promised to continue to marshal all his *resources* to locate Priska.

"She didn't believe it was safe for you on this side of the mountains, Hope. Too many demigods here. Go back and hide where you're safe. I'll let you know the minute I find out anything," he said.

So she'd come back to Goldendale. And back to school.

"Mr. Jeffers will see you now." Ms. Slate interrupted her reverie.

Hope shook off the memories and stood. Opening the door, she walked into a plain, functional office. A metal desk sat in the middle of the room. Wire baskets filled with papers sat on either side of the computer screen in the center of the desk. The overhead lighting was off, but sunlight lit the room. The shades were adjusted so a beam streamed right into the chair opposite Mr. Jeffers's desk.

"Ah, Miss Treadwell." Mr. Jeffers wheeled out from behind his desk in a sleek wheelchair. "Thank you for coming in." He extended his hand. His fair skin contrasted with his curly brown hair, just starting to gray at the temples. He wore a short-sleeved polo, and she could see the cording of muscles in his forearms.

Hope shook his calloused hand. "Of course, sir."

"Pull up a chair." He pointed at the hot seat then wheeled around behind his desk. "You seem to have disappeared for a few days." He glanced down at something on his desk then back at her. "Four, to be exact."

She nodded.

"Would you like to elucidate?"

"My aunt . . . disappeared, and I was . . . worried. I went to see if I could find her."

Mr. Jeffers nodded. "And did you?"

She shook her head.

"Hmm. Are you close to your aunt?"

"Yes, sir."

"But you don't live with her?"

"No, sir. She lives in Seattle." Dang! The seat was uncomfortable as well as warm. Hope shifted, trying to pull out of the light.

"And she's not your guardian, correct?"

"That's correct. She travels, and we thought—" What was he getting at?

"So the responsibility for your education falls on . . ." His head dipped at her meaningfully.

"Me?"

"And here we come to the crux of it, Miss Treadwell. You've been at our school for a little over a month, and you've had six absences. All . . . unexcused." He tapped the paper in front of him. "Are you unwell?"

She swallowed. "No, sir."

"You'll not find me unreasonable." He sat back and spread his arms wide. "But, I don't write the laws, Miss Treadwell. At ten absences, I have to report you to the truancy board. I imagine at that point your emancipation may come under scrutiny." He sighed and wheeled out from behind his desk. "You're skating on thin ice. I would hate for you to get in over your head."

Too late.

"If you need to talk with someone, I can arrange for you to meet with Mrs. Rossi, our school counselor."

Mrs. Rossi, aka Angela's mom. "No, thank you."

"Then I suggest you get caught up in your classes." He indicated the door with a wave of his hand. "Good day." He turned to his computer screen, effectively dismissing her.

Good day? Who said that *anymore?* She left, stopping to get a note from Ms. Slate before heading back to class.

So what was she going to do when she changed?

"**EXCUSE ME?**" *What was her name?* Gods, if only Hope had paid more attention when all those girls introduced themselves. She leaned forward, entering the girl's personal space. "I'm sorry to interrupt, but . . ." She hated to admit it. "I need some help."

The brunette sat up, her eyes wide. "Oh. Hope. Hi." Her smile was tentative. "What can I do for you?"

"I . . . I need to borrow notes . . . from last week . . ." Hope's heart hammered in her chest. The experience of asking for help completely new, and very uncomfortable. "Please?"

The girl's smile spread. "Sure. No problem. I'll print them off for you during computer lab, 'kay?" She leaned toward Hope and made duck lips. "Are you okay? I heard about you having to see Mr. Jeffers. He can be a real jerk."

"No, I mean, yeah." *Why was she asking about what happened with Mr. Jeffers? Why would she care?* "Um, Thanks."

"So where'd you go?" The girl followed Hope out of the classroom and toward her locker.

Great. She didn't need a friend, just the homework. "Over to Seattle."

"Oh." The girl nodded. "The rumor was you skipped town, you know, ran away, but obviously that's not true. I mean, why would you run away? Seattle's awesome. I love it over there. Have you been to Pike Place Market?"

Holy Hades, this girl could talk. "Yeah. But it's been a while."

"Cool." The bell rang. "Well, I'll see you later, 'kay?" The girl waved and walked off.

It was weird to have someone be so friendly. Weird, but maybe a little nice, too.

As promised, the brunette girl gave Hope a stack of notes at the beginning of Spanish. There at the top of the page was her name. Haley.

Hope wanted to start looking at them right then, but Haley lingered at her desk.

"I was thinking," Haley started. "If you're not busy Saturday night, you should totally come to the river with us. I mean, me. I mean, there will be a ton of other people there, but, it would be cool to have you come, too. If you want. I could pick you up."

Was she serious? Hope stared at Haley, her mind processing the request. That was going too far. Hope couldn't accept, even if she wanted to.

"Uh, I—"

The bell rang, saving her from having to answer. The girl had given Hope notes, so she didn't want to be rude, but she couldn't think of a nice way to tell Haley no.

"'Kay then." And Haley walked to her seat in the back of the room.

HOPE TAPPED PRINT and listened as the paper fed through the printer. There was something decidedly satisfying about finishing a paper. She'd spent the entire day on missed assignments, and there were only a couple of worksheets left and she'd be caught up in all her classes.

She stacked the papers then stapled them together.

A glance out the window to the deepening sky told her she had plenty of time to finish her chemistry before bed.

If she wanted. But she really didn't want to. She was over it. Tired of typing. Tired of writing. Tired of balancing and equating. Tired of translating. Over it.

Hope grabbed her phone from the desk and pushed the Power button. Still no messages. Her stomach knotted in worry.

Please call me. Please text me. Please let me know you're okay!

Her finger hovered over the Send button. Every day, she sent a worded plea to Priska's phone. Every day Hope checked for a reply. Every. Single. Day. She clicked send, hoping this one would be the one.

Hoping but not believing.

Knock knock.

"Hey, Hope, it's me, Haley."

Oh blast. Their conversation came back all at once. Clearly, Haley *was* being serious about going to the river tonight. And Hope's non-answer had been misinterpreted.

Hope opened the door a crack. "Hey, Haley."

Haley's eyes widened as she looked Hope over. "You're going in your pajamas? Ugh. I wish I'd thought of that." Haley was wearing jeans, dark leather boots, and a brown fleece jacket.

"Um, no. I wasn't planning on—"

"You aren't going to come?" Haley's shoulders dropped. "Really?"

Hope looked around her house. What else was she going to do?

Everything she'd ever been taught said she shouldn't go. Even her own experiences were evidence that it wouldn't end well. And yet, sitting at home alone, again . . . The self-imposed isolation made her heart ache. She decidedly did not want to sit at home alone doing worksheets.

"No, I'll come. But, let me put some jeans on. Just give me five?"

Hope changed quickly, and soon they were on the road.

"Do you think Tristan's cute?" Haley asked as she drove. "I mean it's okay if you do, but I didn't want to, you know, try and hook up, if you were interested, or something."

Hope squirmed. "Nope."

Haley veered the car to the right as she looked at Hope. "No you don't think he's cute?"

"No, I'm not interested. I guess he's cute." Did it matter?

"Cute, but not demigod cute, huh?" Haley sighed.

Hope's stomach churned.

"Not that we've had one here for, like, a year at least." Haley paused. "Although, maybe Athan is one. He's hot enough, anyway."

Hope nodded. He was definitely good looking. She thought back to the demigod she'd met all those years ago in Kent. He'd been really good looking, too.

"What about you?"

Hope frowned, her thoughts of demigods derailed. "What about me?"

"Are you a demigod?"

Her heart stopped. Was that why Haley had asked her to come tonight? "No."

"I didn't think so. I mean you're pretty and all. But"—she snapped her fingers over and over—"I don't know. You just don't seem the type."

"You've known that many demigods?" A desire to open the door of the sedan and jump clutched Hope. Irrational. She was being irrational.

"A couple." Haley shrugged.

The silence stretched into awkwardness, but Hope didn't know what to say. What could she say? She wanted to change the subject, talk about what normal people talked about. But what did they talk about?

"My best friend was a demigod," Haley said, choking on the words. "But they got her a couple years ago."

Hope's pulse skipped and tripped, and her hands grew clammy. She should've stayed home. Nothing good could come of this, and yet she couldn't help but ask, "Who got her?"

The mood dropped from awkward to somber, and the silence stretched.

Hope began to wonder if she had asked the question aloud or if she'd just thought it.

They pulled into the parking lot, but Haley made no move to get out of the car.

Hope waited. Should she say something? Move to leave? She fidgeted in her seat, her mind racing.

Haley turned to Hope. "Skia got her."

TWELVE

THEY GATHERED AROUND the fire, like bugs to light. Or like cold humans to warmth . . . because they were. Hope stared at the crowd and wondered what she was doing. She didn't know what to say to Haley. Was an apology enough? It wasn't Haley's fault, and probably not the demigod friend's either. Skia just killed. That's what they did. Still, Hope felt bad that Haley had lost her friend.

They crossed the parking lot in silence, and Hope zipped her coat up. It *was* freezing. And dark. And this was stupid. She shouldn't be here. Was there a way to ask Haley to take her home, or would that be rude?

Haley walked over to a group of guys, and Hope knew she'd missed her chance.

Several of her classmates roasted marshmallows, others sipped at cans. People were having conversations in groups of twos and threes, and Hope stood in the shadows watching. She felt the warmth of someone behind her and turned.

"What's the matter? Don't want to mingle with the trash of Goldendale?" Athan whispered.

Hope stepped away from him. "I didn't . . . No. I didn't say that."

"Then why are you over here by yourself?" He smirked.

The cold air nipped at her ears and nose, and her irritation flared.

"Why are you?" She glared at him. He was infuriating. And rude.

"A better view." He raised his brows, and his green eyes flashed fire.

The wind shifted, and with it the smoke. Her eyes stung, and she coughed. Stepping away from the smoke, and using it to get away from Athan, she backed right into a group of girls. Apologizing, she ducked and maneuvered, fighting the urge to just run away.

Tristan stood up and yelled for attention. "Hey! Story time! Everyone quiet down. Athan, come tell us a story."

Out of nowhere, Haley grabbed Hope's arm and pulled her closer to the fire and the large group there.

"Come on, you'll want to hear this," Haley said.

"Uh, okay. But no scary stuff," a freckle-faced boy said.

"Oh, are you scared?" The brawny teen that had tried to help Hope to her locker when she first moved in teased. "Lee, you're such a girl. Better run—"

"No, you pissy harpy, there are ladies here, and maybe—"

"I've got a good story." Athan stepped into the firelight, his presence cutting off the bickering. "I think you'll like it. Even the ladies."

He winked at the group of girls Hope and Haley hovered around. Several girls giggled, as if he'd winked at them.

After several shushes, silence settled, and in its wake the anticipation grew.

Athan began, his lilting accent adding a measure of depth to his story, "When the Olympians were still young and involved in their rule of this sphere, Atalanta was born. Her father, King Iasus, was so disappointed that the babe was not a son that he took his newborn daughter into the woods and left her to die.

"But the gods smiled on the young one, and a mother bear adopted the infant. Atalanta's first years were those of a cub: wrestling, hunting, running, and climbing. When she was still a young girl, a passing hunter saw her kill a doe with only her hands.

"The hunter was married but childless, and he took the girl home to his wife. The couple recognized that Atalanta was strong in mind and body and encouraged her to develop her talents.

"Atalanta became renowned. Famous because of her physical prowess and hunting skills, she was invited to participate in the Calydonian Boar Hunt. Of all the hunters, she won the trophy for drawing first blood. She gained further fame after defeating Peleus in a wrestling match. Peleus was Achilles's father.

"Not only was Atalanta strong and brave, she was beautiful. However, she saw no use for a man—for what could he do that she could not?"

"Hey, hey," Brawny Jock interrupted. "I could show her something."

Somebody snickered.

A male classmate retorted, "Yeah, you could show her your mama's house and your mama's car—"

"Shut up." Haley's soft voice was unusually forceful. "I want to hear the story."

"Of course you do." Tristan laughed and winked at her.

Haley blushed.

Athan waited for silence, and then he continued, "A few tried to take advantage of the young lady; all were injured, most were killed.

"After all her accomplishments and renown, her father, Iasus, finally acknowledged her as his child and brought her home. Once there, Iasus tried to fulfill his parental responsibility and find Atalanta a husband.

"Disgusted with the idea, but not wishing to offend her father, she proposed that she would wed the first man to beat her in a foot race. However, if she won the foot race, the losing suitor would be beheaded. Iasus agreed.

"Despite Atalanta's famed athleticism, there were many suitors. And soon, many heads.

"A young man named Melanion was desperately in love with Atalanta. He knew he couldn't beat her on his own and prayed to Aphrodite for aid. His impassioned plea touched the goddess of love, and she agreed to help the young man. With one condition: Melanion must perform a sacrifice to Aphrodite prior to the wedding. Melanion agreed.

"Aphrodite gave Melanion three golden apples, fruit of the gods. She explained that the apples would be irresistible to Atalanta, and Melanion should carry them in the race.

"The next morning, Melanion sought Atalanta's hand. It had been some time since a race, and the crowd was large. The race began, and Melanion struggled to keep pace with Atalanta. Just as she was starting to pull away, Melanion tossed a golden apple at her feet.

"Atalanta's desire for the ripe, celestial fruit overwhelmed her. She stopped to retrieve the apple and consumed it on the spot. Even with the delay, Atalanta was confident the interruption wouldn't affect the outcome of the race.

"She did, in fact, catch up with Melanion, but not until almost halfway through the race. When Atalanta was about to pass the young man, he again threw a golden apple, this time a bit off the racecourse.

"Having tasted the exotic fruit, Atalanta's desire was heightened, and she again stopped to recover the apple. Unable to postpone her pleasure, she devoured it.

"This cost valuable time, but she was fast. She caught up to Melanion just before the finish line and was set to beat him when he tossed the last apple just out of Atalanta's reach. Atalanta debated for only a second before she claimed the last of the heavenly crop.

"The decision cost Atalanta the race, and Atalanta and Melanion were married that afternoon. In his excitement, Melanion forgot all about his promise to Aphrodite.

"But the gods don't forget. The young couple was walking past a temple of Zeus when Aphrodite struck. The pair was so overcome with desire and passion they consummated their love within the sacred shrine of the god. Offended at this desecration, Zeus turned the lovers into lions."

There was silence.

"THAT'S *IT*?" Brawny Jock broke the silence.

Athan nodded, but his gaze narrowed as he scanned the group of teens, almost as if he were studying them.

"Seriously? That is so . . ." The hulking young man paused as though thinking of an adjective.

"LAME!" Krista exclaimed. "What kind of story is that? Why did the gods have to screw it up?"

"Do you think so?" Athan's accent became more pronounced, his words flowing together. He looked at Krista for a moment and then turned to Hope. His voice dropped, "What did you think of it?"

She shook her head and swallowed the lump in her throat.

"It sounds like typical Greek mythology to me." She hated the story but had been as entranced as the rest while he spoke.

"Hmm." He looked at a couple on the other side of the fire and walked toward them.

"Do you believe the gods are still involved in this world?" Tristan asked Athan as he retreated.

Athan stopped and turned. "Does it matter?"

"What do you mean?"

"If I claimed to be agnostic or atheist, would it change anything?" Athan sighed. "It would be nice to believe gods don't exist, but . . . You know that story about Atalanta?"

Collectively they nodded, but Hope held her breath. Something about the way he spoke was like he knew.

"The gods don't fix problems." Athan paused as if measuring his words. "They make bigger ones. Every story, every myth, every legend ends tragically for a human. Gods have amazing powers, but they leave a path of destruction and never think about the consequences that others have to deal with."

"So you don't worship the gods?" Tristan asked.

"Worship them?" Athan laughed, but the sound was mirthless. "Do any of you worship the gods? Have any of you even been to a temple in the last year to make an offering?"

"I did." Tristan's voice was steady. "Last spring with my dad. We made an offering to Demeter."

"Did it work? Were your crops more plentiful?" Hope couldn't help the words tumbling from her mouth. There was desperation in them, a want so substantial it almost choked her. She hoped that somehow, at least one of them was still good.

Why it was so important she couldn't say, but she needed it to be true.

"It was their best harvest ever." Haley smiled.

There was momentary hope in the words.

And then Tristan shook his head. "We had our best harvest ever, but my dad promised Demeter 'anything.'" He held his hands up and made air quotes. "I don't think he would have made that promise if he'd known the cost."

"What happened?" Hope asked.

"My mom left. Told us all good-bye, that she loved us, and then she left." The words were choked with emotion. "She's a priestess, or whatever they're called, in that temple off Highway 97. We can go see her whenever we want, but . . ."

A heavy weight settled over the group.

"By the gods, you people are such downers!" Krista blasted. "She was probably going to leave anyway." She stood up and grabbed a beer. "Anyone else want to drown that depressing story?"

Several hands went up, and Krista passed out cans.

Someone threw another log on the fire. The wood popped, and sparks floated in the air.

Hope shoved her hands deeper into her pockets and moved toward the orange glow. She was cold, but the chill in her heart wasn't something the fire would fix.

The shadows shifted.

A man walked toward them from the parking lot. At first Hope thought he was another kid from high school coming late to the party. There was something familiar about his stride, maybe she'd seen him before. He crossed under a streetlight, the light reflecting on his pallid skin, and she knew he wasn't from school. His relaxed pace was at odds with the bitter cold, especially considering he was only wearing a black T-shirt and jeans, no jacket.

The girl talking with Athan screamed.

Silence enveloped them as the world stood still.

Hope swallowed, and clenched her hands. She knew exactly what he was, and when her heart started beating again, it was pounding as if trying to run away on its own. She looked around at the crowd of teens, but they were singularly focused on the girl and not the monster from the Underworld.

"What the Hades, Chelli?" Krista glared at the girl.

A few nervous chuckles floated from the group, and Athan smirked and said, "Stop trying to freak everyone out."

He laughed as he stood and put his arm around Brand.

Someone made a comment about Chelli being crazy, and Krista took it one step further with a snide remark about her being off her meds. Conversations erupted, a cacophony of sound, the kids completely unaware of the creature in their midst.

Athan leaned into Chelli and Brand and said more quietly, "You should go. Now."

Then Athan ushered the girl and her boyfriend away with a wave.

The Skia reached into his coat.

Hope should do . . . something. What should she do? What could she do? In the back of her mind, she heard her mother's panic. Her mother's mantra of safety, the reason they stayed home so often. Heard Priska warning of Skia. She should go home. Should she just leave? Should she say something to Haley?

While her mind contemplated what she should do, Hope stood transfixed, her gaze darting from Athan to the Skia. But Athan never even looked at it. He saw the two other students to their car and casually came back to the fire.

And the Skia . . . was gone. She squinted into the night, but the inky blackness was only a void. Her gaze drifted back to the attractive young man. Had he seen it?

"So you're interested in Athan?" Krista sneered.

Hope turned to face the petite girl, staring at her as she flipped her dark hair behind her shoulder. Why would she think that? Hope ran through the last few minutes in her mind. She had looked at Athan, probably several times, but only because it seemed as if he sensed the Skia, too.

"He doesn't even know you exist, you know?"

Hope shrugged. It didn't matter. She wasn't interested in him anyway. Not like Krista.

"You might be kinda pretty, but you're not his type."

People had types? She couldn't even think of what to say to that and thought her best tactic would be to just ignore the other girl. Then maybe she would leave.

"Are you dumb? Gods! Just stay away from him." Krista sauntered past, bumping Hope on the way.

Hope sighed. She had no intention of getting anywhere near Athan.

"It won't work," Tristan said. He and Haley skirted around a couple sitting in the grass and walked up to Hope.

Hope looked out at the parking lot, wishing she'd never come. She steeled herself to deal with whatever else was coming, and then faced them. "What won't?"

"Even if you don't pay attention to her, she'll just take it as a challenge," Haley said. "She really sucks." Her eyes widened, and she turned to Tristan, "Uh, I mean—"

"I don't like her either," he said.

Hope looked down and noticed they were holding hands.

"Anyway," he continued, "you looked like you were going to try the whole ignoring thing. Like, if you pretend she doesn't exist, she'll go away. We just thought you should know it won't work."

Great.

Just great.

THIRTEEN

IT WAS TWO days before she would change, and Hope needed to get some groceries. Mostly, she needed to get some meat so she wouldn't be hungry when she changed. Not that she couldn't eat, but her tastes were definitely different as a sphinx than in human form.

"Hope!" Mr. Stanley smiled as she approached. "It's so nice to see you."

She wanted to smile, but her heart hurt. Loneliness had become her constant companion, and even though she knew it was best, it still sucked. And so did Krista. So much.

Hope surveyed the contents of the meat case. "What's the best today?"

"Hmm. The skirt steak is on sale, and if you slice it thin, it makes excellent fajitas."

She stared at the meat. Fajitas sounded like so much work for just her. And not really worth all the effort.

"Or, you could go with a tri-tip." When she didn't answer, he bent over to meet her eyes. "Are you all right?"

"Yeah." No. Not at all. Haley and Tristan had been correct about Krista. She was making it her personal mission to destroy Hope's new popularity. Unfortunately for them both, it seemed to be backfiring. The tension at school, coupled with tension about Priska, and curse day only two days away . . .

"Well, I'm sorry for whatever has taken the spring from your step."

No argument there. "I'll take the tri-tip. I can just grill that, right?"

"Yep." He pulled on clear plastic gloves and grabbed the roast. "I've got a new riddle for you. Tell me, have you heard this one? I am the beginning of the end, and the end of time and space. I am essential to creation, and I surround every place. What am I?"

She had heard it, but the kindness of his gesture made her smile. "The letter *E*. That's old, Mr. Stanley."

"So it is." He handed her the paper-wrapped package. "I was a bit worried you'd switched stores on me." He was clearly referencing the grocery store on the other side of town and her long absence.

"Nope. I can't believe their butcher would be as cool as you." She held up her meat. "Thanks, Mr. Stanley."

He gave her a wave and turned to the next customer.

Hope stood in line, the blinking 5 marking the only register open. Candy lined one side of the aisle, and beauty magazines the other. Diet, detox, celebrities . . .

A fuzzy photo stopped her heart. THE MONSTER LIVES, read the headline, and there was a picture of her as the Sphinx. Her! It had to be years old.

The desire to flee seized her, and she eyed the exit. With a swallow, Hope looked around. Did anyone know?

"Here kitty, kitty, kitty."

Hope turned to see Mrs. Stephens staring at her. A Hello Kitty T-shirt and yoga pants seemed too young for the woman to be wearing, and too normal.

"Kitty, kitty, kitty . . ." The dainty woman skipped over in her neon-pink flip-flops and pointed at the magazines.

"What do you want?" Hope asked.

Mrs. Stephens closed what little space was left and whispered to Hope, "You don't need to worry." She shook her head. "Not yet. Not yet."

What did she know?

"I, uh . . ." What could Hope say?

But it seemed that the weird lady wasn't interested in a response anyway.

"Be wary of death." Mrs. Stephens drew close, her hand extended. "The reapers will visit, and they will see."

Hope stepped back.

"Is this all for you?" the cashier asked in a monotone voice.

Hope gulped back her fear, nodded at the man, then looked back at Mrs. Stephens.

But she was skipping down the cereal aisle.

"So, ARE YOU going to come?"

Haley bumped Hope's arm as they walked down the hall between classes. Students and conversations flowed around them. Despite Hope's best effort at ignoring Haley, she seemed to believe they were now friends.

Hope instinctively pulled away. "No."

There was nothing appealing about going to the river again. First the Skia, then crazy Mrs. Stephens, and now the change tomorrow. Besides feeling overwhelmed, anxiety was firmly settled in her heart and pulsed through her body with every heartbeat. Disaster was right there, at her door, and Hope's concerns were not who would be at the river this weekend. Tomorrow she would shift into the Sphinx. And miss school. Again.

How was she going to deal with Mr. Jeffers?

"Are you kidding? It'll be epic!"

Haley practically bounced, forcing Hope's attention her way. There was something . . . endearing about the girl's enthusiasm.

"I could get Tristan to set you up with one of his friends. I mean, face it, you could have just about anyone you want." She slowed down and sighed. "Except Athan. I can't believe he's going out with Stacie."

Stacie was best friends with Chelli. Hope snorted her disgust. She could really care less who Athan dated. "Whatever."

Apparently, she was alone in her sentiment.

Haley continued her mooning over him, with big doe-eyes. "He's just so—"

An earsplitting cry for help broke through the din of the hallway. The high-pitched wail was followed by more screaming. And then more.

Hope forgot about Haley, the noise drawing her in, pulling her like a magnet down the hall. A huge crowd of students was gathered around the locker bay, and initially Hope thought someone must have started a fight, but the screams were increasing, and panic charged the air.

"Someone call 9-1-1!"

A tall young man ran by her, brushing her shoulder. And then several more people. They were running away from something. Or someone.

Fear filled her, its icy finger tracing her spine, clenching her heart. She fought the instinct to run and forced herself toward the screams.

Her vision tunneled, and the beige walls disappeared, as did the students in her periphery. As she approached the crowd, her height gave her a view over the other students, and she froze.

There on the ground, a young student thrashed. It was the boy from the campfire—the one Athan had spoken with and made leave. Brand. His name was Brand.

Above him—Oh gods. She couldn't believe it. It just couldn't be.

"Get him off me!" The boy screamed from the floor. "Help!"

Straddling the young man, the Skia held a black knife high in the air. The boy kicked at the creature's legs. A grim look of determination was fixed on the sallow face of the monster from the Underworld. And then, the knife came down.

"Arghhhh!" The boy screamed, his eyes widening. "Boreas! Save me!"

His screams became indecipherable as he bucked and writhed on the pale tile.

The blade came down again and again.

The air thinned, and Hope gasped. A deep heaviness settled in her chest, and her heart pounded a rhythm of terror. But she could not look away.

This was the fear her mother held, the cause of her panic. The reason for their moves. This was the packing, the no friends, the constant hiding. This was rationale for the isolation.

"Oh my gods! Help him!" The auburn-haired Chelli shouted above the melee. "Brand! Brand!" Her wide eyes searched the group, a silent plea for help. Finding none, she stepped forward to her friend.

The Skia shoved her, and, as if shot from a cannon, the girl flew into the crowd, knocking people over like bowling pins. A tangle of legs and arms lay in a heap, unmoving.

Hope stood transfixed by the horror. This . . . This was her mother fighting for her life.

The Skia stabbed, and the boy's thrashing grew weaker with each blow.

"Boreas." His screams turned to pleas then a whimper. Still, the pale hand of death struck, again and again.

No one. Not one person moved to help him. The boy's cries weakened and then stopped. Where the knife had struck there was no blood, no gaping stab wound. Nothing. The boy's body continued to lurch off the ground, seizing and then relaxing.

This was her mother's death.

Cold webs of alarm circled her heart. He could kill her next. And she didn't have her knives. She never even looked for them. How could she forget? And she was defenseless without them.

The Skia turned his midnight eyes toward her.

"You," the demon hissed. "You cannot hide from me. I will come for you." He turned back to his prey, and bringing his pitch-colored blade above his head, he drove it into the young man's chest.

She swallowed a scream and backed up into a solid body. A warm hand held her arm, as if to keep her steady on her feet, and she looked up.

Athan.

He stood, oblivious to her, staring at the seizing boy. His brow furrowed, and the muscles in his neck tightened.

Without another word, she stepped around him and ran.

What a fool she'd been. How could she have been so naïve? Priska had told her to get the immortal blades. Weeks ago, Hope had been warned. And she'd done nothing.

When she got home, she went straight to the spare bedroom. She pulled down the first box with her mother's name on it and opened it. There on top of black velvet sat the heavy leather tome of the history of her curse. With a sigh of relief, she lifted the large book and set it to the side. Her mother always wrapped the immortal blades in velvet. Hope's arms trembled as she grabbed the bundle and hugged it to her chest.

It was going to be okay. She had blades. She was home with the statue of Hecate. She was safe.

Safe.

She went to her room and sat on her bed. Holding the edge of the fabric, she let the weight of the daggers unroll the material. They fell onto her comforter with a clink, sinking into the puffy down. Sliding her hand around the weapons brought warmth to her soul, a sense of confidence.

But it didn't last. Fear drove her to call and text Priska several times over the course of the evening. But the ache in Hope's chest confirmed her fear as her phone lay silent. Nothing. She would call Mr. Davenport's office in the morning. Maybe he'd heard something. As she lay in bed, thoughts sprinted through her mind. Skia had killed that boy. No. Not a boy. Skia only killed demigods.

And now the Skia was hunting her.

FOURTEEN

SEARING PAIN JOLTED her awake. Hope thrashed in the sheets and covers, kicking them away before she ruined them.

The throbbing started in her hips, radiated down her thighs and into her calves and ankles. Cramping, burning, like muscles that were already sore. The shifting had begun. The tingling of her skin, building until pins and needles poked at each pore. She sat up, and just in time. Her wings released, and the early morning rays of sun streaming through the window made her feathers shine.

As the previous day's terror played in her mind, she reached over to the nightstand and checked her phone. No messages.

Should she leave? Move? Was there anywhere safe to go? While fleeing sounded like doing something, would it matter?

Gods, if only she could just get ahold of Priska!

Hope lay in bed, holding her phone, watching as pink streaked the sky, then yellow, and finally, *finally* it was late enough to call.

She dialed, silently praying to any god that might be listening that Priska would be back.

The phone rang only once.

"Mr. Davenport's office. This is Melody."

The musical lilt reminded her of Sarra, and Hope's question caught in her throat.

"Hello?" The woman practically sang. "Anyone there?"

"Um, hi. This is Hope . . . Treadwell. Is Priska there?"

"I'm sorry, Ms. Treadwell." The chipper voice didn't sound the least bit sorry. "Priska is still on vacation. We aren't expecting her back for a few weeks. Is there something I can help you with?"

On vacation? Right. "Uh, is Mr. Davenport available?"

"No. He's in with a client. I'll tell him you called, if you'd like?"

Hope's heart sunk, and she sagged back into her pillows. "Yes, please."

"Will do. Thank you."

Ten minutes later, her phone buzzed with an incoming text.

No news from her. Be careful.

Careful. With a long, slow exhale, she thought of Priska's advice. Hope would keep a blade with her when she left the house. But would it matter?

She stumbled out of bed and made her way to the kitchen.

After breakfast, there wasn't much to do. She was caught up on homework, and her house was spotless. So that left watching crummy daytime television, reading a book, or surfing the net.

The claws on her back legs clicked on the floor as she went out to the study. After drawing the blinds, she booted up her laptop and entered *demigod* into the search engine.

Eight hundred thousand results.

There were quizzes to find out if you were a demigod. She wasn't. Quizzes to find out if your boyfriend/girlfriend was a demigod. She didn't know enough about anyone to answer the questions except for Priska, who according to the test wasn't a demigod either!

Hope typed in *Skia*.

Two hundred fifty-nine thousand results.

She scrolled through the first two pages. A lot about fonts, art graphics, an art gallery . . .

There!

Strong's Greek Site. Skia—shadows of the Underworld, minions of Hades.

Hope read through page after page after page.

There was information about the dark immortal blades Skia used to kill demigods and Hades's deal with Themis that gave him power to *create* living beings from the dead to restore balance. Could that be right? There was sense to it, but then . . .

Where did monsters fit in with divine balance?

SHE CALLED THE school to let them know she was "still sick, but feeling better today." She expected to be back Monday. Ms. Slate informed Hope that her absences were being noted and she would need to make up her work with her teachers.

After she hit End on her phone screen, she stuck her tongue out at the black rectangle.

She was reading when a knock startled her.

"Hope?"

A man was at her door?

The knocking became pounding. "Hope, are you in there?"

Adrenaline pumped through her body. Who in the world? Was that . . . Was that Athan? What was he doing here?

She slid off the couch, her gaze focused on the door.

Another knock. "Hope?"

The deadbolt was engaged. The curtains and shades were drawn.

The next knock rattled the window, and his words came in fragments. "Car here . . . two days . . . no way . . ." His voice faded around the side of her house.

She scanned through her home and noticed, for the first time, that the window above the sink in the kitchen was bare.

She needed to hide.

She crept down the hall toward her bedroom, the clicking from her nails shattering the silence and making her cringe. She was halfway there when she noticed the light coming from her doorway. She must have left the blinds open in there.

The spare room? She couldn't be sure if the blinds were open or closed. That left only . . . the bathroom?

Ugh. She grimaced with the thought of sitting in the bathroom for the next few hours, but a tapping coming from her bedroom window made the decision for her. She opened the door, relieved to see the muted light came through a frosted window. There was no way he could see in.

She shut the door and waited.

And waited.

The silence was strained, even after her heart rate slowed. When she heard the crunch of gravel, followed by a vehicle pulling away from her house, she began to relax. Even so, she stayed in the bathroom until she changed back to her human form.

Cleaning up the fur was the worst part. When she went to take the garbage out, she froze, her foot just missing the small package.

On her front doorstep lay an envelope. On top of the envelope was a small bouquet of daffodils.

He'd come by and left her algebra assignments. And flowers.

Why would he bring flowers?

HOPE NEVER USED to count the days. Oh, sure, she would count how many days since their last move, but time as a Sphinx wasn't a burden then. It meant she could fly. Now, it was one more weight, an ever-present secret, a stressor she couldn't afford to forget. She counted down, like a time bomb, waiting for the explosion that would kill her. Because she knew—*she knew*—sooner or later, she would be discovered, and then she would have to run for her life.

But until then, she'd better be on time for school.

"Oh, craptastic! You came back."

She'd just walked through the double doors into the school. A shove from behind, and Hope turned to face her mortal nemesis.

Krista's features were contorted into an ugly sneer. "I thought we'd gotten lucky and you moved . . . or died." She pushed past Hope, followed by her entourage. "Too bad."

The words drifted back with a chorus of snickers.

Hope shook her head and tried to dislodge the words as she went to her locker. What Krista said didn't matter. She was just an irritation to be ignored. They all were. And yet, the venomous words still pierced the wall around Hope's heart.

"Oh. My. Gods. Where were you last week? And Saturday? I totally called you, like a hundred times. Why didn't you answer?" Haley verbally ambushed Hope. "You totally disappeared after the"—Haley held her hands up in air quotes—"Skia attack, which the teachers are all calling a seizure, by the way. I thought maybe . . . Well, anyway, here you are."

"Yep." Hope closed her locker and offered a tentative smile. She shouldn't care that Haley came up to her. Shouldn't care that she wanted to talk to her. In fact, after the Skia attack it was probably better if Hope pushed everyone away. So even while she told herself she shouldn't care, she knew. She shouldn't, but she did.

The bell rang, and both girls jumped.

"Okay. I'll meet you for lunch." Haley furrowed her brow. "Where do you eat lunch?"

She started walking backwards, forcing others to watch out so they didn't get bumped by the thin Asian girl.

Hope waited, debating. The idea of hiding, by herself, brought a heaviness to her chest that threatened to crush her. In that moment, she decided having one person to talk to wouldn't be wrong. She would still keep all her secrets. "The library."

"I'll come find you," Haley yelled, and then she sprinted down the hall.

"So, WERE YOU really with Athan last week?" Angela whispered.

Hope sat in chemistry with her book open, trying to get her make-up work done. There were a few more minutes before class started, and she was scribbling down answers. Maybe if she ignored Angela, she'd leave Hope alone.

"Hope?" Angela interrupted. Again.

Hope looked up at the girl. No, that wasn't fair. She glared at her. Angela was like Krista's minion, and while Hope didn't hate her, she definitely didn't want to have bonding girl time.

"Were you?"

Hope grimaced, deciding she'd do everything she could to make it hard for Angela. "Was I what?"

"Were you with Athan Friday?" Angela's eyes were alight with curiosity.

Hope recoiled and wanted to remind the girl what happened to the curious cat. And what she was asking was preposterous. "Why would you ask that?"

"It's just a rumor. You were both gone, and someone said you skipped together." She gave a slight shrug.

Skipping with Athan? That was insanity. "Uh, no. I was home sick. Thursday *and Friday*."

"No biggie," Angela said, holding her hands up defensively. "I was just asking."

Right. Just asking. Hope shook her head and tried to focus on her work, but the chemical equations now refused to be balanced.

Students shuffled in, and the bell rang. Mr. Burgess stood, and Krista came running through the door.

"Sorry. My locker was jammed." She slid into her seat, tossing her thick curls over her shoulder.

Hope turned away from the sickly-sweet, honeysuckle scent of Krista's hair. Hope hated that smell. Something about it made her stomach turn.

Mr. Burgess started class, and Hope stared dutifully at the board. But her mind wasn't on chemistry. Instead her mind repeatedly played the same questions over and over in her head. Who started that rumor? And why?

She could ask Athan in algebra, but just the thought made her palms sweat. No, she would ask Haley at lunch.

FIFTEEN

"**I HEARD THAT!**" Haley squealed, and then she clapped her hand over her mouth.

They sat in the library in the overstuffed chairs in the back corner. The air was musty and smelled of old paper.

Haley leaned toward Hope and whispered, "Tristan said Lee and Scott were talking about it in gym."

Lee and Scott. The freckle-faced boy and Brawny Jock. Why would they care? "I don't get it."

Haley bobbed her head up and down. "I know. It's so weird. And did you hear about Chelli?"

Chelli was at home with several broken ribs and a broken leg. Allegedly.

But if she'd seen the Skia that Saturday at the river, wouldn't that make her a demigod? And if she was a demigod, wouldn't she have already healed?

Hope nodded. "Is she going to be okay?"

"No one knows. She hasn't answered her phone since the attack." Haley arched her eyebrows. "You know what I think?"

Hope leaned forward.

"If Chelli could see the Skia attacking Brand . . . that would make her a demigod, too."

"Do you think Skia got her, too?" She shouldn't care. But for some reason, she really didn't want the other girl hurt.

Haley shook her head. "I think someone rescued her. Took her to a conservatory, maybe."

"Athan?"

Haley shrugged. "He'd be my guess if he doesn't come back."

"Why wouldn't he come back?"

"Um, duh." Haley laughed. "If he's a demigod searching for other demigods, what is there to come back for now?"

Of course. "Right."

Hope actually wished he was a demigod, if it meant he wouldn't come back.

HOPE HAD JUST turned in her make-up assignment in mythology when Ms. Slate called her down to the office. She'd known it was coming, but when no one called her to the office yesterday, Hope had thought she might've escaped unnoticed. She should've known better.

"Miss Treadwell." Mr. Jeffers pointed to the seat across from his desk. "Back so soon?"

"Sir?" She stood to the side of the chair, wanting to avoid the uncomfortable heat.

"Have a seat, young lady." His tone brooked no argument.

She gulped and sat. The sun's rays began to warm her immediately.

"I'm a little disappointed to see you again. Are you all right?"

"I . . . I was sick, sir." It was the best she'd come up with.

He nodded. "I see. And do you by chance have a doctor's note?" He leaned forward and rested his elbows on his desk.

"No." She shifted to the left, trying to avoid the sun. "I didn't go to the doctor. I don't have one here, yet."

"Well, I suggest you get one. If you are sick again and miss school, you will need to bring a doctor's note for your absence to be excused."

She nodded. It was so unfair. He was being such a stickler to the rules. And it wasn't like she wasn't doing well in her classes. She was getting straight *A*s.

Jerk.

"That will be all, Miss Treadwell."

Her frustration pulsed, but there was no release. Nothing she could do.

So she went to algebra.

"I'm glad you caught up." Mr. Romero took her assignment and set it on his desk. "We're moving on to quadratic equations this week, and I'd hate for you to get behind."

She nodded and went to her desk. The room filled in the minutes before the bell. Hope bowed her head and focused on the numbers and letters in her book. A tapping on her desk drew her focus, but she kept her head down.

"Are you okay?"

She glanced up into Athan's green, green eyes. Why was he talking to her? He smiled, and she noticed a scab the size of a quarter on his cheek, like the skin had been rubbed off but hadn't quite healed. She'd taken enough Tae Kwon Do as a kid to recognize a punch to the face. Hmm. He didn't really seem the fighting type.

"You missed school last week."

Gods. Why was he talking to her? "I was sick."

"I heard. But you're better now?"

She couldn't help the furrow that creased her brow. Why wouldn't he just leave her alone? "I'm back at school."

His hands were scratched up, too. And he looked tired.

"What happened to you?" The question slipped out, and she had no idea where it came from. She wanted to follow it up with a never mind, but the words stuck.

He chuckled, a low deep sound at the back of his throat, and his gaze travelled over her face, to her lips and then back to her eyes. "Why, Hope, I never thought you'd ask."

She wanted to laugh at him, but her blush was short-circuiting her brain.

"Whatever," she managed and turned away.

"I'm fine. I had a little misunderstanding, but things are resolved now." The tips of his fingers brushed her forearm.

She flinched. "Did you start that rumor?"

Athan frowned and shook his head. "What rumor?"

How had he not heard? "Uh, about you and, uh, me hanging out."

Could a blush kill you? She could feel it all the way down to her toes.

He smiled. "Maybe we should."

Halfway through class, Athan brushed by, dropping a note on her lap.

She unfolded the paper and read: *What about dinner tonight?*

She clenched her hands together, crumpling the note into a ball. What the Hades? He was with Stacie, right? And even if he wasn't, there was no way! She must have given him the wrong impression at some point in their conversation. He needed to leave her alone.

Hope was the first one up when class was dismissed. She dropped the wad of paper into the garbage on the way out the door.

"**You're staring at** him again," Haley said.

Hope dropped her head into her locker and grabbed her chemistry book.

"What happened? I mean, you look seriously hacked, like he stole your last cookie or something."

"Nothing." She slammed the locker closed. "It's whatever. He's a total 'taur."

"Did you just call him a 'taur, as in Minotaur? Gods, Hope, you're so weird."

Hope ignored the ribbing. "You know he asked me out. To dinner. Yesterday."

"*What?*"

Several kids looked over at them.

Hope rolled her eyes. "I know. What a loser."

"No. Like. Wow. That is—"

"Super lame. He's with Stacie, right?" Her outrage was totally justified. He should get dropped in a pit somewhere.

"I don't know. I mean, they're always together, but, maybe . . ."

Hope shook her head. "Total 'taur."

"I'm so going to ask Tristan. What if you're wrong?" The bell rang, and Haley turned to go. "Crap. I can't be late again. I'll see you in Spanish, 'kay?"

Hope nodded.

She wasn't wrong.

And it didn't matter.

THAT NIGHT THE cool air wicked the heat from her body as Hope ran. She turned left on Columbia for another loop around the town.

The sun had set hours ago, and the streetlights cast an eerie glow in the shape of hourglasses on the ground.

It had been twenty-two days since Priska disappeared. Three—freaking—weeks.

And Mr. Davenport had been worthless. He didn't even know what city she'd been in. Why had she been so secretive? How was Hope supposed to rescue Priska—

Hope stumbled over the uneven sidewalk. With a curse, she righted herself. When she looked up, she saw him.

He stood just outside the yellow glow, the same pallid skin, eyes dark as pitch. The Skia that had killed Brand.

She gasped and stepped back. He could kill her! And she'd left the immortal daggers at home.

She stared at his obsidian eyes.

He narrowed his eyes and beckoned her, fingers waving at her in invitation.

Her muscles tensed. Her breathing became shallow, and her heart raced. She reached for a dagger, and in the time it took her to blink . . .

He was gone.

What the Hades?

She swallowed down her panic. She should go home, go straight home. But he was gone. How was he just gone? She stepped up to the shadow he'd been under.

Nothing.

The concrete was solid. There was nothing to explain what she'd seen.

"**HE'S SO HOT**, and if he was interested in Stacie, he's not anymore." Krista looked like a cat that got the cream. "I saw her in the bathroom crying this morning."

"Did they hook up?" Angela leaned forward.

Hope rolled her eyes, but her interest was piqued nonetheless.

"They hung out and everything, but . . . Get this—he never even kissed her."

"Right." Angela's disbelief colored her tone.

Hope was with Angela on this. Hope had seen the couple sitting in the library last week during lunch. Stacie was on his lap.

"*Seriously.* And Athan said they were never together. Like, not at all."

Right. If they weren't together, then why was Stacie on his lap? Boys were idiots, and Athan was the king of them all.

The bell rang. Hope gathered her things and shoved them into her backpack. As she walked out the door, she glanced back at Krista and Angela, heads bent toward each other, probably still gossiping.

Thud!

"Easy there."

Warm hands gripped her arms, steadying her, and she looked up into dark-green eyes.

"You all right?" Athan stepped forward even as he continued to hold her upright.

"Yeah. Sorry." She stepped back, but his grip prevented her from going anywhere. She pulled back, but he held tight.

"You're not hurt, are you?"

She snorted. "Uh, no."

She looked down at his hands, still holding her arms. Why was he not letting go?

"Right." His hands dropped, but he continued to stand in her direct path.

Krista and Angela gushed as they came out the door. "Oh my gods!"

"Could you be more clumsy, Hope?" Krista rolled her eyes and turned her attention to Athan. "She practically ran you over. So lame."

Krista stood on one side of Hope, Angela on the other, hemming her in. Krista tossed her hair over her shoulder, the ends whipping Hope in the face.

She was boxed in, her anxiety about the attention pushing in on her as much as the proximity of the bodies surrounding her.

"Sorry about that," Hope mumbled, stepping back in an attempt to escape. But all she did was step back into the classroom.

"No need to apologize." Athan frowned and stepped out of her way. "I should have been more careful, too."

She said nothing more and fled to the library.

Five minutes before lunch was over, Hope hurried down the hall to algebra. She wanted to be in her seat before Athan came into the room. In her seat with her head down. Maybe even catch a few minutes of the sleep she'd lost last night.

She even beat Mr. Romero to the room. With a sigh of relief, she slid into her chair and dropped her head into her hands.

"Do you have a headache?"

Athan's strange accent shattered her mental block, and her head shot up. It felt like he was everywhere. She glared at him while she answered, "No."

"Are you tired?" He crouched down so they were at eye level. "Are you not sleeping well?"

"I'm sleeping fine." She clenched her teeth, then forced her jaw to relax. "Not that it should matter to you."

Instead of looking offended, he smirked. "But maybe it does."

He reached out, his hand halting just before touching her arm. He rested his fingertips on the edge of her desk, just millimeters from her arm.

She shook her head and snapped at him, "Go away, Athan. Find someone else to annoy. We aren't friends."

She dropped her head back onto her arms and waited for him to leave.

She felt his hand move off her desk, but his presence remained. Why would he not just leave?

"I am not your enemy. And maybe, someday, you will see just how much I would like to be your friend," he whispered, and then he left.

SIXTEEN

HOPE'S HEAD FELT tethered to her desk. She'd woken up late and barely made it to school before the bell. The morning was dragging, and so was she.

She was supposed to be balancing chemical equations, but the Cs, Hs, and Os were a jumble on her paper. She closed her eyes and couldn't help but overhear Angela and Krista.

"So, I heard he joined the track team."

Krista snorted. "Hmm, for the last month of school? Well, that's super interesting."

"And nothing is going on with him and Chelli." Angela sounded like she was giving a book report. "Her dad's got her enrolled in some private school. I guess Athan took her out, but just as friends. You know, because of Brand."

It was amazing that Angela's mother was a licensed counselor. Seriously.

"Whatever." Krista dismissed her friend's information. "Guess what I heard?"

Angela said nothing.

"He told Scott that he doesn't have a curfew. At all. You know his aunt is insane, and he can come and go as he pleases."

Hope peeked at the two girls. Angela stared at Krista with wide eyes, while the dark-haired girl held up her hand as if to stop her friend from speaking.

"Anytime." She raised her eyebrows as she continued, "Mmm. This weekend is my chance, and I'm totally taking it."

"Is he going to come down to the river Saturday? Did Lee invite him?" Angela asked.

"Yeah. I was there when Lee asked him, and he looked at me and asked if I'd be going. I was like, 'Yeah, I'll be there,' and then he said he'd come." Krista smirked, as if she'd just won the lottery.

By the end of class, Hope found herself fuming with irritation. Three days ago, Athan wanted to be buddies, but since then he'd been out with three other girls. Three. No, if he was going out with Krista, make it four.

What was with him? He took player to a whole new level.

Hope headed back to her locker, alternately thinking about Athan and forcing herself to not think about him. Consumed with her thoughts, she didn't notice him until he spoke.

"Hey. How are you today?" His voice was light, but the intensity of his gaze was incongruous with his tone.

She wanted to hit him. After three days, he was talking to her again? "Fine."

"Hmm. Okay." His gaze flitted from her eyes to her lips and back to her eyes. "I was just wondering, well, two things, actually. First, are you running tonight?"

He reached out as if to touch her, and she pulled back. She refused to fall under his spell. "No, I'm not." *Not that you should even care.* She glared at him. "What else?"

"Oh. Um, well." He reached for her again but pulled back before she had time to react. "I was wondering if you were going to the . . ." He glanced down for a moment, and then took a deep breath. His gaze searched her face. "Hope . . ."

He was thinking, but what about, she couldn't tell.

"Never mind. That's it." He shifted to leave.

Her curiosity was piqued, but she told herself she didn't care. Besides, even if she did care, it was better to avoid him. He brought chaos. And way too much attention. She grabbed her algebra book and headed to the library.

"So he's talking to you again?" Haley sat in the library with Hope and picked at her sandwich. "I can't keep you two straight."

Hope glared at her friend. "There is no us two. Just me. Athan is just . . ."

There weren't even words to describe how irritating he was.

"You know what I think? He's trying to make you jealous. And I think it's working."

'Ugh. No way." There was no way Hope was jealous. Was she? Is that what this ugly feeling was? But she didn't even like him. Just thinking about him made her frustrated, but that wasn't jealousy. Nope. She just hated him. "What about you and Tristan?"

"Oh, man." Haley took the bait and flopped back into her seat, her sandwich dropping into her lap. "He's all nice and everything, even wants to meet at the river tomorrow, but here at school he acts like we're just friends. I mean, he won't even hold my hand."

"Maybe that'll change tomorrow." Hope puckered her lips. "Maybe he'll kiss you, or—"

Haley snorted. "Yeah. He kissed me two weeks ago, and then, BAM!" She clapped her hands together. "Nothing."

"Shhh!" someone whisper-yelled. Probably the librarian. No one else was ever in the library at lunch.

Hope giggled but stopped when she looked back at Haley.

"What if he's playing me?" Haley looked up, her face lined with worry.

"I don't think he's like that." Not that Hope knew him well, but he wasn't like Athan. He didn't hang out with other girls at school. "He seems friendly enough, but not really flirty."

At the end of the day, as she crossed the school parking lot, she saw Athan, Tristan, Lee, and Scott out by the hugest truck she'd ever seen. A bright iridescent blue, it was bigger than any other vehicle in the lot. The tires were oversized, and there was an inordinate amount of chrome; it was the most ostentatious thing.

She went to duck into her Civic, and someone laughed. She glanced at the group of boys again, and her gold eyes locked with green ones. As Athan regarded her, the corners of his mouth lifted.

Something foreign pulled at her heart, and for the briefest moment, she wanted to join them.

HOPE AWOKE TO the muted light of the sunrise. Despite the emotional strain of the last few months, she felt rested and oddly at peace. She ran her loop around the town twice before getting ready for the day.

She tapped out a quick text to Priska.

I miss you. I hope you are safe. If you get this, plz call me.

For the first time, Hope didn't wait to see if there was a response. It wasn't that she didn't want Priska to rescue her. But as the days turned into weeks, and into over a month, Hope no longer expected it.

Preoccupied with her thoughts, Hope didn't hear the approach of the vehicle until the crunch of tires rolling over the road slowed beside her.

"Do you want a ride?" Athan leaned over the seat toward the passenger window of his flashy truck.

And just like that, her mood darkened, and her chest tightened. "No thanks. I'm enjoying the walk."

"Of course." His shoulders dropped. "It is a nice morning." When she said nothing, he continued, "See you at school."

"Sure." She stepped back on the sidewalk, but her lungs wouldn't release. Butterflies swooped and swarmed, and she wondered at his persistence.

Minutes later, she bounded up the steps of the school, an unfamiliar sense of buoyancy adding a spring to her step. The smile that played on her lips twitched as it pulled and tugged long-unused muscles.

Hope walked toward her locker, feeling a little brighter about her day, but then she stopped. Right in the middle of the hall.

Athan . . . and Krista. Hope sucked in a breath. For a moment, she thought they were kissing. Krista's back was against the lockers, and Athan's hands framed her face.

Hope wanted to throw something.

No, she scolded herself. He could flirt with whomever he wanted. It didn't matter. Not to her. She'd turned down a ride from him that very morning, only minutes ago. He was a jerk. But it meant nothing to her.

Three hours later, she was still fuming.

"I can't *wait* until tomorrow," Krista gushed to Angela in chemistry.

Hope's pencil stopped, all her attention drawn to the two girls. No, really just the one. Was it wrong that she wanted to physically hurt her?

"Single today, hookup tomorrow. By Monday, my name will be tattooed on his arm. That's my prediction."

Hope dreamed that the girl would be struck by a stray lightning bolt. Right there in class.

Angela looked just as stricken. "He seems really—"

Krista tossed her hair. "Yummy. I know. He smells so good I could just lick him. I can't wait to . . ." Krista must have felt the weight of Hope's stare, and her eyes narrowed. "What are you looking at?"

Fire danced into Hope's cheeks. "Nothing."

"Nothing? Really? If you're looking at nothing, why don't you turn around and look at nothing that way." Krista waved a pink polished finger at her. "Go on. Turn around."

The hot pulse ran from Hope's heart to her toes. Her body tensed. "Excuse me?"

"You heard me. Turn around."

She clenched her hands under the desk. A sharp splinter of wood dug into her palm, and the pain bit through her haze of rage.

"Whatever," she said, through gritted teeth.

"Back at ya, harpy." Krista leaned toward her friend, and her voice dropped to just above a whisper. "What's up with her?"

The bell rang, and Hope shoved her binder and book into her bag. She needed to get out before she lost it. But as she hurried out the door, someone shoved her from behind.

"You're in my way." Krista glared. "Hurry up."

Something inside Hope solidified with a snap. She lowered her head till she was looking Krista in the eye. "Back off." She took a deep breath and continued, "Now."

"Really?" Krista sneered. "Are you, like, telling me what to do?"

"Only if you, like, value your life." Hope tossed her head back and forth, mocking Krista. "Like, seriously, like." Dropping her voice to a growl, Hope narrowed her eyes and said, "Seriously. Back. Off."

Krista drew her small hand back and slapped Hope across the face.

Before the sting fully registered, Hope caught Krista's wrist and ducked behind her, twisting the girl's arm up her own back. Hope pushed the hand inward and torqued the wrist until she heard Krista gasp with pain.

"Don't ever, *ever*, do that again," Hope fumed. "Or I will make it my personal mission to destroy you."

She had no idea where the words came from, but they felt strong on her lips. She yanked Krista's arm again, eliciting a whimper. "Do you understand me?"

Krista bobbed her head in shaky, jerky movements.

Hope pushed her away and strode out the door and down the hall. She could hear the curses drifting after her, and they still rung in her ears even when she sat alone in the library.

Whispers followed her the rest of the day. Any empowerment she felt dissipated before lunch was over. Embarrassment washed in and took its place.

In algebra, as the other students shuffled in, she kept her head down, pretending to review her completed assignment.

And then laughter rang out, uproarious and mocking, and a group passed by on its way to the back of the room. A pang of longing zinged through her, then a sensation that was overwhelming and bitter.

As soon as the final bell rang, Hope fled.

SEVENTEEN

SHE WRAPPED HER loneliness around her like a shawl and trudged toward home. A desperate need for some kind of connection drove her into the Red Apple and back toward the meat department.

"Hi, Hope." Mr. Stanley's smile was a ray of sunshine.

But even he could barely pierce the gloom.

"Do you have anything good for me?" Her voice was flat, and she looked at the case in front of her.

"Okay," he said, rubbing his hands together. "I spent some real time finding this one. I think you'll like it." He concentrated then recited: "If you break me, I do not stop working. If you touch me, I may be snared. If you lose me, nothing will matter. What am I?"

A smile pulled at the corners of her soul when Mr. Stanley started the riddle. He'd misunderstood her question, and yet given her exactly what she needed. Distracted by the puzzle, everything else disappeared.

As she leaned against the meat case, Mr. Stanley went back to work, helping customers, packaging meat, and cleaning his area. She thought of watches and rabbits, money and health. She thought of flirting girls and stupid boys. She thought of Priska, and Paul and Sarra. She thought about her mom.

After more than a half an hour, Mr. Stanley cleared his throat. "I know what it's like to try and sort out a riddle, but I don't think I've ever seen you take this much time."

Her memories of love lifted her spirits. And he was pleased that he'd stumped her; she could hear it.

"I hate to put you on the spot, but I'm going home a bit early today. Do you want to come by tomorrow and give me the answer?"

"Sure," she said. "Or maybe Sunday."

"Right. Hang on a second." He stepped through the double doors and then returned with a large parcel, her name written across the top.

Hope accepted the meat with a smile. "Thanks, Mr. Stanley."

With a parting wave, she turned to leave. The riddle went to the back of her mind as she thought about dinner. She stopped in the produce section to get vegetables to roast with the meat. She stocked up on apples, bananas, grapes, and when she smelled the strawberries, she grabbed a container of them as well. She needed eggs, milk, and bread.

Halfway through the checkout process, she remembered.

"I'm so sorry." Her skin flushed as she looked at the clerk. "I . . . I don't have my car. Would you mind if I pay now and then run home and get it? I'll only be about fifteen minutes. I could just leave the cart right up front here?"

The matronly clerk merely nodded. "Sure, honey. We'll bag it, and you can pick it up when you get back."

She thanked the woman and gazed out the window, calculating how quickly she could run home. Then she saw Athan approaching. Her heart jumped, and she shifted her gaze. Maybe he hadn't seen her. Hopefully, he wouldn't.

"Hey," he said seconds later. Athan stood at the end of the lane, blocking her exit. "Didn't you walk to school? I didn't see your car outside, and"—he stared at the bags being piled back into the cart—"that's a lot of groceries."

She delivered a tight smile. Of course he saw her. "I'm going to run home and grab my car right now. No worries."

She swiped her credit card and waited for the transaction to process.

Athan continued to stand and stare. "Um," he paused for a second, "Can I give you a ride?"

While Hope contemplated how to best refuse the offer, the clerk grinned up at both of them and said, "That's perfect timing, huh?"

Hope wanted to growl her frustration. It wasn't perfect timing. What would've been perfect timing is for Athan to have missed her by five minutes. But how could she say that? She couldn't. And it didn't matter. A ride wasn't going to kill her. "Su-sure," she stammered. "That would be very . . . great."

As she signed the receipt, Athan grabbed the cart. He waited for her to finish, and then they walked out to his truck in silence. He unlocked the doors with a button on his key ring, opened the passenger side for her, and then started to load the groceries in the back.

She should help him unload the cart, but she'd have to walk all the way around . . .

"Go ahead, climb in." He interrupted her thoughts and nodded at the passenger door.

So she did. But she couldn't help the hyper-vigilance pulsing through her. Once inside, she was surprised by the luxuriousness of the truck. The cream leather was soft, and the windows were tinted. There were several buttons and dials, as well as a large screen on the dashboard. She could smell the newness of it. She took a deep breath, and something rich and sharp tickled her senses.

While Athan stuck the last two bags in the back, Hope tried to place the scent. Something warm but familiar. She took another deep breath, watching him out of the corner of her eye.

He moved smoothly, almost gracefully, like a dancer, spatially aware of how he fit in the world. He pushed the cart, and it glided through the lot, finding its way into the rack. Excellent aim. Of course.

When he climbed up into the vehicle, she realized what she'd been smelling. The scent in the car was him. *His* scent.

With the door closed, she was overwhelmed. Leather, mossy woods, and a hint of citrus. She suppressed a smile.

Athan started the truck, and a strange blend of pipe and drum sounds emanated from the speakers, reverberating through her body.

She turned, her eyebrows drawn down in question.

"I know. I know." He turned the volume down. "My dad loves all types of music, so I got to hear lots of different styles growing up. I usually only listen to this when I'm alone; not many people appreciate it." He reached again for the dial.

"No." She reached out to stop him, but withdrew before touching him. "Don't change it. It's different, but I like it."

He pulled up to the curb outside her house and turned the engine off. Before she was able to push the door open, he was there, pulling it open for her, extending his hand to help her down.

Hesitantly, she took it. His skin was warm, the tips of his fingers calloused. The contact filled her with fluttering discomfort. She released his hand as soon as her feet touched the ground.

He said nothing but turned and reached into the bed of the truck, pulling out two bags of groceries.

She grabbed one from him, and their hands brushed. Her breath caught, and her heart somersaulted in her chest. Hope managed a mumbled thanks but couldn't look at him. What was it about him that put her so on edge? Whatever it was, she needed to get over it. Because it didn't matter.

While she unlocked the door, he set two bags on the porch and went back to the truck to get the others. She deposited her school bag and the groceries on the kitchen table and was on her way back out when Athan passed her. She grabbed the last two bags off the porch and went back inside. When she walked in, she noticed him looking around in awe, two bags sitting on the floor at his feet.

She looked around at her home. There was nothing amiss. The statue of Hecate was on the mantel. She'd recently vacuumed and dusted. "What?"

"Nothing," he replied, but he continued to study the small interior.

She stared at her home and tried to see it through his eyes. There was nothing wrong with it. "Nothing?"

"Yeah. There's nothing here. No pictures, no art, nothing . . . personal." He stopped talking and examined her. "It's like no one really lives here."

He stepped closer to her, studying her.

She stepped back, and, for the first time, saw her house as he was describing it. She'd never thought of her home as a reflection of her. A home was just functional, just temporary. The less she had to pack, the better. But that didn't mean she was empty of character. It didn't mean that she was nothing. Her palms itched, and her feet begged to run. "Um, thanks for helping me. I'd better get started on putting things away . . ."

She hoped he would take the hint and leave. She moved toward the kitchen, the two bags still in hand.

"Sure, no problem." He grabbed the bags off the floor and followed her.

"No," she protested, "I got this." She set the bags on the table and turned to face him.

"I don't mind. It's not like I have some place I need to be." He smiled as if he knew he would have his way.

"Fine," she huffed. "But look, before I let you help me, I get to ask you a few questions." She planted her feet and crossed her arms.

He set the bags down again. "Shoot."

"Are you stalking me?" She glared at him as if she could somehow see through his lies if she focused hard enough.

"Stalking you?" He mimicked her pose, crossing his arms and glaring at her. "Seriously?"

The words sounded ridiculous, she knew it, but it wasn't about how rational it sounded. "You're just always . . . around."

"Hope." He laughed. "It's not exactly a big city. Besides, is it so hard to believe that I'm interested in you?"

She swallowed. "I thought I made it clear that I'm not. Interested, I mean. In friends. Or dating."

"But why not?" He took a step toward her, and his voice softened. "Will you just . . . let me be your friend?"

"I'm not looking for friends."

"Well, I am."

Hope snorted. "I've seen your parade of friendships over the last week." She grimaced. "I'm not interested in cuddling in the library, or meeting you at my locker."

He chuckled. "*That* is not what I meant. Besides, not one of those girls was looking for friendship." He tipped his head at her. "For being so uninterested, you sure notice a lot."

"Noticing and caring are hardly the same thing."

"Hope," Athan countered softly, almost pleadingly, "if I promise not to hit on you, or be creepy and weird . . ." He paused for a moment. "Well, I won't be creepy or weird *again*." He grinned. "Please. Can we try to be friends?"

"It's just . . ." Fissures and cracks dissolved the mortar encasing her heart. The bricks crumbled. His simple plea was impossible to refuse.

"We can try, I guess." But she had serious doubts, and she let it leak into her voice.

A slow smile spread across his face, and somehow it made her feel like warm honey was spreading through her heart.

"That's all I'm asking for," he said, his expression brightening. "Now, *friend*, why don't you let me help you put away your groceries?"

The question was rhetorical as he was past her and into the kitchen before she had a chance to come up with a response.

They spent the first afternoon of their tentative friendship sitting at her kitchen table doing homework. Shortly before six, Athan stood up and, with an apology, announced that it was time for him to go.

"I'll see you at school Monday. Unless you want some company running tonight?"

She shook her head. "I ran this morning."

"Okay." He crossed the room but then turned back toward her, his hand on the doorknob. He studied her, looking for something . . .

"What?"

He sighed. "Just, try not to be weird next week, okay?"

The brick wall was immediately back up. She knew it, he was a jerk. "What do you mean? Are you being condescending?"

"I'm just saying, at school I'll probably talk to you." His lopsided smile didn't quite hide the anxiety in his eyes. "Please don't be hostile, okay?"

She snorted. Maybe not a complete jerk. "Yeah, okay. I'll be nice. Wouldn't want to break your heart."

It was at this exact moment that Hope knew the answer to Mr. Stanley's riddle. "Oh," she said, and then she slapped her hand over her mouth.

"What? What is it?" he asked, stepping toward her.

Her blush crept up her neck, and she wished there was some way to take back her exclamation. "Umm, nothing. A riddle . . . Mr. Stanley, the butcher, gave me earlier. I . . . I just got the answer."

Athan stood, eyes wide, waiting. "Well? Tell me."

Awkwardly, she stared at her hands as she wrung them. "All right, but don't laugh."

She took a deep breath, and still staring at her hands, she recited, "If you break me, I do not stop working. If you touch me, I may be snared. If you lose me, nothing will matter. What am I?"

After a few seconds of silence, she looked up at him.

He shrugged. "I suck at riddles. What is it?"

Flushing a deep red, she wondered why she'd ever told him. She should've said something else. Made up a different riddle. Breaking eye contact, she stared at the floor and whispered, "One's heart."

"Clever."

She looked up to see if he was making fun of her, but there was no hint of mockery crossing his features.

"You can tell me riddles anytime, Hope." He smiled and continued, "Except right now. I've got to go." He winked, said goodbye, and then left, closing the door behind him.

Suddenly, her home seemed very empty.

EIGHTEEN

IT WAS NOT that Hope was depressed, although maybe there was some of that. All of her life, she'd listened to her mother and done what she was told. And her mother was probably right. Wasn't what happened in Bellevue the perfect example of why forming attachments was destructive? And yet, part of Hope refused to believe it. Part of her wanted, so badly, to believe it could be different. Because she had nothing else.

When her stomach finally protested against spending any more time in bed, Hope meandered to the kitchen in her pajamas. She scrambled eggs with cheese, and fried the bacon. She rinsed the strawberries, snacking on their juicy sweetness even after her hearty breakfast.

As she walked back to her room to change, her eyes drifted to the spare bedroom. She'd walked past the door countless times, avoiding the memories stored there. The door was ajar, and inside the room were the stacks of boxes that would never unpack themselves. With a deep breath, she affirmed the truth: If she didn't go through them, no one would. It was time to move forward, even if it was only by inches.

Trepidation fluttered in her chest as she pushed open the door. The darkness smelled stale and faintly of ash. She flipped the light switch, and artificial light flooded the room. Brown moving boxes covered the beige carpet, some stacked two or three high. Except for the one that had contained the knives and book, they were all still sealed with packing tape.

She cleared some space in the center and grabbed the nearest box. She ripped the tape off and opened the flaps to find stacks of clothes, the pungent smell of smoke clinging to the fabric. She sunk her fingers into a thick sweater. It was her mother's sweater, though it no longer carried her scent. Hope set the garment to the side and pulled out a pair of jeans. She patted the pockets and folded the pants. Shoving her emotions aside, she grabbed an entire stack of clothes from the box.

After unpacking and then repacking several boxes, she got a marker and tape, resealed them, and wrote *For Donation* on the side. Someone would appreciate all this stuff. As the number of boxes in the bedroom dwindled, the ones marked *For Donation* in the hallway grew. When she came across something significant, like the photo album of her mom, she set it aside. That would require more . . . emotional space.

In the end, there was only one box that held things she wasn't willing to part with; the rest she moved to the living room.

She stood at the doorway, appraising the products of her labor. The second bedroom was almost completely empty, the box in the corner looking forlorn and lonely. The only light was from the overhead bulb, the single window revealed a small square of the night sky. The sun had set and she hadn't even noticed. With a sigh, she closed the door behind her.

Her stomach gave a rumble of neglect, and she glanced at the clock. Just after ten! Almost eleven hours—whoa! No wonder she was hungry. She crossed into the kitchen and grabbed a jar of peanut butter and a loaf of bread. The rich smell of ground peanuts made her mouth water, and she licked a spoonful of the sticky spread and sucked it from the roof of her mouth. The salty sweetness tasted like nirvana.

After finishing her makeshift meal, she stepped back into the living room. Accomplishment and pride thrummed in her veins. And in that moment, she knew she would do what she could to stay in Goldendale for as long as she could. She'd keep her secrets, but she'd find a way to make friends.

If the Skia attacked, she'd be ready for them. She had her training, and her knives.

This was her home.

Baby steps indeed.

"WHERE WERE YOU last night?" Haley asked. "I thought you said you would come."

Hope could imagine Haley's pout. "I never said that." Hope lay on her bed, her feet up on the wall, the phone to her ear. "You said you wanted me to come, but I never agreed."

It was Sunday afternoon. Hope had spent the day cleaning house, grocery shopping, and washing her car. All the boxes from yesterday were still stacked in the living room. She'd need to take them into Yakima or the Dalles next week, but she was done being responsible.

"Fine. But you missed out. Krista—"

"Want to go see a movie? Or go shopping?" She didn't really want to hear what happened with Krista. Especially if it had anything to do with Athan. Yes, they were just friends, but Krista was the spawn of Tartarus. No one deserved her.

"Oh, did you see the new *Pirates* is out? I love David Arturo." Haley sighed. "He is so hot."

"Okay. Do you want me to come get you?" Hope couldn't care less about David Arturo or how hot he was, but if that meant she got to leave, she was on board.

"No, I'll come get you. Give me a few minutes to tell my dad then I'll head over."

Hope changed into a hoodie and jeans and tucked her wallet under her arm. Just as she grabbed her phone it rang.

"Hey, what's up?" Hope answered.

A long silence was her first clue it wasn't Haley. She was just about to hang up when she heard a man ask, "Who is this?"

"Ex . . . excuse me?" Her grip tightened on the phone. Who would have this number? "Who is this?"

"I found this phone and was wondering if you could help me locate the owner. What's your name?" The guy rushed through the words.

Not for one second did she believe him. Alarms went off in her head, and Hope looked at the screen. Priska's number flashed back at her.

"Hello? *Hello*? Who is this?" he demanded.

Panic coursed through her. "You . . . must have the wrong number."

She hit End. Someone had Priska's phone! And Hope's phone number! Oh . . . oh gods!

"Hope?" Haley pounded on the door.

Hope unlatched the deadbolt and pulled the door open. She tried to force a smile, but her hands were clammy, and her heart was racing. "Hey . . ."

Haley scrunched her nose. "What took you so long?"

"Uhh, I was . . . on the phone." Hope's voice went up as if asking a question.

"Oh." Haley frowned. "You okay? You look . . . stressed." She stepped in and looked around the room. "What's up with the boxes?"

Hope took a deep breath. "Just cleaning out some stuff." She shook her head. "I'm fine. Let's go."

Because what could she say?

"So, you cut me off, earlier," Haley said with raised brows as she drove through the parking lot. "But I'm going to make you hear this."

A car was backing out farther up the row, and she put on her blinker and eased up to the space.

Hope slouched down in the seat, waiting for a bomb. Because really, what more could go wrong?

"Yesterday at the river . . . Athan was talking about you."

Hope sat up. That wasn't what she was expecting. "What?"

"I knew it." Haley smiled as she pulled into the parking stall. "You're all, 'whatever, I hate him,' but really . . ." She nodded. "Yeah. I knew it."

"No. Friday he gave me a ride home from the grocery store. He asked if we could be friends; I said yes. That's it."

"Friends?" Haley glanced at her before climbing out of the car. "Well, maybe that's it on your side. But I don't think that's all he wants."

Hope closed the door, and the two of them crossed the lot toward the theater. It seemed very important that Haley understand this. "No, he just asked about being friends. Besides, I saw him with Krista Friday. They were practically kissing."

"Oh, Krista wants him all right." Haley laughed. "She was all over him, but I can tell you he doesn't care a bit about her. I think he's into you."

Great. That was all Hope needed. More wrath from the she-demon. "Maybe I should just tell him I changed my mind. Maybe I don't want to be friends."

"No. Don't do that. Tristan was saying that we could go do something together. The four of us. It would be so cool. Please?" Haley batted her lashes.

Hope laughed. Haley barely had lashes, so it looked like she was blinking something out of her eye. "Fine. But if Athan hits on me, you totally owe me."

Haley snorted. "You mean if he doesn't hit on you . . ."

They bought their tickets and went in.

"**I DON'T THINK** I'll ever look at pirates the same after those movies. Gods, I would love to be kidnapped by David Arturo. Wouldn't you?"

Hope frowned. "That's sick."

"What?" Haley turned to look at her. "Really?"

"There is nothing sexy about being kidnapped. There's like a whole syndrome about people who fall in love with their captors." Hope thought of Priska being tortured somewhere by demigods. "Seriously, that's messed up."

Haley rolled her eyes. "I'm not serious. Well, I am about the David Arturo part, but not pirates. I mean . . . No one really wants to get kidnapped."

Hope fiddled with her phone, turning it over and over in her hands. Five missed calls. All from Priska's number. Five.

"Can I ask you something?" Hope didn't know what to do. And she didn't have anyone else to turn to . . .

"Sure. As long as you aren't going to bash on David Arturo."

Hope smiled. "No. It's just . . . My aunt . . . kinda disappeared a month ago."

"Kinda disappeared? What does that mean?" Krista gasped. "Oh, gods. Was she kidnapped?"

Hope's eyes welled. Tension that had been building for weeks ballooned, and she couldn't keep it in. She wiped away the tears before they could fall. "I think so. Can . . . can you keep a secret?"

"I'm such an idiot," Haley murmured with a face-palm. She took Hope's sleeve and pulled her to the car. "Of course I can keep a secret. You can tell me anything."

They got back in Haley's blue sedan.

Once the doors were closed, Hope gave an edited history of her mother dying in a fire, her aunt's recent disappearance, and the strange phone call. "I don't know that they're all related, but . . . What if they are?"

Haley blew out a breath. "Well, maybe someone was just trying to be nice. I mean, he didn't threaten you or anything, right?"

"No. But he's called like another five times."

Haley was silent as if contemplating her answer. Finally, she said, "Well, I'd let it go. Unless you keep getting calls, or if the guy threatens you, or something."

It was sound advice. No need to freak out about one more thing.

"How was your weekend?" Athan asked.

He stood at Hope's locker, staring at her. It was the oddest sensation. A mixture of pride and anxiety coursed through her, and she wanted to giggle and run away. "Fine. I hung out with—"

"Hey, Hope." Haley bounced up. "How are you?" She smiled at Athan as if just noticing him. *As if.* She turned back to Hope. "Oh, I was going to ask you, have you had any more phone calls?"

And so much for secrets.

"Phone calls?" Athan frowned. "Who's calling you?"

Hope rolled her eyes at Haley and answered, "No." She turned to Athan. "It was nothing. Just a wrong number, but they kept calling back. Kinda freaked me out."

Hope snapped her locker shut.

"You two hung out?" Athan asked, looking back and forth between the two of them.

"Well, yeah," Haley said. "That's what friends do, you know."

"Yes, so I've heard." He gave Hope a hard look.

"What?" she asked him. "We hung out on Friday." Why was he acting all weird?

"I bet she didn't have to coerce you to hang out," he grumbled.

The three of them walked down the hall, drawing several stares. It felt like every single person in the hall was watching as they passed. Hope had never felt so conspicuous in her entire life.

"Of course not," Haley responded to Athan. "My motives aren't questionable."

Hope laughed and ducked into mythology, but she still heard him . . .

"There is nothing questionable about my motives, either."

NINETEEN

"ARE WE EATING lunch or what?" Athan asked. He'd met Hope at her locker right after chemistry, before she had a chance to disappear into the Library.

Hope pushed down anticipation—if that's what fluttering in her chest was—and took a deep breath. The commons was out because of the rain. "How about the cafeteria?"

He nodded. "You got it."

He held the door open for her and then led them to the table where Tristan, Lee, Scott, Haley—and Krista—were sitting.

"Hey, guys," Athan said, setting his stuff down. "Can we join you?"

Haley smiled at Hope from the other end of the table, and Tristan scooted his tray over.

"Yeah, of course," he said.

Athan sat next to his friend and patted the seat next to him.

This was not quite what she'd been thinking, but not knowing what else to do, Hope slid into a chair next to him.

As soon as she was seated, he stood up and leaned to whisper into her ear, "I'll be right back. I need to get some food. Stay put."

He pushed her hair back, exposing her ear, his hand cupping the back of her neck. Leaning closer, his lips brushed her ear as he spoke. "They're more scared of you than you are of them."

Her head and heart swirled as he walked away. Scared of *her*? What was there to be scared of? And he shouldn't be allowed to do that almost-kissing-ear thing. Friends didn't do that. Did they? She was pretty sure not.

"So, Hope, what did you do this weekend?"

Startled, she glanced up to find Tristan studying her expectantly.

"Uh, homework. Went and saw a movie."

"Lame," Krista muttered from across the table.

Hope glared at the petite girl.

"With me!" Haley's stare shot daggers at Krista until she looked away.

Hope wanted to say something. Anything. She just needed them to focus on something else. "I heard you guys had a great time down at the river."

It worked. Conversation erupted all around her. She tried to stay involved, nodding, smiling, answering questions, and by the time Athan returned, she no longer felt the need to run and hide. It was overwhelming, but . . . nice.

Tristan was telling her about the observatory when she heard a high-pitched whizzing sound. Something incoming, at high speed . . . Instinctively, she glanced at the sound and caught a roll of bread midair just before it hit Athan. The stinging of her hand told her just how fast the roll had been travelling. Someone hooted their approval, and someone else cheered.

Her stomach churned, and she dropped the roll like it was on fire. That was why she was supposed to stay invisible. Isolated. Not stand out. Not get noticed.

"Nice catch." Tristan leaned over and bumped her shoulder.

"Thanks," she mumbled, curling in on herself. How could she have been so dumb? That wasn't normal. Would they put it together?

"Impressive skills." Athan picked up the roll as if weighing it.

"Freak," Krista spat.

All Hope could think of to explain her reflexes in the most normal way was, "Twelve years of Tae Kwon Do."

No need to mention the supernatural hearing and reflexes.

"Tae Kwon Do teaches you how to catch?" Tristan asked.

She shook her head. "No, but it improves hand-eye coordination and reflex time."

"*Twelve* years?" Athan asked, his gaze boring into her.

She swallowed. "My mom wanted to make sure I could defend myself."

When the bell finally rang, Hope threw her barely eaten sandwich away. Without saying anything, she started to her locker. Athan kept pace next to her.

"Tae Kwon Do, huh?"

She nodded, wishing he would drop it already.

"Well, they loved you," he teased. "You just got twenty new BFFs and a starting position on the football team if you want it."

He didn't get it. Obviously. He seemed to thrive with all the attention he received.

Hope blew out a breath of frustration. "Yeah, sure," she said with a shake of her head. "Did you not notice the shade Krista was throwing?"

"Aww Hope, she's just jealous. You can't let her get to you."

She scratched at her palms, as if that could erase what had just happened. When Hope parted with Athan in algebra, she slumped into her seat with relief. But he was persistent and caught up with her after Spanish.

"I'm meeting Tristan in a few minutes, but what are you doing later?" His stride matched hers as they walked toward the lockers.

"Same old." There was homework and dinner in the solitude of her quiet home. Far away from the stares of her classmates.

Haley stood at her locker waiting.

"Same old is so boring. Let's hang out." He bumped her arm.

Tingles shot up from the contact, and Hope shook her head. "It's too much."

"What?" He tilted her chin so she was forced to meet his eyes.

"I . . . I don't know if I can do this. It's too much." She was exhausted. All the attention, all the scrutiny . . . It was overwhelming in a way she'd never experienced.

"You're too much," he teased. "See you soon." He turned and jogged down the hall.

"So, you gonna hang out with him?" Haley asked as they walked out to the parking lot.

"I don't know." Hope sounded like a broken record. "All of this . . . activity . . ."

Haley laughed. "Hope, this is normal."

"Not for me," Hope muttered.

"Where did you live before here? A cave?" Haley twisted her deep-brown hair into a bun. "Seriously, you should hang out with him, or we could do something together."

"Tomorrow. I have homework tonight. We can do something tomorrow."

Because Hope could not handle one more thing today.

SHE STILL HAD more than a week before the change. A week that seemed like forever away, and yet every day was a reminder of the time ticking away. And as the time grew closer to the change, the constant reminder that she was different than everyone she hung out with began grating on her. Her curse was a burden, and she resented it more and more every passing day.

But she pushed it aside, her fear and her worry, because today was going perfectly. It was early afternoon, and they were in her Civic heading south on I-82 to the fish hatchery. Tristan and Haley sat in the back seat, their constant conversation lulling Hope's nerves. Athan chimed in occasionally, mostly to give her directions.

Today had been different than any she'd ever had at school. She sat with Haley, Athan, and their friends at lunch and found herself laughing at Tristan's jokes. Haley invited her to come to the river Thursday night for a bonfire, and Hope contemplated going. Krista had left her alone. There'd been no further phone calls from Priska's number. And no Skia. If Priska would just let her know she was okay, life would be perfect.

"You look awfully pleased."

Athan's comment pulled Hope from her reverie. "Oh, just thinking. Are you going to the river Thursday?"

Part of her wanted to hang out with her new friends, and she recognized the shift. She was even referring to them as her friends.

"Do you want to go?" he asked.

Unwilling to commit, Hope mumbled, "Maybe."

The revelation that she'd settled enough to have friends was a bit disconcerting. It warred with what she'd been told over and over: connections were to be avoided. At some point, she would have to move, and . . . She didn't want to leave.

"I think you'll have a great time if we go, but I'll leave it up to you."

She caught his wording, and her heart fluttered. She would deal with leaving later. Once Priska came back.

They pulled off the freeway, and Hope followed signs to the Bonneville Fish Hatchery.

Hope looked out the window, assessing the surroundings. She could see picnic tables, benches, and a water fountain from the car. Trees and shrubs lined the concrete landscape; small pink petals floated in the breeze.

"How did you know about this place?" she asked as they walked past a couple industrial pools.

The group wandered down a path that wound alongside a natural-looking creek and several smaller ponds. The flowers bloomed in white, pink, and lavender. The smell from the blossoms mixed with the scents of the nearby river and the large pine trees. Overhead, small birds chirped.

Haley laughed. "Seriously, this isn't really a dude kinda place."

"Oh, I asked Scott what there is to do around Goldendale."

"Scott?" Surprise was written all over Haley's face.

Tristan chuckled. "Scott loves to fish. They have monster sturgeon here."

"Come on." Athan gave Hope's arm a little tug further down the path.

Hope could only stare when she first saw them. She had no idea that fish in a river could be so big and so *ugly*. They reminded her of the picture of catfish that she'd found in an encyclopedia when she was younger.

"Can you believe that Poseidon created *that*?" Athan leaned against the glass tank, looking at Hope.

"It's disgusting," Haley said, wrinkling her nose. She turned to Tristan. "Let's go feed the fish. I saw fish food thingies . . ."

The two of them wandered off.

Hope continued to stare at the glass window. The gray fish circled through the tank, coming through the murky water to pass the glass every few minutes. She thought of Athan's statement, hung up on his mention of Poseidon. Since starting public school, Hope rarely heard anyone mention the gods outside of a curse or a plea for a blessing. Athan seemed well versed in all their mythological history.

"It's like a giant albino catfish." She stepped up to the glass and tapped on it as the large fish swam past.

Despondency gripped her heart, a pity for wild creatures held within strict confines, their freedom limited by someone more powerful. Was it any different for the fish than it was for her?

A soft pressure at the small of her back brought her attention to the present. Athan stood beside her, his hand grounding her in the moment.

He stared into the tank and asked, "It's sad, don't you think?"

It was like he was feeling the same thing she was. "Do you ever feel like that?"

"Trapped?" He turned to face her; his eyebrows furrowed then released. "Do *you* feel trapped?"

She swallowed and bit her lip. Hedging, she responded with, "Doesn't everybody sometimes?"

He pinned her with his gaze, and the rest of the world disappeared.

"You didn't answer my question," he whispered.

Hope crossed her arms over her chest and set her chin in what her mom would call her defensive jut. Something deep in her wanted to avoid exposing vulnerability. Was that wrong? "I asked first."

"Fair enough." He laughed, relaxing back onto the glass. The smile still played on his lips as he said, "Yes. Sometimes I feel very trapped."

She exhaled, releasing her tension. Maybe he wouldn't judge her too harshly after all. "Me too."

The light in his eyes dimmed, and he took a deep breath. "I didn't want this to be such a downer. Come on, let's go feed the trout."

He took her hand and led her from the sturgeon tank. Stopping at a vending machine, he fed coins into it, filling their hands with little brown pellets of fish food.

Her mood lifted as she tossed the stinky bits into the ponds and streams. Silver-sided fish slid over each other as they came to the surface, their mouths opening wide as they gulped the small particles of food.

It was peaceful, with just the occasional splash from the fish, the sun warming her through her dark sweater. For one minute everything was right.

"Penny for your thoughts?" Athan nudged her with his elbow.

"You'll feel ripped off," she warned him. "It's peaceful here."

She brushed off her palms over the water.

Hope and Athan watched as the trout slid back into the darkness and the water calmed. They walked through the park, and when they didn't see their friends, they went back to the entrance.

"Hey, guys!" Tristan yelled. "Are you almost done? We're starving."

He stood by the storage ponds in front of the gift shop. Haley sat on a picnic table out by the parking lot.

She held her hands out as if begging. "Please . . . I'm dying . . . I . . . must . . . have . . . food."

The sun disappeared behind a cloud, and a chill blew in on the breeze.

"*Skata!*" Athan breathed the curse under his breath, startling Hope.

Tugging her hand, he dragged her toward the car. "What would you say to some seafood?"

Instinctively, she pulled back, dropping his hand. The chill felt ominous, and she scanned the picnic area. A flicker of movement by the flower beds drew her attention, and her eyes widened, as she froze in her tracks.

The Skia stepped from behind the budded trees. Staring at Hope, he made no move to come closer.

"What is with you, Hope?" Haley asked. "Don't you see I'm withering away?"

Hope didn't even look at her friend. Could she reveal what she saw? Should she? She wanted to yell at him to leave her alone. She wanted to fight him so he couldn't bother her again. She gritted her teeth.

"Hope?"

She felt Athan next to her, and glancing at him saw he'd bent down, fiddling with his shoe and pant leg.

Her gaze went back to the Skia, but he was gone.

Again.

Athan dropped his pant leg and stood up. "I'm starved. Let's go eat."

"Finally!" Tristan said.

Haley grabbed his hand and turned toward the car.

Hope wouldn't ask Athan what made him curse. Had he seen the Skia? Did he know that she'd seen it? Had she been obvious?

She thought the best thing would be to say nothing. No reason to scare her friends. And more importantly, she didn't want to reveal she could see them.

TWENTY

HOPE SET HER bag on the table and grabbed an apple. A light rap at the door brought a smile of expectation. She and Athan had talked about getting together, and he hadn't forgotten.

"Grab your homework. Let's go," Athan said, poking his head through the door.

"Where are we going?" she asked from the kitchen as she grabbed her backpack.

"My aunt wants to meet you, so I thought we'd have dinner with her. I hope you don't mind skipping your run?"

She thought of the strange meeting at the grocery store weeks ago and shook her head.

"No, you don't mind, or no you don't want to go?"

The latter. But of course she couldn't say that. Athan seemed so earnest, and she didn't want to offend him. "I don't mind skipping the run."

"Good." He grabbed her bag and slung it over his shoulder, then led Hope out the door.

"She's great, but a bit odd," Athan said as they wound through the quiet town toward the highway. "If she starts singing, or talking in rhyme, it's okay to ignore her."

"Does she do that a lot?"

He shrugged. "Sometimes. She's also likes to talk about the future."

"Can she tell the future?" Maybe she was a witch. Hope had read that there were still visages of Hecate that roamed the mortal realm. As goddess of crossroads, maybe her subjects could see into the future.

"Sorry, what?" He turned but never met her eyes.

"I asked if she can see the future."

He snorted. "You don't believe that, do you? Fortune-tellers?"

She shrugged. Maybe. Probably. Why wouldn't she believe it? She was a monster, after all.

They pulled into the driveway of the old bed and breakfast, and Athan faced her. "I know she's a little . . . odd, but she's always been there for me. I told her about you, and she wanted to meet you."

Hope nodded. She could do this. "Let's go see your aunt."

White azaleas and pink rhododendrons lined the walkway, complementing a fresh coat of paint.

"Been doing a bit of work?" Clearly someone had.

"My aunt thinks it helps keep me from being idle." Athan laughed. "'A teenager shouldn't have too much free time or he'll find trouble.'" He wagged his finger at her.

Just before opening the door, he gave Hope's hand a squeeze.

"Aunt Myrine?" Athan called out as soon as they crossed the threshold.

The inside of the house was the exact opposite of the out-side. It was a complete mess. Boxes lined the entryway, hall, and glancing into the other rooms, every available space. It made the house feel like a maze. As they walked down the hall, Native American masks, statues of Greek gods, and stacks of books drew Hope's attention. Some looked like they'd just been set down, others were covered in dust.

A door opened, and Myrine stepped out of a darkened room. Tinted goggles covered half her face, and her white hair escaped the confines of a bun at the top of her head.

When she removed her goggles, Hope's gaze was drawn to her unlined face. If her hair had been any color besides white, she could easily have been in her twenties. She glanced at Athan and then the gaze of her pale-blue eyes converged on Hope. The look was piercing.

"Athan"—his aunt addressed him but kept her focus on Hope—"you've brought me a riddle." Extending her hand to

Hope, Myrine added in a singsong voice, "A riddle, a joke, lots of fun to poke, poke, poke."

Hope cringed but took the woman's hand. It was dry and cool.

"Cats and bats and lots of boys," Mrs. Stephens chanted.

"Excuse me?" Hope stuttered.

Athan put his hand at the small of her back. He muttered something unintelligible under his breath, then cleared his throat. "Aunt Myrine, what are you talking about? This is Hope, the girl I was telling you about."

The two exchanged a look, and Myrine nodded. "Oh, yes. Yes, yes, yes. Here for dinner. Hello, my dear. Manners, manners, manners. I'm Myrine, but of course you know that. And you are Hope. But of course you know that, too." She turned and addressed him. "Locks of gold, and eyes that glitter, touched by gods . . . I can see why you are intrigued."

Hope said nothing, and Myrine prattled on.

"Come for dinner; come to eat. What a treat . . ." She squinted her eyes and nodded. "Yes, yes. Athan, go start the grill." She waved at him in dismissal. "Hope, my dear, help me in the kitchen?" Myrine bounced down the hallway, rhymes dribbling from her lips. "Greens are good, bread and butter, need some meat, yes, beef is better."

"Are you freaking out?" Athan asked, holding Hope back with his slow pace.

"She's . . . odd." She *was* freaking out, but clearly it meant something to Athan for her to be here. And the weird verses seemed harmless. "I think I'll be fine."

Athan ran up a set of crowded stairs, leaving Hope to follow Myrine.

As Hope walked down the hall, she looked into the open doorways. Artifacts littered the house: a golden pomegranate, a wooden birdcage carved with doves and roses, a small harp . . . an anvil and tongs.

When Hope stepped into an immaculate, completely updated kitchen, she stood momentarily blinded by the incongruence.

"Thou art the great cat." Myrine nodded at her. "Avenger to the gods . . ."

That was too close to the truth. Anxiety spiked Hope through the gut, and she glared at her hostess. "What are you saying?"

"It's on the royal tombs in Thebes." Myrine shook her head. "You . . . you have told him nothing."

Hope's jaw dropped. "I don't know what you mean."

"As you wish, as we be." Myrine smoothed her hair back, then went to the sink. "Do be a dear and help me with the broccoli, Hope." She set a paring knife and cutting board next to a produce bag on the counter. "I'll get the corn ready."

"Are you a witch?"

"A seer, a sage, a sibyl, a witch—call me what you want, take your pick."

Was that a yes? Hope cut broccoli, placing it on a sheet pan. Athan passed through the kitchen and went out the sliding glass door to start the grill.

Myrine turned to Hope, blue eyes bright with interest. "You have many roads before you, kitten. Choose wisely where you step, for that is where you will walk." Myrine closed her eyes. "Here kitty, kitty, kitty."

"Stop!" Hope clenched her fists, and her heart hammered. "Just stop. Why are you saying all that? What do you want?"

The clanking outside ceased, and as the door slid open, Myrine shifted, singing about being close to where the watermelon grew.

"How's it going in here?" Athan looked from Hope to Myrine.

Hope tried to smile, but the movement was forced, almost painful.

"Myrine?"

The older woman said nothing, and he turned to Hope.

"Are you okay?"

She shook her head. There weren't words for exactly how *not* okay she was.

"Do you want to go?" His warm fingers brushed her chin, and she looked up at him.

"Athan!" Myrine's voice was sharp. "If you play with a cat, you must not mind its scratch."

"Good gods!" He turned on his aunt. "Is this what you've been saying? You promised!"

Myrine bowed her head. "Cats and bats and lots of boys."

Athan grabbed Hope's hand, practically dragging her as he strode from the room.

In the doorway, Myrine's face was cast in shadow, but her head was downcast, her shoulders slumped. She waved weakly. An apology or merely a farewell?

The drive home was silent.

"I asked her if she was a witch," Hope confessed as they pulled up to her house. Maybe she'd actually triggered something and Myrine would tell him it was her fault.

Athan sighed. "She was in one of her moods. I should have checked in with her before I took you over. It's my bad, Hope, nothing you did."

"What's wrong with her?"

"She thinks she's an oracle. She has visions, hears voices . . . She thinks she's called of the gods and that she can see the future. But really, she's insane. When she's on her medication, she's docile. I'm sorry."

Hope knew there were people with mental illness, but she'd never met anyone. She also guessed that there had to be actual oracles out there, and witches, and who knew what else.

"I'm not mad," she said in an attempt to reassure him.

"But it scared you."

She wore her emotions like a coat, all on the outside. "Yes. But—"

"No. I don't want you defending her, or apologizing." He took a deep breath. "I'm sorry I let that happen to you."

But if Myrine was crazy, how did she know what she knew?

THERE WAS LESS than a week before the change. Soon enough, Hope would need to figure out how she was going to pull it off. Leave or stay home? And what would she say to Mr. Jeffers?

"So, are you coming tonight or not? It's a three-day weekend . . ." Haley tapped her pen against the lockers. "You only came that one time, and I promise—"

Hope shook her head as she turned her attention back to her friend.

"You didn't even hear what I was going to promise." Haley pouted.

"It doesn't matter." Hope grabbed her math book and slammed the locker door shut. "I'm not going back to the river."

"Of course it does. Athan will be there." Haley waggled her brows. "You don't want him to get distracted by some other chica."

Hope snorted. Since the disastrous dinner at his aunt's house last night, she'd done her best to avoid him this morning. "Athan can get together with whoever he wants. It's not like—"

Haley cleared her throat, and her eyes told Hope *someone* was behind her.

"Really, Hope?" Athan stepped around to face her. "I thought you said you wouldn't break my heart."

The blush went from the tips of her toes to the roots of her hair.

"We're just friends," she muttered, her gaze dropping to the floor.

"Yeah, but there's friends, and then there's *friends*." Haley pursed her lips and made kissing sounds.

"Shut up." Hope pushed Haley with a laugh. "You're acting like you're Eros-touched."

Haley rolled her eyes. "If the god of love had shot me, I promise I wouldn't be making kissing sounds at you. I would be getting all hot and sweaty with . . . uh, never mind." She grimaced. "Think about coming tonight, 'cause you should." She turned and started running down the hall. "I'll call you!"

Hope shook her head.

"You're not coming to the river?" He leaned against the wall of lockers, blocking her immediate path.

"Not you too." Hope stepped around him and ran down the hall to class just as the bell rang.

TWENTY-ONE

THE PIECE OF solitude was balm to her harried week. Hope responded to Athan's and Haley's texts with a definitive no. There was no way Hope was going to the river tonight. She needed a break.

But as exhaustion faded, worry wormed its way in.

If only Priska had said where she was going . . . Maybe they could find her. Mr. Davenport had sent a text Monday, telling Hope the same thing: stay put, no news. Was there anything Hope *could* do?

Useless . . . She was completely useless.

She blew out a breath and looked around her living room. The boxes from last week still sat stacked against the wall by the door.

It was dark out, but purpose burned through her. A few taps on her phone showed there was a Salvation Army in the Dalles. It was late, but not that late.

Hefting the first box, she fumbled at the front door and again as she pushed the button to release the trunk. The cool air tickled her skin, bringing goose bumps to her warm arms, but by the time the car was full, sweat ran from her hairline and soaked into her T-shirt. There were still four boxes inside, but nothing more would fit into her compact car. She'd just have to make a second trip later.

As she sang along to the radio, the thirty-mile drive went quickly. Once off the freeway, she followed the directions to the alley behind the Salvation Army. It wasn't until she sat the third box down that she actually assessed her surroundings. She crashed from the high of her impulsiveness, suddenly tempered by the risk of being alone in an alley at night. Stupid, stupid, stupid. While the Dalles wasn't a big city, it was certainly larger than Goldendale.

With the car off, she could hear music and loud, raucous clamor. At this time of night, and that kind of noise . . . There must be a bar nearby. Her heart beat a rhythm of anxiety, and she sped up to finish her task.

The largest box of clothing was wedged into the middle of the back seat. Hope pushed the box to the side then went around to pull it out. As unease raced through her veins, her palms became clammy. The large box was awkward, obstructing her view, and she stumbled over the uneven ground. As she bent to set her donations down, inebriated chortling roiled down the alleyway.

The box slipped from her hands, the contents spilling on the asphalt. The sleeve of her mom's sweater landed in the gutter, the splash of red contrasting with the darkness around her.

Even before she turned to the car, the fermented stink of alcohol wafted on the breeze. Two men, just more than shadows, came from the left, their drunken gait slow as they ambled toward her car. Even if she ran, she couldn't get in the car before they reached her. She sucked in a deep breath.

Adrenaline washed through her, and her muscles tensed. The sound of her heartbeat pounded in her ears, pages of a book rustled in the wind, and then the sharp intake of breath from a man.

The shorter man leered, and his brown eyes bespoke his mortality, and his smirk promised pain. In his fist, he clenched the handle of something. A hammer? No, a wrench.

The taller man's gait was steady, and something about his features was . . . off. Wrong. Washed out. And . . . his eyes! Two solid orbs of pitch.

Skia.

She swallowed back fear as it clawed up her throat. Hope grabbed for the golden dagger in her back pocket but came up empty. In another second, they would be in striking distance.

The human raised his arm, and instinctively, she moved. Stepping to the left, she hooked his wrist as he moved to strike, rotated her grip, and lunged behind him. She brought his arm with her, applying torque until she heard the snap. Before he had time to register the pain, she kicked his knees with the heel of her foot, buckling him to the ground. Not even a second later, he screamed. He dropped the wrench and clutched his shoulder.

She spun to face the other attacker and dropped back into a defensive stance, her arms up in a guard position. The Skia chuckled, a ghostly wheezing sound. They circled each other twice, and Hope struck. She jabbed twice, measuring his ability. Fast and hard. He knew how to fight.

"You are not as you seem," he rasped.

He reached as if to grab her, and she swung her left leg up in a crescent kick, clearing his arms. Before she brought the leg completely down, she shifted her stance and kicked him in the ribs. Sliding close, she delivered a hook punch where his liver would be, as if the dead still had their organs.

He bent over, exposing his left side, and she slammed her elbow into his jaw. The Skia crumpled to the ground.

Her legs trembled, and it felt like she was running through water, her movements lethargic and contorted. The man wrapped his warm hand around her forearm, and she stumbled.

Panicked, she lashed out with the heel of her palm, bringing her right hand back at the same time as she struck with her left. Over and over and over again. Using every ounce of force, she struck. Bones crunched and warm wetness covered her hands. Only when the man released her arm did she stop.

Hope looked around for the Skia.

The tall figure leaned against the wall of the alley, the shadows lapping at his feet, the weight of his gaze fixed on her.

She shifted back into a defensive stance, waiting for him to attack.

"Interesting." He tipped his head. "Little monster . . ." He stepped into the shadow and disappeared.

Hope gasped. Just like the other Skia, he was gone. Staring at the shadow, she inched forward.

The Skia stepped back out and grabbed her arm.

"Your presence is requested by my master," he hissed.

She screamed and yanked her arm away.

He cursed and, with a blade black as pitch, he swung at her.

Hope dropped to the ground, the air above her whistled. As soon as the knife had passed, she jumped up and ran to the car, falling into her seat. Her hands were slick with blood, and she struggled to get the key in the ignition.

She glanced out the side mirror and saw the Skia standing over the body of the man.

"Come on, come on . . ." she whimpered.

The engine turned over, and she put the car into reverse.

She was almost to the bridge when she realized she was shivering.

She turned the heater on full blast, but her teeth continued to chatter. Too afraid to stop, she drove until she was outside her house.

Safe, safe, safe, she chanted in her mind. But she did not, could not, get out of the car. She sat debating her fear, trying to talk herself out of her shock. She knew that's what this was, and it was to be expected, even normal, considering. But it was all useless; she couldn't move.

Unconscious of time passing, she eventually became aware she wasn't shivering or cold anymore. She glanced at the dash. It was well past two in the morning.

She should go inside, wash up. The thought of the gore on her hands was motivation enough. She turned the car off, and as she pulled the keys from the ignition, she noticed her golden dagger in the cup holder. Right where she put it when she climbed into the car. She grabbed the blade, opened the door, and stepped out into the chilly night.

I'm home. It's okay. One foot in front of the other.

In a sort of shell-shocked trance, she didn't hear her name being called at first. When she did, she instantly recognized the voice and looked around for the source.

Athan crossed her lawn in long strides.

"Hope? Are you all right?" His approach slowed as he got closer.

"Sure." She attempted to mask her weariness. "What are you doing out so late?" She needed to distract him, to steer the conversation away from her. Her gaze darted to his truck parked on the street right next to her house. How could she have missed it?

"I was down at the river, remember? I dropped Tristan off, and I was heading home when I saw your car running with the lights on. I wanted to make sure you were okay."

He was close enough that she could feel the heat rolling off his body. Unconsciously, she rubbed her hands over her chilled arms.

The silence was uncomfortable. Had he asked her something? "What?"

"I said, are you okay?"

"Yeah, I'm fine. I dropped some boxes off at . . . at the Salvation Army." She shuddered and forced herself to continue. "Just doing some house cleaning, trying to make the place look lived in."

It seemed like forever ago that he'd been in her house.

She took a deep breath to steady herself and smelled him, the sharpness of his soap, and the campfire that clung to his skin. He was staring at her with wide eyes, his head shaking. He took another step forward and touched her lightly, his fingers brushing her forehead. He withdrew his hand and looked at it.

"What is it?" she asked.

"Hope." His voice throbbed with anxiety. "Why do you have blood on your face?"

She reflected briefly, but words failed to come, and she stood dumbly looking down. The ground started to shake, and it wasn't until Athan put his arms around her that she understood. She was trembling.

He pried her keys from her fingers and led her inside. Turning lights on as he went, he guided her into the study and pushed her into the overstuffed chair.

"Shh, shh. You're okay. You're safe. You're home," he whispered, the cadence of his voice a soft lull.

Eventually, she stopped shaking. She stuffed the dagger in between the cushions and grabbed the edge of her sleeve to wipe her eyes, but the moisture was sticky. One glance and her stomach rolled. Her sleeves were saturated with blood, and maroon splattered the front of her shirt, too.

She pushed herself up and stumbled past Athan and into the bathroom. She dropped to the floor, and her stomach heaved. She vomited again and again as tears rolled down her cheeks. She yanked off her shirt. She had to get the blood off.

"Hope?" Athan came through the doorway and knelt next to her.

He handed her a wet washcloth, and when she didn't take it, he wiped down her face and hands, rinsing the cloth after each pass.

She lay her head down on the floor and started to cry, a soft whimper, pleading for relief from the horror of her memories as they flashed through her mind.

"Shh." He rubbed her back, the contact of his hand warm and comforting. "Shh."

When her tears stopped, he stood up. "I'll be right back."

He returned shortly with a clean T-shirt and pajama bottoms.

"I'll wait out here while you get changed." He closed the door behind him.

She stood, looking down at the gore on her sweats. She peeled them off and threw them into the corner behind the door. She dressed and pulled herself out of the bathroom.

TWENTY-TWO

ATHAN SAT ON the couch and patted the spot next to him. "What happened?"

She sat close enough that she could feel his warmth, needing the reassurance that could only come from another human being. With a deep breath, she tried to explain. "When I dropped off that stuff, there were . . . two men. I hit . . . I hit him. I must have gotten some of his blood . . . on . . . me."

She looked up to see Athan gaping at her.

"But you're okay?" He crouched down, cupping her cheeks in his hands.

She forced herself to focus on his eyes. Such a strange green. Like the moss on the trunks in Bellevue. What was he saying?

"Are you okay?"

She brushed her tongue over the roof of her mouth. It felt like sandpaper. "Water. Please. I'm . . . so . . ."

Too exhausted to think anymore, she curled into a ball. When he returned, she took the cup gratefully and drank the contents.

He sat next to her, his arm circled around her, his hand resting on her back. He brushed a tendril of hair back behind her ear. With his touch came warmth, and she involuntarily leaned toward him.

"Just . . . sit here . . . a minute?" If he would just stay for a minute or two, she would be all right.

"Sure."

He took her hand, and she felt comfort. Peace. Her lids became heavy, and she fought to stay conscious.

"Thank you," she mumbled. She knew she should ask him to leave, or see him out, but she couldn't make herself move. She felt the light touch of him tracing his fingers over her hand, and as she drifted off to sleep, she was vaguely aware of him humming.

WHEN HOPE AWOKE, her thoughts were already racing.

She sat up, the memory of the previous night's events crashing into her. She glanced down at her clothes, and while they were clean, she could see flecks of blood under her fingernails. Her attacker's blood. Her victim's blood.

Her stomach lurched, and she dashed to the bathroom. Throwing up bile, Hope retched until her muscles hurt, then rested her head on the floor until the churning stopped. The sharp tang of bleach burned her nostrils.

Willing her rubbery legs to hold, she stood at the sink and brushed her teeth. Then, she filled her hands with liquid soap. With the water running, she scrubbed her fingers with her tooth-brush, and then her palms. Suds dripped into the water, disap-pearing down the drain. Her skin was raw, and the water stung as she rinsed the last drops of her fight down the drain.

Her body ached, and she was overcome by the urge to clean every part of herself present at the attack. She turned on the shower and then remembered Athan. Was he still there? She turned off the water and tiptoed out into the hall.

"Athan?" Her voice broke, and she cleared her throat. "Athan?" She looked in the study, the kitchen, the spare bed-room, and the living room. Finding herself alone in her own home and the front door locked, she went back to the bathroom.

She bathed fiercely, scrubbing until her skin was tender. When the water ran cold, she climbed out. While she dressed, she remembered her clothes from last night, still behind the door.

But the clothes were gone, as was the washcloth and towel she'd used last night. Sharp as the scent of bleach, understand-ing cut through her. She shivered as icy fingers of dread crawled over her scalp and down her back. She shut the bathroom door and climbed onto her bed. The panic made her ache for the familiar. She called Priska's number, hoping but not believing. It went to voicemail on the first ring. With a sigh, Hope disconnected. Why bother leaving another message?

What to do? She should leave Goldendale, move to another part of the state, or maybe another part of the country. She left all those boxes at the Salvation Army, and, no doubt, the cops would link her to the crime. She thought of the Skia and then . . . The man travelling with him was definitely alive. But humans couldn't see Skia, which meant . . . Her head swam; there was a pounding, a constant thumping, and she closed her eyes in an attempt to seek relief from the incessant noise.

The pounding stopped, and she let out a sigh of relief. Then the floor creaked, and her heart stuttered.

"Hope?" Athan tapped on her bedroom door.

A sob escaped her lips.

"Hey." Athan sat on the bed next to her and wrapped his arms around her, pressing her into him.

She couldn't control it. She sobbed into the warmth of his shirt.

Her comfort turned to embarrassment and then horror at the reality swirling around her. What did he know? What could she say?

She ducked her head and pulled away from him, mumbling something akin to an apology, if it had been coherent.

He scooted close to her again. "What?"

"I'm. Sorry." She said it slow so that she wouldn't have to repeat it again.

He wrapped his arms back around her, and his chuckle rumbled through his chest. "Yes. I can see that you are."

She felt brief pressure on the top of her head, and then he pulled away.

"I'm staying with you today. All day." He picked up her hand and threaded his fingers through hers. "And before you protest." He tightened his grip. "You do need me to."

Hope frowned, her eyebrows pulling down in a grimace.

"I saw the news this morning. There was an attack last night in the Dalles. Some guy named Antony Kohl who was out on parole. A real dirt bag."

She felt like she couldn't breathe.

"There's speculation that he was a demigod, and Skia killed him. The police are looking into it."

Her vision spotted, and the room spun.

"Hope! Breathe."

She gasped.

"Don't *do* that." He cupped her face in his hands, forcing her to meet his eyes. "I can't help if you pass out."

What was he talking about? Help her? Help her what?

"Have you eaten today?"

She shook her head and looked down at their hands. Hers lay in his, but even with his fingers wrapped tight, she could see the tremor.

"Stay right here, okay? I'll be right back."

"Okay." She leaned back into the pillows, her eyelids heavy. She had been up for just over an hour. Why was she so tired?

She could hear him pulling dishes from the cabinets, opening and closing the fridge. Lulled into a sense of security, she closed her eyes.

"Here you go, Sleeping Beauty." He set a plate with two slices of cinnamon toast in front of her. "I would have made you more, but I think it's best we make sure you can keep this down."

She took a bite and savored the sugary spice flavor. She inhaled the rest. "Thanks."

He took the plate and set it on the dresser, then sat at the foot of her bed. "I burned your clothes this morning. I think the only link anyone will have to last night will be the boxes you dropped off. Do they have your name on them?"

She thought about it. "Yes, just . . ." Just Nicholas, her last name. But that wasn't what she was going by. "Just my last name."

"Okay. That's okay. Donating stuff doesn't tie you to the . . . incident."

Incident? Is that what he was calling it? "Do they have a security camera?"

He shook his head. "Nope. It was on the news." He sighed. "I think today will be the hardest. We need to make sure it's like nothing happened. Just in case."

Just in case. The swallow was almost painful. She could do this. "I could drop off the rest of the boxes."

"Let's do it." He tilted his head toward her. "Anything else you need to get done today?"

"Homework."

He smiled. "Let's get started. Just like any other day." He stood, collected the plate from the dresser, and stepped into the hallway.

SHE SNACKED ON dry cereal while she peeled and cut vegetables. Finished with a mound of onions, carrots, and potatoes, she dropped them into the large Crock-Pot. The mundane movements helped steady her heart rate. After filling the bottom of the pot, she seasoned the chuck roast she'd bought earlier that week and put it on top of the vegetables.

Athan sat quietly at the table, looking between her and his math homework.

"What happened last night?" she asked. "The last thing I remember was drifting off on the couch."

"You fell asleep. I moved you to your bed, then I slept out here on the couch till about seven. I checked on you before I left to shower and change clothes; you were still asleep."

She noticed his hair was still damp. "And the bathroom?"

"I thought it would be better if you didn't have to face the cleanup."

She blushed and nodded.

"Oh." He dug into his pocket and then put her keys on the table. "I'm sorry. I took these. I wasn't sure how else to lock up when I left."

She shrugged. "It's okay. Thanks for your help. I think . . . I might have gone a little crazy." Her emotions simmered inside her, threatening to boil over, and knew she'd better change the subject.

He stood and reached for her hand. "What do you say we take the rest of the boxes to the Goodwill in Yakima?"

Instinctively, she stepped back. "No. Let's drop them at the Dalles. I . . . I need to not be afraid."

His hand dropped to her waist. "Do you want me to load everything into my truck?"

"No. There's room in my car. The trunk is still full, but the last few boxes should fit in the back."

"All right." He lightly pushed her aside. "Let me get a drink of water, then I'll go load. Meet you at the car?"

The heat from his hand was still there, and she wanted to soak in that warmth. She shook herself free from the trance. "I'll go get my shoes." She dropped the keys onto the table for him and went to her bedroom.

He was loading the last box into the back seat when she came out. She got the keys and locked up the house. Athan walked over to the driver's side.

"Hey, I'll drive," she protested.

With a shake of his head, he said, "I don't think you should be behind the wheel today." He slid into the car and then looked up at her and grinned. "Besides, I'm a male chauvinist. I always drive."

The joke made her smile. She climbed into the passenger side.

When he started the car, the radio blared, and he quickly shut it off.

Funny, I don't remember hearing anything on the way home last night. She remembered the blood on her hands, and her eyes locked on the steering wheel.

"I cleaned up in here, too," Athan explained. "It wasn't bad, but . . . Hope?"

"Hmm?"

"If anyone ever asks . . ." He fiddled with the keys for a moment before meeting her eyes. "I want you to tell them we were together last night."

"But you were at the river."

"Yes, but I was back in Goldendale before midnight."

Midnight? "But that would mean . . ." She couldn't say it. He sat in his car, watching her for over two hours?

"I promise I'm not stalking you. I drove around for a while. When I passed your place, I saw you sitting in your car. I wanted to make sure you were okay."

A strange feeling warmed her chest. Unsure of what it was, or what it meant, she was certain of one thing: She was glad to have him here.

He lifted his hand from the wheel, and gently wove his fingers through hers.

She looked down at his dark olive skin and her own, pale gold. In her chest, hundreds of butterflies emerged from cocoons. She slid her hand away.

"I don't . . ." She struggled not only with what to say but how to say it. "I don't understand you."

"What do you mean?"

"I . . . I don't know if I can trust you. How do you know if you can trust someone?" She wanted to, and was so, so afraid.

"You just decide." He grabbed her hand again. "Trust me. I promise you won't regret it."

His warmth seeped from her fingers up her arm and into her heart.

She took the leap. "Okay."

TWENTY-THREE

THE CLICK OF a seatbelt awoke her, and Hope sat up rubbing her eyes. They'd arrived in the Dalles.

Athan leaned toward her, his hand on her leg. "Why don't you just sit tight? This will only take a second."

She nodded. When he left the car, she sat up and stared at the empty alleyway. Memories flashed through her mind like pictures. The Skia standing there watching her. What did he mean his master wanted to talk with her? Why would Hades want her?

She leaned back in her seat and pulled out her phone. She wanted to send a note to Priska. *Crap.* Someone else had Priska's phone. Oh, gods, Hope had called her this morning. Did she leave a message?

"So." Athan slid back into the driver's seat. "What else do you have on your agenda today?"

There was nothing she could do about it now. She sighed and concentrated on what needed to happen today. "I need to finish my algebra and Spanish. What about you?"

The right corner of his mouth turned up in a half smile.

"Same." He paused briefly. "Is it going to bother you if I crash and do homework with you? Maybe stay for dinner?"

"Um, did you just invite yourself over for dinner?" Inside, relief washed over her. The last thing she wanted was to be alone.

He chuckled. "Yes. Yes, I did. Is that okay?"

"Yes." She smiled. "Actually, it's a great idea. I owe you more than dinner for all your help."

"It's called friendship, Hope. You don't *owe* me anything. But I will be your best friend if I can have some of that roast."

They stopped for lunch at a sandwich shop, and when they headed back to the car, she slid into the passenger seat.

Once they were on the interstate, she turned to him. "What was your mom like?"

Athan was quiet.

Had she offended him? Should she apologize? "You don't have to tell me if you don't want to—"

"She was the greatest." His voice was soft, as if he was living among his memories. "She was beautiful. She had dark hair, almost black, and I got her green eyes. She loved to laugh, and she would try to play jokes on people, but she could never keep a straight face. She loved to dance. When I was little, she would turn on music, and we would dance in the living room. She was a great cook, too. She was . . . she was the best mom."

"What happened?"

His gaze hardened, and he took a deep breath. His exhale was slow and measured. "She got sick. The doctors didn't know what it was. My dad went crazy trying to find someone to help her, but no one could." His words were strained. "One night she went to bed and didn't wake up. We knew it was coming, but still . . ."

"Do you miss her?" She stared out the windshield, trying not to cry.

"Every day."

"Me, too." Her tears fell, and she wiped them away choking back her emotion. Athan took her hand, and a portion of her pain lifted.

"What about your dad?" she asked.

"He's gone, too," he whispered.

Hurting for him and his loss, she wanted to give him some of the same relief, and Hope squeezed his hand. He had to know she was there for him, too.

He continued to hold her hand while they drove to Goldendale.

They spent the rest of the day on homework. And Hope found her perspective shifting even more. Athan was actually smart. Really smart. Especially in math and science.

When it started to get dark, Hope unwound herself from her chair and headed into the kitchen. She diced a tomato to toss into a salad and rinsed grapes from the bunch. She grabbed a couple of plates, silverware, and glasses and brought them to the counter. She dished up their dinner, just like she would for her and her mother, and brought the plates to the table.

Athan looked up from his homework as she came in and then jumped up out of his chair.

"I'm sorry. I should have been paying more attention. I could have helped." He ran into the kitchen and grabbed napkins from a holder on the counter.

When he joined her at the table, her heart thudded, and she gulped a deep breath. All the stability she'd tried to build in Goldendale was shattered, and Athan was sitting at her dinner table. She'd hated him, and now—

"Hey. What's up?"

The warmth of his voice broke through her reverie, but she could only give him a blank stare.

"You don't look so good." He waved his hand in front of her. "You feeling okay? Is the shock getting at you?"

His words registered, and she looked at him with horror.

"Yeah." Her appetite dissipated, but she sat down. "I'm sorry. I'm just not feeling myself."

"Want to talk about it?"

"Maybe another time." Or another lifetime. There was no way to explain it without revealing everything. Which she would never do.

She picked at her meal, worrying and overanalyzing her actions and his behavior. She could tell Athan knew something was up, but he didn't press.

When he scraped his fork on his plate, Hope noticed he'd devoured his food.

"Do you want seconds?"

He grinned. "If you aren't going to finish yours, just pass me your plate."

He did the meal justice, eating all of his food and most of hers.

"Go set up a movie," he said when they were done. "I'll load the dishes."

She went into the living room, turned on the television, and scanned through the titles. There had to be something Athan would enjoy, or at least tolerate.

He came up behind her, reading over her shoulder. His body was so close the heat filled the space between them. She was no longer reading titles but trying to regulate her breathing.

"Hmm, what's that one about?"

His voice was soft and low, and his breath tickled her neck. He placed his hand on her waist at the same moment she turned to ask him which movie he was talking about. Her breath caught. They were almost face to face. She moved to step back, but he held her close.

"Hope." He breathed her name so softly it was a caress. He removed the remote from her hand and then brushed her hair away from her face. His green eyes were just inches from her gold ones, and she could feel the tension of his body, his muscles taut, the vein in his neck pulsing. "What are you thinking?"

Their breath mingled, and her emotions whirled. Her desire to lean into him was so overwhelming she struggled to form a coherent response. "What movie . . . should we watch?"

He laughed softly and clicked through the titles. "How 'bout this one? *Some Like It Hot*?"

It took all her focus to pull herself together. "Yeah."

The knock at the door felt like a jackhammer, startling them both. Hope jumped away as if they'd been caught, her heart pounding against her chest. Eyes wide, she looked at him, but the same confusion marked his features.

She thought of the dead man. Had the police found out about her? How could she explain?

The knock came again, this time a bit harder.

"Wait, Hope." Athan grabbed her wrist. "Remember. We were together. No matter what they ask. We were together last night."

She nodded at him, and with a deep breath, she opened the door.

Scott and Krista stood on her doorstep. Scott shifted from foot to foot, a grimace on his face. Krista looked like a cat that had just caught its prey.

"Oh. Hi." Krista gave her a too-sweet smile. "Is Athan here? We thought we saw his truck outside, and he's supposed to come with us to Lee's tonight."

"Sorry, guys. I totally forgot." Athan moved toward the door and put his hand at the small of Hope's back. "We were just getting ready to watch a movie."

"Come on. You promised last night you'd come, and we need even numbers to play." Krista was wheedling, her voice honey, but the hint was hardly subtle.

"Well, do you mind if Hope comes?" He looked to Hope with expectation and desire, and he nodded at her encouraging her to agree.

Krista rolled her eyes.

Before Krista could respond, Hope shook her head. "Actually, I think I'll call it a night. I could use a little extra rest."

Athan frowned. "Really? I could—"

"No, you should go ahead. I'm tired. I don't think I'll be much fun tonight."

Krista beamed.

Athan looked at Hope intently. "No, really, Hope. I'd be happy to stay."

"Come on, Athan. She already said she wanted you to come," Krista said while waving him toward the door.

Gods, she was really putting on the pressure.

Athan put his palm to Hope's cheek, drawing all of her attention to him. "Are you sure?"

When she nodded, he sighed.

"All right." He turned to the two on the porch. "Why don't you guys head over? I'll be there in a few minutes."

Krista shook her head. "It's okay. We'll just wait for you."

They stepped off the porch and wandered in the yard. But, of course, they'd left the door open. Hope would admire Krista's persistence if she didn't despise her so much.

"If you'd feel better having someone here, you know I'll stay, right?" Athan took Hope's hands, his thumbs tracing circles over her palms.

"Thanks. I'll be okay." She pulled away. "I'm so tired. I'm sure I'll go right to sleep."

"Will you call me if you don't? I mean, if you're scared, or need something, will you call me?"

She laughed because she felt like she should, but there was nothing funny. She *was* scared.

His lips pulled up into a sheepish grin. "I'm being ridiculous, huh?"

She offered a wan smile. "You'd better go before Krista comes and hauls you off."

"You're probably right." He started toward the door but stopped halfway, returning to cup her chin in his hand. "Please remember to call me if you need anything," he whispered and then he gently kissed her forehead.

Hope locked the door behind him and stumbled into the kitchen, feeling like the energy had been sucked from her body. She prayed to Hypnos for sleep and Artemis for protection before placing a small plate of the roast by the shrine of Hecate. But she grabbed her daggers, just in case.

TWENTY-FOUR

HOPE SLEPT LATE Saturday. She told herself she deserved it. In fact, she deserved to spend the entire day in bed if she wanted to. But with a glance at the calendar, she saw there were only four days left before she'd shift. At the very least, she should take a shower.

She knew it was the shock taking a toll, but by the time she got out of the shower, she was exhausted. So she got into a clean pair of pajamas and spent all afternoon watching movies on the couch.

The knock at her door caused panic to flutter through her chest until she heard Athan's voice calling her name. She opened the door and took him in. His hair was still damp, and she could smell the citrus from his soap. His moss-colored T-shirt made his eyes bright.

He pulled an envelope from his back pocket. "My aunt asked me to give you this."

Hope stepped aside to let him in. "Everything okay with her?"

The disastrous dinner seemed ages ago.

Athan rolled his eyes. "Hades in hell. She's been off her meds the last couple of weeks. I didn't know. Usually she's so . . . Anyway, she wanted to give you this, like an apology or something."

He pushed the thick cream envelope into her hands.

Inside was a golden coin. One side was embossed with the figure of a woman holding a cornucopia and a set of old-fashioned scales. *One favor* was stamped on the other. The image reminded her of Athena, but neither the cornucopia nor the scales were Athena's symbols.

"Is this for real?" Hope held it up.

His eyes widened and then closed. He shook his head.

"Gods. That is so embarrassing." He offered a wan smile. "Do you want me to get rid of it?"

Maybe it was crazy, but intuition zinged, quick as lightning. There was something odd about the coin, and if felt powerful.

"No, I'll keep it." She tucked it back in the envelope and the envelope under her arm.

"You better hope you never need it," he muttered.

What was that supposed to mean? "It's not like I could spend it anywhere."

He shrugged. "Not in this realm."

She stared at him, trying to figure out if he was serious.

He laughed, but it sounded forced. "Just in the Land of Make-Believe."

But the weight of the coin and its intricate detail spoke of its value. Maybe he didn't know anything and he was just embarrassed about his aunt.

"Hey." Athan leaned against the doorframe. "Do you want to go get dinner?"

"That sounds great." She'd barely eaten all day and was starving. "Where do you want to go?"

"I know this place in Yakima." He smiled. "Birchfield."

"I've heard it's good. Just let me get dressed." She pulled at the front of her tank top.

"And get a jacket. It's a little cool out."

She went back to her bedroom and opened her closet. She put the envelope with the coin in the *Book of the Fates*. Then she slipped on jeans, and as she reached for a T-shirt, she thought better of it. Instead, she pulled on a black camisole and wrapped a sheer black blouse over it. She pulled her hair back into a messy knot and clipped in a couple of black gem bobby pins. A little bit of makeup, and she grabbed a pair of black heels.

"Sorry that took so long." Her heels clicked on the floor.

He said nothing.

"If you think it's too formal, I can go change." She turned to go back to her room.

He grabbed her wrist, his grip soft and warm.

"No, no." His voice was husky. "Don't. I just . . ." He stroked the inside of her palm with his thumb, and his gaze travelled her. "By the gods, you are beautiful." He shook his head. "I'm sure you hear that all the time." A muscle in his jaw jumped, and he continued, "We'd better go or we're going to miss our reservation."

He'd made a reservation? Nice.

They chatted about school, music, and movies, and the drive passed quickly. They arrived at Birchfield just before six. Athan handed the keys to the valet and offered Hope his arm.

Inside, the maître d' looked up at the young people with disdain.

"Can I help you?" His voice was barely civil.

Hope looked to Athan and was surprised at the change in his countenance. Gone was the relaxed young man. He stood tall and, looking down on the maître d', spoke evenly. "I have a reservation for six o'clock. Mr. Michael. Is our table ready?"

The man staggered, almost as if he'd sustained a physical blow. He shook his head, then looked back up. "Yes, sir. Right this way, sir." With several glances behind him, all with wide eyes and fawning smiles, the maître d' led them to a secluded table marked *Private*. "I trust this will do." When Athan nodded, the man finished with, "Enjoy your evening."

The coup de gras came when he bowed at them before leaving.

Hope had never seen someone so smitten and eager to please. "What was that?"

"What?" Athan raised his eyebrows as if nothing odd had happened.

Hope tried to put it into words. "He was so rude, and then all super nice. Like a complete change of heart."

"Don't you know the phrase 'money talks?'"

He helped Hope into her seat and then slid into his. The waiter was prompt with their drink order, and the service was consistently superb. The food was exquisite. The plates disappeared as they finished each course, only to be replaced with the next. The experience was unlike anything she'd had before.

As they made their way back out to the valet, she took a sidelong look at her date. While he was dressed casually, he carried himself with poise and confidence unlike anyone she'd ever met. As soon as the thought crossed her mind, she froze. That wasn't true. She *had* known confidence like his.

But she pushed the thought away.

Impossible.

As he helped her into the truck, she thanked him.

"Did you have a nice night? Wasn't the food great?" He was grinning.

"Yeah. The food was fabulous, and I love not having to do clean up." She laughed at the thought of the number of dishes that would be required to make such a meal. "Seriously, thank you."

"No, no. It was my pleasure. Really. I'm so glad you enjoyed yourself."

"I did. Very much so."

On the stereo was a soft piano medley, and Hope stared out the window at the night sky. When they pulled off onto Highway 97, the lack of lights made the stars bright.

"What are you looking at?" He reached out and touched her hand, drawing her attention to him.

"The stars."

She rarely took the time to enjoy the night sky anymore. She used to love it, flying with her mom at the new moon. Hope closed her eyes, and with a deep breath made a decision to focus only on the present moment, the now. As she opened her eyes to the sky before her, she saw the waning moon was brilliant—only the brightest stars could compete. Still there were millions of them in the sky, and without city lights, it was breathtaking.

She turned and looked at him, but he was glancing up at the night sky, smiling, and then he turned back to the road.

"Do you know very much about astronomy?"

"Orion, Cassiopeia." With his index finger, he traced the constellations in the sky. "There's Hercules, and Taurus. Over here is Gemini and Ursa Major and Ursa Minor." As he traced the constellations, his voice grew wistful.

Hope shifted in her seat so she was nearly facing him. "Are you an astronomy whiz, or all-around nerd?"

He laughed. "I'm a nerd. Seriously. My dad, he loves astronomy. He would keep me up late pointing out the constellations. My mom would come outside and act put out, saying I should be in bed already. He'd just laugh and invite her to join us."

He paused, but Hope had no intention of interrupting him.

"My dad said that if you knew the map of the constellations, you could never get lost."

His reverie became soundless, and she waited in until he came back to the present.

"He seems like he was a great father," she finally said.

"He tries to be."

There was momentary silence as he allowed her to digest the words.

"He's still alive? But you said . . . he was gone. You had to come live with your aunt?" Her voice was tight with incredulity.

He accepted her scrutiny without interruption. "My father travels a lot, and his schedule is not always his own. It's easier to just say he's gone than having to explain." He averted his gaze as he spoke. There was tension in the muscles of his jaw, and his grip on the steering wheel tightened. "It sounds terrible, I know that, but I understand now. I didn't when I was younger; it used to make me so mad. He takes me with him when he can."

She could hear there was more. "What does he do?"

"He has a courier service of sorts."

"Like FedEx?"

"Kind of. Messages are part of it. He also does some guide work."

"So he's self-employed?"

He snorted. "I guess you could say that."

"He doesn't like it?"

"Oh, mostly he likes it. He complains sometimes, but I guess that's probably true regardless of what your job is, huh?"

"So, what's the name of his company? Maybe I could use them sometime." She thought it would be amusing.

"He doesn't really do local deliveries; it's all long distance. Besides, he's unbelievably expensive. The only reason he still has a business is because no one else will do what he does."

"But you said he's really busy, so he must have some good customers, right?"

Athan sighed. "Yes. He has a group of loyal customers, and then a lot of one-time clients."

"I don't get it. They use the service once, but they don't like it?"

"No, more like they only need his services just the one time." She felt like he was talking in riddles.

She inhaled, ready to lob another question when he cut her off.

"It's not that interesting. Really."

With that, he closed the subject.

She nodded. "I'm sorry. I wasn't trying to pry."

"No worries." He took her hand.

"So you like to run?" Surely, this would be a safe topic.

"Hmm." There was a brief pause. "You already know that. Usually when I move, I join the track team."

"You like to compete?"

"Not really." He laughed. "I know what I can and can't do. I'm not really trying to prove it to anyone."

"So then why join the team? Why not just run by yourself?"

"I guess I could, but track is a good way to get my running in and get to know people. You know, new in the area, find people with common interests."

She laughed. "I noticed you're pretty friendly."

"But you're not so much."

His tone was teasing, and even though there was no malice in the comment, it struck a chord. Her back stiffened, and she attempted to pull away.

After a moment of hesitation, he released her hand. When he spoke, his voice was soft, conciliatory. "You seem to put a lot of effort into . . . not letting people in."

She wavered. His touch was comforting and gentle. She flipped her palm up and wound her fingers back into his embrace.

"Hope?"

"Yeah." Her whisper was an attempt to restrain the emotion bubbling in her heart.

"Why is that?" He looked sad.

"What?"

"Why do you work so hard to push people away?"

She was unprepared to answer his question; she'd never had to explain. She thought about lying, but then what was the harm in the truth. At least for most of it. "We moved a lot, my mom and me, for most of my life. I guess I already knew I'd be leaving soon, so it was easier to not get attached. I tried having friends once, but it . . . was . . . a disaster. It didn't seem worth the effort."

But it was more than that. The reality was, she didn't believe *she* was worth the effort. Not if they knew what she really was.

"Besides," she continued, shoving her dark thoughts deep into her soul, "it wasn't like I was alone; my mom and I were really good friends."

Her eyes filled, threatening to overflow.

"What happened to your mom?"

"There was an accident." She waited until she could swallow the lump in her throat before continuing. "I went to school one morning, but when I came home . . ." She shrugged, unable to say more.

But the lie felt horrible. Someone had *killed* her mom, and she wanted to shout from the rooftops that she would make them pay for what they did.

"I'm so sorry." He was silent for a moment before continuing. "What about your dad? Isn't he around?"

"No, he left before I was even born." Hope shrugged his question off. "I don't think he's even listed on the birth certificate."

She told him how her lawyer had helped with the emancipation, her time in foster care, and the move to Goldendale. It felt good to share. Really good.

They pulled up to her house, and he turned the ignition off. The light from across the street was muted through the tinted windows, and they sat cocooned in his truck.

"I didn't realize it was so late. I should get to bed."

She gathered her clutch and jacket and was surprised when Athan got out of the truck and headed toward the passenger side. Before she could get her seatbelt off, he was opening her door.

"You don't have to walk me to the door."

"Of course I do. Otherwise, it wouldn't be a date."

The word brought heat to her cheeks. It was a date?

When they reached the porch, Hope looked at him, seeing him as if for the first time. His green eyes blazed with live flame, and his tawny hair fell forward just enough that her fingers itched to push through it. With his proximity she could smell him, a hint of soap and the richness that was completely him. Almost like a magnet, she inched toward him.

He gently stroked her collarbone with just the tips of his fingers, his eyes filled with wonder as he studied her.

Was he feeling it, too?

"I have to say, Hope Treadwell, I'm interested in you." He circled her neck with his hand, his fingers winding into her hair. As he leaned in, his lips brushed her ear. "Very interested."

He leaned back, searching her face. She said nothing but forced herself to meet his eyes. Her heart pounded, running its own race, and her knees trembled. He reached out slowly, giving her time to pull back, but she wouldn't move. Holding her chin, he stroked her lower lip with his thumb. Slowly, achingly slowly, he brought his head low enough that their breath mingled.

Her eyes fluttered.

Waiting.

Athan closed his eyes, and with a swallow he pulled back, his hand dropping to his side. He turned and was down the steps before she was able to gather her thoughts.

"See you tomorrow." His voice was rough.

Dumbfounded and confused, she stood staring at him. She should say something, but words failed her. It took a concentrated effort for her to turn toward the door and not chase him out to his truck.

It took several seconds to gather herself enough to focus on the door and get it open. When she finally did, she was surprised to see Athan still waiting at the curb. She forced a smile and waved before she closed the door.

Seriously . . . What *was* that?

He was going to kiss her, but then he pulled back? Did she have bad breath? Something between her teeth? Did she smell like an animal? Could humans tell?

No biggie, she told herself, trying to discount his obvious dismissal. Really, was *she* even interested in him like that?

The answer was instantaneous.

TWENTY-FIVE

HOPE LIMPLY HELD the green basket in one hand, the wrapped steaks rolling from side to side. In her other hand, she held a large piece of poster board. She stood in line at the Red Apple. The one cashier today had to be approaching sixty, and her burgundy hair clashed with the red employee vest. By the time Hope got out, she might be sixty, too.

She glanced at the racks of candy and gum and then turned. The other side of the aisle was lined with glossy covers featuring cakes, swim-suit clad models, and airbrushed movie stars. Interspersed were matte covers of *news*papers reporting alien babies and talking animals. Although, maybe there was some truth to the talking animal thing.

Oh. Sweet. Hera.

Monster Tore Up My Orchard

Hope set her basket down and grabbed the *Daily Star*.

Danny Graves awoke early that March morning to get the cows out to pasture. The birds were chirping, and the weather was unusually mild for early spring. That's when he heard the terrible screams. "Sounded like someone cryin' and dyin' all at the same time. They was hollerin' and such something awful." What he found when he went to investigate left him speechless. "My orchard was just destroyed. Big ole trees all torn up, like someone was pluckin' weeds—roots hanging upside down and all."

Hope swallowed. This could not be happening. How could she have been so careless? After all the warnings from her mom. The disappointment was sour and hard to swallow.

Graves claims to have heard the banshee-like screams for several minutes. He was shocked when, as the sky was lightening, he witnessed a large beast flying out of his orchard. "I must have been right scared 'cause I didn't even think to use my shortie," Graves said as he patted a sawed off shotgun beside him. According to Graves, the monster had the wings of a bird, the legs of an animal, and a top half that looked human.

"Do you want to get that?" The clerk looked over her glasses at Hope.

"Oh, uh. No. No, thank you." Hope put the paper back in the wire bracket, face down. If only it were that easy to bury the story.

"Readin' about the Sphinx, huh?"

"What?" Anxiety rolled from her neck through her chest, leaving her skin prickled with chill.

"That's what they're calling it. That monster that tore up that man's orchard."

Hope nodded. Hades in hell.

"Seventeen eighty-two."

Hope handed her a twenty.

"Then he got a bunch of ancient coins worth a fortune in the mail. He'll never have to work again, they say." She held out Hope's change. "You have yourself a nice day, and don't worry none. They'll catch that monster soon enough, just you see."

Hope nodded and left the store. That was *exactly* what she was afraid of.

The information on the internet confirmed everything the grocery clerk had said and went further. There was even a petition at the end of the article asking for demigods to hunt down the beast.

Great.

Hope didn't sign it.

By late afternoon, she was restive and cross. She hadn't heard from Athan, and Haley was out with Tristan. Hope needed to get out of her house. More than anything, she wanted a run.

It's fine. You want to run, so run. She decided that, despite her fear, she would. She changed her clothes and strapped on the Velcro belt that held the leather sheath. She'd improvised a casing for an immortal dagger and strapped the golden knife to her hip, tucking it into her shorts. It felt odd, but she wasn't running without one of the blades.

The sun was setting as Hope took her second lap around the small town. She waved at Tristan and Haley who were having dinner on the patio of Sal's Pizza, the smell of oregano and yeasty bread heavy in the air.

She rounded the corner and slowed to a jog and then a walk. The anemic streetlights did nothing to light the path at dusk, and the sidewalk around her house was broken and uneven.

In four days, she would change again. Tuesday was going to suck. Hard. She needed to come up with something to tell Haley and Athan before she left—

A man walked from the darkness between two homes.

Oh gods.

"Little monster," he rasped.

The Skia was the same one that had killed the demigod, Brand. Her heart raced, and she pulled out the golden blade, waving it in front of her.

"Stay away from me!" Her voice trembled.

He chuckled. "You don't even know how to use that, Sphinx."

Her stomach churned. She couldn't deny it. "Don't come any closer, or you'll find out how well I use it."

He stepped back and put his hands up, but the leer plastered on his face showed no fear.

"I'm not here to hurt you," he said.

"Then what do you want?" Her gaze darted to the shadows, then back to him.

"My master would like to invite you for an audience. He would like to speak with you." His laugh was a dry wheeze. "The gods are all astir . . . Because of you."

A door slammed, and someone cursed.

"You tell him no. I have no interest in talking with Hades." She took a deep breath. "And leave me alone. You might think I'm harmless, but I'll kill you if you threaten me."

The Skia nodded, as if accepting her answer. He pointed to the home behind her. "Be careful, Sphinx. Your curse will not protect you from . . . everything."

Hope turned to see a man in cutoff jeans and a dirty tank top coming off his dilapidated front porch.

"Who's there?" He slurred the words.

Hope turned back to the Skia, but he was gone. Hope said nothing as she slunk past the man dragging his garbage can to the curb.

What did it say that she was more afraid of the drunk man than the Skia?

Once inside her house, Hope locked the door behind her and looked at the statue on the mantel. She had no idea how it worked, but she was grateful for the protection of Hecate.

Anxious and filled with nervous energy, Hope focused on tasks over which she had control. She showered, dressed in pajamas, ate the rest of the steak she'd grilled earlier, texted Haley then started on her last bit of homework.

In black marker, she outlined the endothermic reaction of citric acid and baking soda on the bright-pink poster board.

Her phone buzzed, then rang.

Finally. She tapped Accept and brought it to her ear.

"Hey, are you done with your chemistry poster, yet?" Hope asked.

A man chuckled. "I had no idea you'd be so young."

Her stomach dropped.

"Who is this?" She held the phone out and looked at the screen. Priska's number. No. No, no, no!

"We know what you are . . . Sphinx." He hissed the last word, as if a curse.

She clenched the phone, her knuckles turning white.

"Who are you?" She pushed the words out in an anxious whisper. "Where's Priska?"

"We will destroy you. And we will send you to Hades."

"Where's Priska?" she screamed.

The man laughed.

Her hand shook, and she tapped End over and over and over. Could they trace a cell phone?

Her phone rang again. And again. And again.

What could she do? What should she do? Her panic overwhelmed her, and she sat immobilized.

Thud, thud, thud.

Hope screamed.

"Hope?" Haley's voice came through the door. "I know you're home!"

Hope jumped from the chair and raced to the door. Her hand trembled as she undid the deadbolt. Pulling open the door, she tugged Haley inside.

"So, did I see you run by Sal's earlier?" Haley closed the door behind her. "I thought I saw you." She stopped at the kitchen table. "And how much more homework do you have? I wanted to go to Portland tonight, but we'll never make it back by ten. Maybe we could go to Yakima. I'm dying to go shopping." She turned and looked at Hope. "Holy Hades, what happened to you? Was . . . Was that you screaming?"

Hope couldn't stop the tremor, and she nodded. "Yeah. I . . . just . . . uh . . . Remember those prank calls I was getting? Well, they've been calling, again. So . . . I need to get a new phone."

"Don't tell me you're getting the new iPhone." Haley's shoulders sagged, then she straightened. "Wait, did you say those guys are calling again? Oh. My. Gods. For real?"

Hope nodded. "Do you know if you can trace where a phone is? Like the physical location?"

"Maybe. I don't know." Haley frowned. "We can ask at the store. And if they can, we'll just dump it in the river. Are you all right?"

Hope nodded and grabbed her coat. "Yeah. Let's go. Now."

Hope locked the door while Haley went out to get the car started. As Hope turned, she saw the short Skia standing in the shadow of a tree. He nodded once and faded away.

Her heart couldn't take anymore.

She ran to the car.

HOPE LAY IN bed and thought about Athan. Two days ago seemed like forever. And that moment at the door? She was sure he was going to kiss her. But then, why didn't he? And why did he never call her? She hadn't imagined that date, and he'd even called it that. Was it normal to be all hot and cold like that?

She kicked off the covers, eager to see him at school. At least there he wouldn't be able to avoid her and she could find out what was going on.

A couple hours later, she pulled into the back parking lot of the school. Her phone buzzed, then rang, and after checking the screen, she answered it with a frown.

"Hello?"

"Hi, this is Melody at Mr. Davenport's office, will you please hold for Mr. Davenport?"

Hope rolled her eyes. She'd called him not even twenty minutes ago with her new phone number. "Of course."

The sounds of classical music filled her ear, and then: "Hope?"

"You called me, Mr. Davenport."

He laughed. "So I did. How are you holding up?"

She told him about Mr. Jeffers and her worry about getting in trouble with the truancy board, and her emancipation being threatened. "I need to change again in two days, and . . . I just don't think I could go back into foster care."

"I won't let that happen. If he files a truancy order, just forward it to me."

"Okay. Have you found anything? About Priska?" Hope asked.

Mr. Davenport sighed. "No. That's partly why I'm calling. Priska was the trustee over your assets. With her . . . disappearance, I've got to redraft the trust. I think the easiest thing to do is make you the trustee, now that you're emancipated."

"What does that mean?"

He explained in great detail that she would have sole discretion over her money. "Just like it's been, except this will make it official."

"So what do I need to do?

He chuckled. "Just come sign a bunch of papers, or I could mail them, or even email them."

"No. I'll just come over. At least this way I'll have an excuse to be gone." She thought about how she could tell her teachers she had a meeting with her attorney. That was a good reason to be absent, right?"

"Hello?" Mr. Davenport asked.

"Sorry, sorry. I was looking at the calendar. Could I come on Friday? Nine o'clock-ish?"

"Sure. That would be fine. See you then." He disconnected the call, and Hope let her arm fall. Now she would need to talk to her teachers and get the makeup work.

She looked around the parking lot. Where was Athan?

TWENTY-SIX

"**What the Hades**, Hope!" Haley slammed Hope's locker shut. The bell rang, and Hope was collecting her homework so she could sneak off to the library. "You can't go and hook up over the weekend and not tell me. I mean, we were out all last night, and you said nothing about your date." Haley air-quoted the word *date*.

Hope rolled her eyes and started her combination.

"We didn't hook up," she grumbled.

"What?"

"I said we didn't hook up." Hope glared at her friend.

Haley's eyes narrowed. "Are you sure, because I heard—"

"For real? Like I wouldn't know?" It was so frustrating. Athan hadn't even called since their almost not kiss. Hope pursed her lips, the epiphany breaking slowly. She wanted Athan to like her. Oh. Gods. That was so not okay.

Hope turned and punched the locker behind her.

"Whoa. You're totally right. You would know. Sorry."

Hope leaned back against the wall. "No. I just . . ." This was so much worse than breaking a taboo on friendship. She couldn't have a relationship with him. Or even if she did, she wouldn't be able to tell him everything. It was just . . . wrong. She pushed away her feelings because they didn't matter. There was no relationship. They hadn't kissed. "Where were you this morning?"

"What? What just happened in your head? Did Krista tell you that she and Athan . . ." Haley waved her arms together and apart, then shook her head. "Okay. She's psycho. I'm going to have to talk with Tristan. Because I seriously can't be around that harpy anymore. It was. Disgusting." She batted her eyes at rubbed up on Hope. "Oh, Athan, you big, strong man, let me sit on your lap and lick your face. I just want to see if you taste as sweet as you look. Oh, yum, yum."

She licked Hope's face.

"Oh, gross!" Hope pulled away.

Haley started laughing. "It was sick."

Tristan walked up to them, staring intently at Haley.

"How come you don't do that to me?" he asked with a chuckle.

"You like *that*?" Haley pursed her lips and inched away from him.

"Ah, no," he said with a snort then he turned to Hope. "Was she telling you about Saturday?"

Hope nodded. Is that what they were talking about? Hope flinched as her memories of Saturday batted around in her head.

Tristan tilted his head toward her and whispered, "You don't have anything to worry about."

Before Hope could correct him, or question him, he straightened. "Come on, Haley, let's go get something to eat."

Haley left with a wave.

It took Hope a few more minutes to gather her thoughts and her books.

She went through the day in a funk. Athan was a no show, and she couldn't help but think it had to do with her. And the not-quite kiss. Maybe she'd read him wrong.

She drove to the Red Apple after school and was relieved to see Mr. Stanley behind the meat counter, weighing hamburger for a customer.

"I'll be with you in just a moment, Hope." Mr. Stanley greeted her with his usual warmth.

She nodded.

Mr. Stanley finished wrapping the man's dinner and then turned to her.

"How are you? It's been a few days." He acknowledged her absence in a way that made her feel missed, not guilty.

"Yeah." She deliberated for only a second. "I've been hanging out with Mrs. Stephens's nephew, Athan."

Mr. Stanley nodded. "Is he nice?"

She found herself telling Mr. Stanley almost everything, starting at the Red Apple the previous Friday up to the dinner last night. She edited out the attack in the Dalles and the almost kiss. He definitely didn't need to know those details, and she really wasn't sure what to make of them anyway.

They were interrupted several times by customers, but the tale seemed to hold his interest, and so Hope continued talking. When she finished, she looked up at the butcher, standing still in contemplation.

When it was clear she was finished, he said, "Well, you've had a lot going on."

He didn't offer advice, nor did he pry.

And the talking had made her feel better and helped clarify her feelings. She liked Athan, but she'd rather be friends than nothing at all. With sincere gratitude, she thanked Mr. Stanley.

"Sure, anytime," he said. "I've got three daughters, and even though two of them aren't home anymore, I still hear about their days plenty." He paused momentarily as if considering something. "I found a great riddle online. Do you want to hear it?"

She nodded. "Of course."

"Okay, here it is. I make you weak at the worst of all times. I keep you safe, I keep you fine. I make your hands sweat and your heart grow cold. I visit the weak but seldom the bold. What am I?"

She thought about the riddle for a few minutes. It seemed vaguely familiar. Then she remembered. It was one her mom told her a couple years ago after an especially bad day at school.

"Fear," she answered confidently.

"Yep. Boy, that one threw me. How is it that you are so good at riddles?"

Her smile was wistful and brief. "It's in my blood. My mom and grandmother studied them for years. In fact, one of my grandmother's passions was riddles."

"Excuse me." An older woman tentatively looked from Hope to Mr. Stanley. "Can I get some pork chops?"

"I'll let you go." Hope waved as she turned to leave.

"Bye, Hope," he called after her before turning to the shopper.

She got home and sat at the kitchen table, doing homework for the rest of the afternoon and into the evening. She ate leftovers and finished her work. She was restless after sitting for so long. A short run was just what she needed. The night was brisk, but after the first mile, the cool air felt delicious on her bare arms. She modified her loop, going up and down side streets to increase the distance of the run.

Which was the only reason she ran into him.

He was walking past the community hospital, dressed in jeans and a pale-blue T-shirt. The light shirt was a beacon in the dark night.

As if on cue, he turned.

That can't be . . . There were worry lines that didn't seem to fit his face, his shadowed features told of sleeplessness, and instead of his normal teasing smirk, his lips were drawn.

As she drew closer, she could see the lines fade as if shadows.

"Athan?"

"Hope." He said her name as though it was a life raft. His eyes met hers hungrily. His shuffling turned to a determined stride, and he closed the gap, but he stopped just short of her.

"Are you all right?" Her concern was a presence between them.

"Oh. Yeah." He sighed, sounding defeated. "There was a lot I needed to sort out, and it all hit me today."

She nodded. The first couple of months after her mother died had passed in a fog of despair. Maybe it was the same for him. He seemed so well-adjusted she'd almost forgotten he must still be grieving.

"Is it about your mom?" she asked.

"Oh, no. No. My mom . . ." He sighed again. "I haven't been totally honest. My mom passed away a while ago. I've been living with extended family for years. But, when I move . . . It's easier than trying to explain my family situation."

As she listened, she found herself nodding. His quick adjustment hadn't been so quick. "But then, what *is* wrong?"

She braced herself just in case it was about her.

"Actually," he continued, "I was thinking about change."

"About change?" She swallowed.

"Have you ever," he started and broke off. A deep breath. He met her gaze. "Have you ever felt so comfortable and then your world turned upside down?" He waved his hands at her while he continued, "I knew what my responsibilities were, what was important, and how to accomplish what needed to be done . . ."

"Like, you thought you had all the answers, only to find out you didn't even know what the questions were?"

"Exactly." He practically simmered with emotion.

"That first month after my mom died," she started softly, her voice just above a whisper, "I pretty much sat in my room. I felt bewildered. Then I got angry. When I finally grasped that it was just me, I started moving, thinking, doing again."

She thought of leaving Bellevue, living in foster care, and coming to Goldendale, the changes each had been painful. Even now, if she thought too much, the memories felt like picking off a scab before the cut was healed. Hope took a deep breath, pulling her focus to the now. Because now didn't hurt nearly so much.

"So what kind of change are you having a hard time with?" She brushed a sweaty strand of hair back from her face.

His gaze clouded, and he rubbed his chin. "It's. . . What I thought was important doesn't seem to be so important anymore."

What did he mean? He wasn't talking about her, was he?

He glanced at her sweaty figure. "You were out for a run. May I walk with you?"

As they approached her house, they bumped shoulders. Hope laughed as he pretended to stagger from the impact. When he drew close again, his hand grazed hers and caught it.

When they were on the porch, Athan leaned against the wall, his gaze drilled into her.

"What?" She breathed.

Athan brushed loose strands of hair behind her ear, and then he traced his fingers down her neck to her shoulder. He tilted his head and focused on her lips. "I want to kiss you, Hope."

He leaned in, his hand cupped the back of her neck, his fingers threading into her hair. His lips brushed her skin as he breathed in her ear. "And I want you to kiss me back." His lips touched the hollow behind her ear, then traced a path across her jawbone.

The world stopped. Her heart exploded in a sensation that was wholly unfamiliar but completely wonderful. A breathy sigh escaped her lips.

His breath was warm on her skin, and her lips parted to breathe him in. She wanted to say yes, wanted to tell him she wanted the same thing—for them to be together. The words wouldn't come. Instead, she closed her eyes and leaned forward in anticipation.

He wound his arm around her waist, his hand resting at the small of her back then he pulled her to him. His lips brushed hers lightly first, then with more pressure. His lips were soft and warm. The kiss tender and sweet.

Athan pulled away, and Hope was left off balance.

"Hmm." He looked almost sleepy, but his smile was mischievous. "Again?"

"Please." She ran her hands ran up his chest and to the back of his neck, trailing her fingers into his silky hair. Their lips brushed again and again, and then more deeply.

When they broke apart, both were breathing heavy.

"What are your plans tomorrow?" He continued to trace the back of her neck with his hands then trailed them over her shoulders.

"School." She blushed at her incoherence.

He chuckled, and his laughter radiated through her, bringing a smile to her lips.

"Then I'll see you at school."

"Okay."

He touched his lips to hers again, skimming them back and forth. "I'll see you tomorrow." He pressed his lips to hers briefly then released her and stepped down to the walkway.

The hot shower felt great, and so did the coolness of her sheets, but all of this was lost. As she snuggled down under her blankets, she was giddy from the high, and her lips tingled with the bliss of her first kiss.

TWENTY-SEVEN

FOR THE FIRST time since her mother passed away, Hope felt excited. She alternately floated and buzzed through her morning routine. On the short drive to school, she envisioned what it would be like to have a friend—a boyfriend. At what point did you call someone your boyfriend? The thought made her giggle.

She opened the door and walked into the crowd of students.

"Oops." Someone bumped into her, hard. "Excuse me."

Her smile froze and then faded as she turned and looked down to Krista's venomous face.

"I totally didn't see you there. You just kinda blend. Almost like you're invisible." The girl's lips curled into a sneer. She sauntered off, giggling, with her gaggle following behind.

CURSED BY THE GODS

Something ugly bubbled inside Hope, but she shoved it down. Krista had nothing Hope wanted. Nothing. Sure, he'd gone with Krista and Scott on Saturday night. But it meant nothing. Hope had told him to go. And he'd kissed her last night. That had to mean something.

She got to her locker and started to turn the dial when she heard a familiar voice.

"Hey, I forgot to ask you last night, where were you Sunday?" Athan drew close; his fingers separated a lock of her hair that he curled around his finger. "I called and called, but you never picked up."

"Oh . . . yeah, sorry." She pulled out the new phone in its bright pink case. "New phone. I texted you, though." She frowned.

"New number, too?" He pulled out his phone. "*Ouai.* Sorry. I didn't look."

"Uh-huh."

"Swapping digits, huh?" Haley bounced up in a new denim skirt and flip-flops. She looked ready for the beach. "I bet you're so glad those creeps won't be calling anymore."

Hope shook her head and tried to signal Haley to shut up.

"So freaky . . . What?" Haley looked back and forth between Hope and Athan and settled again on Hope. "You mean you didn't tell him?"

Athan frowned. "Tell me what?"

Hope pursed her lips. "It was nothing. I got a couple prank calls."

Haley grimaced. "Nothing? You looked like you'd been chased by Apollo's army. Freaked. Out."

"You got a new phone because some guys were prank calling you?"

"Not just some guys," Haley continued. "Some guys that were threatening her, like 'We're going to hunt you down—'"

"Do you know who they were? That's harassment." Athan's nostrils flared, and he looked like he wanted to hit something, or someone.

The bell rang.

"Come on. It doesn't matter now. New number. They don't even know who I am."

Haley waved goodbye, and Athan walked Hope to class.

"Seriously, if something like that happens again, Hope, you've got to tell me. It's not right to keep secrets from me. You don't keep secrets from your boyfriend."

Did he just say . . .

Athan leaned over and kissed her on the cheek. "Come on."

When they got to the door, he paused, holding her back as he continued the conversation.

"Please don't keep things from me. I'll see you at lunch?" He held her with his gaze; his cadence wrapped her in silk.

"Um, okay."

"I'll meet you by your locker." He turned to leave but looked back with a wink.

She heard a nearby student giggle, but she didn't care. She smiled and went into class.

"How many of you have seen this?" Mrs. Biggers held up a newspaper and waved it in the air. "I'm shocked. It's just so exciting!"

Hope slid into her desk and looked around the room. Heads were down; a couple people were texting on the phones in their laps. A few students had glassy stares fixed on their eccentric teacher.

"Let me read this to you," she continued. "This is the second sighting of the monster many think is the ancient Sphinx. Mythologists around the world are flocking to Eastern Washington to hunt for the creature." She looked up, her face alight. "Can you imagine?"

Hope forgot all about Athan. A second sighting? Her face grew hot, and she looked to see if anyone was staring at her.

"If I didn't know better, I'd say you were a monster," Krista whispered.

Hope glared at her. "Who cares what you think?"

"*Everybody.*" Krista tossed her hair over her shoulder.

"Do you have something you need to share?" Mrs. Biggers stared from Krista to Hope.

Hope shook her head.

"Then I suggest you let me finish my lesson, ladies." Mrs. Biggers took a deep breath in. "Now, where was I . . . Oh, yes. The sons of Apollo have been petitioned to hunt the monster. But some say there is no such organization. It's most exciting. Krista, what are your thoughts?"

Krista looked from Mrs. Biggers to Hope. "Personally, I think all monsters should be hunted and slaughtered. Even if they look human."

"Interesting. You aren't the only one who feels that way, Krista. So, class . . . What defines a monster? And who should make that determination?"

Hope waited until the students filed out of class to address Mrs. Biggers.

After a deep breath, Hope went up to her teacher's desk. "Um, Mrs. Biggers?"

"Yes?"

"I'll be out the last half of this week. My lawyer, Mr. Davenport, called, and I need to see him about the trust." She wanted to sound confident, but her statement sounded more like a request.

"Of course." Mrs. Biggers nodded. Students filed into the room. "You have the assignments. You can keep up."

Chemistry was next.

While Mr. Burgess was doing a "dangerous, don't try this at home" demonstration, whispers from Angela and Krista floated across the aisle.

"Did you and Athan have fun at the river on Thursday?"

Hope's breath caught. She told herself it didn't matter what they said, but her focus zeroed in on the two girls.

"So. Much. Fun. You should've come. Tristan and Lee were there, and Scott showed up later, too. Haley and Heather came, and Heather brought some friend of hers from the Dalles." And then, louder: "It was perfect."

Hope felt hot, and her stomach dropped.

"What did you guys do?" Angela asked, clearly more than a little jealous.

"Oh, you know, just hung out. Lit a campfire, told scary stories, roasted marshmallows. Did you know that Athan can play a whole bunch of musical instruments? And he can sing." Krista's voice dropped further, "He's so incredibly . . . sexy."

"Did anything happen?" Angela asked.

Hope shifted in her seat to get a better look at the two girls.

Krista looked like she'd won the lottery. "Well, he took me home, and do you count kissing? And, Friday for Twister." She giggled, and her voice dropped. "And Sunday for poker."

"You guys played poker?"

"Mm-hmm." She raised her eyebrows. "Strip poker."

Hope couldn't wait for class to end.

Angela's eyes went up. "Really? Who won?"

Krista rolled her eyes. "Uh, when you play that game, everybody wins."

"So, did he pick you up Friday?"

"Uh, no. He was over at . . ." Krista inclined her head.

Angela followed Krista's gaze, and her eyes locked on Hope's.

"What was he doing at her house?" Angela whispered.

"I don't know. It was kinda weird. I think she was trying to get him to stay." Krista shook her head. "So pathetically sad."

Hope gritted her teeth to stop herself from saying anything. It was torture to pull her focus back to Mr. Burgess, and despite facing front, her attention kept drifting. Had Athan just played her?

When the bell rang, she collected her books and headed down the hall. She saw Athan standing at her locker, playing with the dial. When he looked at her, her heart rate picked up.

"What's the matter?" Concern danced across his features.

Hot with emotion, she responded, "Krista and Angela were talking about the weekend in chemistry."

She looked at him, expecting him to understand.

He grimaced. "They're not your friends, are they?"

"No way." As if! She glared at him. Did he not know her at all?

"Okay. Are you mad because you weren't invited to the river? I tried to invite you, but—"

"No," she cut him off, frustrated. "Krista said that you kissed her. And you took her home, and played strip poker . . ."

Athan suppressed a chuckle, a grin stretching across his face.

He thought it was funny? She clenched her fists. Before she could hit him, Athan held up his hand.

"Let me explain . . . just a little." When she nodded but said nothing, he continued, "I told Scott and Tristan I would go with them last week. I tried to invite you Thursday, but you made it clear that you didn't want to hang out."

She remembered the abrupt text she'd sent him and nodded.

"We played a game about truths and lies, and I'm not sure winning is really best. Anyway, I did take Krista home then, and Tristan. I dropped her off first. I'm not interested in her. Not at all. And Sunday night? I had to take off my shoes and socks. That's all. I promise I wasn't the one who lost that game." The smirk remained, like he was enjoying an inside joke.

"What's so funny?"

He shook his head. "You can't call what happened a kiss, either. And that was all before there was an *us*, Hope."

She dialed her combination, dropped in her books, and grabbed her lunch without glancing back at him. Was that supposed to make her feel better? She closed the locker, and he was still staring at her, his smile just playing at the corner of his lips.

Because it didn't.

Hope slammed her locker shut, then looked around for Athan. He'd left in the middle of algebra, and she thought he'd be back by now.

She stared down the hall, willing him to appear. A group of students passed her then started laughing. Then another group.

The smell of overcooked vegetables and beef gravy wafted down the hall from the open doors of the lunchroom.

A group of girls pushed past, bumping her shoulder. A couple of them snickered as they passed.

Someone shoved her, and she lurched forward. Hope turned and faced Krista.

"I'm sick of you always putting your face where it isn't wanted," Krista spat.

"Excuse me?" Hope could hardly believe Krista's hostility. "What are you talking about?"

"You're disgusting, you know that?"

Hope shook her head. "What did I ever do to you?"

"Ugh. Your entire life is offensive. And not just to me." Krista looked back at her friends with a nod. They were like a horde of wannabe Barbies. "You're a monster, and we've already sent a message to the sons of Apollo."

Hope's heart stopped. Krista couldn't be serious. Was she?

"You don't even know what you're messing with." Hope took a step forward, ready to . . . What? What could she do?

"And when the demigods find you," Krista sneered, "they'll rub you off the face of the earth."

With all the bravado Hope could muster, she closed the gap separating them and looked down on Krista. Hope wouldn't hit the stupid mortal girl, but she wouldn't lay down either. "You're just jealous because Athan picked me."

Krista drew her hand back, and this time Hope knew what to expect. She caught Krista's wrist before she could strike.

"I told you not to do that again." Hope released Krista's arm with a little shove.

"You have nothing that I want," Krista shrieked. "Nothing."

She drew her leg back, and Hope could see the projected course of the kick. Swinging her arm low, Hope blocked, changing the trajectory of Krista's leg.

Hope could see it before it even happened.

Krista was too close to the lockers. She spun, wind-milled her arms, and lost her balance. Her face bounced off the metal as she went down. Crimson gushed, and Krista's hand flew to her nose and lip.

Hope backed away, hands up.

"What's going on?" A cafeteria worker came up to the gathering crowd. "Oh. Oh, no." She looked at Krista and yelled for someone to get ice. Then, surveying the group, the woman's gaze landed on Hope. "You. You did this?"

The other students backed away.

"It was an accident." Hope's fear warred with her pride. "She tried to kick—"

"And yet," the lunch lady said, "she's the one bloodied on the floor."

Krista sobbed hysterically.

"To the principal's office." The matronly woman's voice was steely. "Now." Then, she bent over Krista. "All right now. Let's get some ice on that and get you to the nurse."

Could this day get any worse?

TWENTY-EIGHT

"MISS TREADWELL, YOU seem to be causing quite a stir today." Mr. Jeffers waved her into the office.

Hope sat down on the edge of the chair and leaned away from the sunlight. "She tried to kick me, sir, and when I blocked her, she fell."

He nodded, as if considering his words. "Do you want to tell me what the fight was about?"

Not really.

"She was with a group of her friends, she pushed me, called me a monster, and told me that she was going to get the demigods to kill me." Hope rushed through the explanation, afraid that Mr. Jeffers would cut her off any minute.

"I see." He took a slow, deep breath. "Normally, we suspend instigators, but you're not really in a position to be missing any more school."

Had he not heard a word she'd said?

"Sir, I didn't start the fight. You can ask anyone in the hall. They *all* saw it." And she was hardly flunking out. Her lowest grade was ninety-seven percent in algebra. Last time she checked, that was still a solid *A*.

"And Mrs. Biggers said you will be out the rest of the week?"

"I have meetings with my attorney in Seattle," she bit out. Hope was trying to keep her frustration in check, but she was seething.

His leaned forward on his elbows and templed his fingers. "That's a lot of time to meet with your lawyer."

What was she supposed to say to that?

When she said nothing, he dropped his hands. "Well, you better go get your homework for the rest of the week. I'd hate for you to get behind."

Hope stood and walked to the door.

"Oh, and Miss Treadwell?"

She turned and looked back at him. "Yes?"

"No more fights in my school."

For real? "Yes, sir."

She escaped the office and leaned against the wall facing the cafeteria. Students pushed their way through the halls, a sea of oblivious humanity, and Hope resented their ignorance and freedom.

"Hope!" Haley yelled over the ruckus. "Oh. My. Gods! I just heard what happened. Did you kick her butt? I can't believe she did that to you."

Hope turned to her best friend and wearily responded, "Word spreads fast."

Haley wrinkled her nose then waved at the crowd of students. "She sent the picture to *everyone*."

Hope froze. "What picture? What are you talking about?"

Haley's slack expression mirrored Hope's confusion. "What are *you* talking about?"

Hope couldn't stand it. There was more? How much more could go wrong today? "No. You first."

Haley pulled out her phone and turned it to Hope.

There she was. Hope's face amid a mass of writhing snakes. She looked every bit a Gorgon. Part of her felt outraged, but another, albeit smaller, part was relieved. At least Krista didn't know the truth.

"Now, what are *you* talking about?" Haley dropped her phone back into her purse.

"Just a few minutes ago . . . Krista tried to kick me, but when I blocked, she fell."

Haley laughed. "Poetic justice."

"Sadly, Mr. Jeffers didn't see it that way. What's up with him? He keeps lecturing me on missing school, and it's not like I'm even a bad student."

Haley snorted. "Oh, yeah. He would totally hate you. You get good grades but miss classes a lot. You're like proving how wrong he is, how school doesn't even matter."

"What?"

"His grandmother is Athena," Haley said by way of explanation. "He thinks the school is his way to get her approval or something."

"Where did you hear that?"

"My dad. He's big into mythology."

Haley Stanley. The dots connected. "Your dad is Mr. Stanley? The butcher?"

Haley shook her head. "I know. I know. But, really, he's pretty cool. For a dad."

"He is cool." Hope felt a pang of jealousy. The bell rang, and she looked around. "Where's Athan?"

Haley grimaced. "Sorry. I was supposed to tell you. He had to run home, but he told me to tell you he'd be back before school got out."

With a sigh, Hope went to Spanish.

"HEY, BEAUTIFUL." ATHAN leaned against her locker, his head resting on the metal door. He stood up, almost as if peeling himself off. "Sorry I missed your fight today."

Hope rolled her eyes. "Nothing like the fight you got in. This wasn't even a fight. No one got hit."

"I got in a fight? When?"

"Like a month ago, I think?" Hope grabbed the books she'd need for homework for the rest of the week, which was all of them.

"I never got in a fight . . . Whoa! Why are you taking all your books? Are you . . . running away?"

She slammed her locker shut. "If I was running away, I wouldn't be taking homework."

"True. All right, I'll bite. Where are you going?"

"If you'd been here for more than five minutes today, you would know that I have to go to my attorney."

"For a month?"

"No. Just a couple days."

Athan nodded. "Bummer. I was going to ask if you wanted to go to Portland. Maybe we should get together tonight?"

They got to her car, and he leaned against the driver's door, blocking her entrance. As he reached up and twisted the loose strands of hair back into the knot at the nape of her neck, his shirt hem lifted above his waistband, revealing taut golden skin.

It took a moment to gather her thoughts. "Won't you be tired after your work out?"

"Hardly," he said with a chuckle. Hooking his finger in her jeans, Athan pulled her closer. "If you'd like to go for a run, I promise I'll have plenty of energy for you."

Despite the cold fingers playing with the hem of her shirt, Hope felt heat emanating from him.

She shivered and put her hands on his chest. A gust of wind swirled around them. The smells of spring carried possibilities and hope. He took her unruly hair, tucked it behind her ear then trailed his hand down her neck. Her heart, already a staccato drumming in her chest, surged into cardiac arrest territory.

The sun peeked out from behind the clouds. The light touched Athan's shoulder, revealing a silvery spot, almost like a scar. As Hope traced the odd, irregular mark, it took shape. It seemed unlikely, but it looked just like a lyre.

She shook her head. "What is this?"

He shrugged. "A birthmark. Weird, huh?"

The light dimmed as the wind blew more clouds over the sun. The mark all but disappeared.

"It looks like a harp, kinda."

"Yeah—" A thumping bass sound from Athan's pocket interrupted him. "Just a sec." He pulled out his phone. "Hello?"

Hope watched as he grimaced, then his jaw clenched.

"All right. All right! I'll be right there." He disconnected and sighed.

"Who was that?"

"My dad," he said. "He came into town this morning." He frowned. "Do you really need to go away this week?"

Was he using her as an excuse to get out of seeing his dad?

"You don't want to spend time with him?" She would give anything to spend just an hour with her mom again.

"No. It's not that . . ." He pulled her close. "Could we still do something tonight?" The small gap between them disappeared, and their legs touched. His hands moved to her hips and kept her hostage. "Can we go have dinner, or just spend some time . . ."

Her breath hitched as he kissed the hollow below her ear.

"I wish . . . I could," she managed to say with an uneven breath, "but I've got to get stuff ready for my appointment." She stepped back. "I'd better go."

His eyes shifted, his gaze intent on her face. His phone started ringing again, and he ran his fingers through his hair, ignoring the incessant sound.

"Yeah, me too." Touching her chin, he whispered, "Please, be careful." His jaw clenched, and a vein pulsed in his neck. "Please." He took a step back, painted on a smile, and added, "And have fun."

She stared at him, something pulling at her consciousness. "Thanks." She unlocked the door and slid into the car. "See you in a couple of days."

He wasn't looking at her anymore, and his fists clenched then released. "Yeah, see you soon."

HER INITIAL PLAN to stay home till her Friday appointment with Mr. Davenport seemed oppressive. She didn't want to be cooped up for the next two days as a Sphinx. No. She would drive toward Seattle and find an uninhabited area to stop. A place where she could fly. Far away from civilization. She couldn't afford another sighting.

She ate, gorging herself until she felt like she would burst if she took another bite. Then she packed a couple sandwiches for the morning. It was all she could do to prevent the need to eat over the next two days.

There were some things she appreciated about being the Sphinx. She loved being able to see at night, as well as over long distances. Her reflexes were better than a human's, and some of the physical capabilities were fun, like leaping from a tall building and landing on her feet, just like a cat.

Up until her mother's death, Hope had enjoyed these skills. How had she forgotten that? She could see it clearly now. For months, she had wallowed in self-pity. While she went through the motions of living, it had been a mere existence.

Over the last couple of weeks, she'd drawn strength from her emotions. Her life was a mess, but the choices were hers. She'd felt happy, sad, confused, hurt, angry. Most important, she'd *felt*. She didn't want to lose that.

She packed an overnight bag with a change of clothes and toiletries, took her homework to do during the day, then glanced around her house. All set.

She climbed in bed, hoping to sleep before her alarm went off at four o'clock.

It was dark as pitch when she got up.

Eastern Washington was sparsely inhabited in places, and she expected to find somewhere that would serve her purpose. She drove, her mind wandering, and when she hit Toppenish, she glanced at the clock. Plenty of time. She continued toward Yakima.

When she hit the freeway, she glanced again in her rearview mirror. *Was that Athan's truck?* She slowed to get a better look but wasn't able to see more than a few cars behind her through the early morning traffic. *I must be delusional, or really obsessed.*

The fuel light came on. Flipping on the blinker, she swerved across the three lanes to get to the exit. The early morning hours were cold and dark. Unwilling to leave the safety of the bright lights over the gas pumps, she huddled by her car. She exhaled a sigh of relief when she got back behind the seat and clicked the locks.

As she drove up I-82 toward I-90, she started scanning for a good place to stop.

A sign indicated no services for fifty miles. The pressure in her back was building. She had about twenty minutes before sunrise. This area would have to do. She just needed an exit.

TWENTY-NINE

SHE DROVE ANOTHER ten miles before she saw an exit sign, then followed ramp to a four-way stop. The road to the left had grass growing up through the asphalt, and she took several odd turns until she saw a dilapidated barn off a dirt road. She sighed with relief.

The decaying structure smelled of old hay and rotting wood, but lacked any recent evidence of human use. As she pulled the sagging barn door closed, she noticed the sky lightening. She undressed and stretched upward.

The first rays of the sun broke the horizon, and the tension in her back released as her wings expanded with a whoosh. Heaviness pulled at her hips and knees, and she gritted her teeth as the muscles in her legs cramped and seized. After another heartbeat, it was over, and Hope sat on her haunches. She beat her feathered wings twice, reveling in the strength.

The soft downy fur that covered her skin was the same golden honey as her hair, and she ran her hand over the silky coat.

She grabbed her backpack and left the barn before the sky got any lighter. It was always risky leaving cover, but she wasn't waiting.

Instinct took over. She pulled her wings down hard and let them float back up, again and again, creating the change in pressure that would give her lift. When her body left the ground, she laughed. She rose high into the sky, past the low-flying birds, up to where the eagles flew.

She flew north, toward Wenatchee and then Leavenworth. It was too early in the spring for tourists, and the locals were still warm in bed, but she flew high, just in case. Despite the covering of fur that kept her warm, the temperature at this height was biting.

Scanning the ground, she looked for a suitable landing place. There were plenty of wooded areas, and she finally saw one with a small clearing. She circled in closer. No roads, no hiking trails—Hope went through her mental checklist. She landed on her feline feet and padded through the clearing. Satisfied with the isolation it provided, she curled up in the sunlight and slept.

She awoke in the early afternoon. After stretching up toward the sun, she contemplated the rest of the day. Homework first, she decided, and grabbed the bag she'd used as a pillow. Without distractions, she hammered through the work, finishing just before sundown.

With the sun setting, and nothing else to occupy her, her thoughts turned to Athan. In the past, he'd made it sound like he enjoyed spending time with his dad, but yesterday it was all he could do to get out of it. She wondered about their relationship, but when her thoughts went to whether or not Athan's dad would approve of her, she shifted her focus back to Athan. With the cover of dark, she'd be almost invisible. She could fly by his home.

The air was crisp, and she circled high over the sleepy town. Then she wound her way in and out of the windmills dotting the hills on both sides of the Columbia River, making a game of speed and maneuverability. When she got to the river, she dropped lower and ran her hand through the water. Her mood lightened with the thrill of flying.

She dove down, pulling up just so her haunches dragged through the cold water. Laughing, she dove again and again. She flew west to Portland, following the river out to the ocean. As she got closer to the city, she increased her elevation, and after briefly admiring the city lights, she turned around.

On the return trip, she pushed her speed. It was only a few hours before the sun would come up, and she took her cues from the landmarks to cut the travel time. As she came over Goldendale, her heart beat rapidly in anticipation. From up above, she saw Athan's truck in his driveway, and her heart expanded. A light flicked on in the kitchen, and she pulled higher into the darkness. Laughter bubbled from her lips, both nervous and relieved. He was safe at home.

The night was drawing to a close, and she flew north to the mountains where she'd be safe from human eyes.

She spent much of the next day sleeping. She reviewed her homework, finishing the outline for a paper. She'd decided to write about the curse placed on King Minos's wife, which led to the birth of the monstrous Minotaur. Unsurprisingly, another depressing tale of the gods taking revenge on a human.

As the sun fell, the trees cast long shadows across the wild grasses. Hope shoved her books into her backpack and glanced over the small area. Clinging to the straps of her bag, she beat her wings and lifted into the cool air.

Icy-cold needles encircled her ankle, and she was yanked from the sky. With a cry of pain, she crashed to the ground. She pulled her wing away from her face, and time slowed.

Skia. The one from the Dalles.

"It will be your fear that destroys you," he rasped, stalking toward her. "And you should be afraid."

"What do you want?" she asked, even as she pushed her wings out and curled her fists, the best she could do for a defensive stance.

He laughed, a sound akin to nails on a chalkboard. "You will come with me."

She fixed him with a glare. "No, I won't. I told your buddy I'm not going to the Underworld. You need to leave me alone."

He pulled out blades dark as night. "I will take you myself if I need to."

Hope had never fought in this form. Not as the Sphinx. She shifted on her haunches, testing reflexes and maneuverability.

Crack.

Her chest lit with pain, and she doubled over with a gasp.

"You are too slow, beast. This will be easy."

She glared at the Skia, even as fear licked at her heart. He'd gotten in and out fast. Really fast. And the sun was setting. She needed to get off the mountain before she changed.

There was no time for fear. No time to think. Only time to act.

She took a deep breath and stared at the torso of her attacker. He feigned left. But she saw his weight shift right. He was coming in. This was it.

His fist extended as he closed the gap between them.

Hope rotated her hand as she blocked with her forearm. With a fluid movement her opposite elbow followed through, connecting with his leg, just below the hip. A crunch of bone, and he collapsed with a scream.

Hope backed away and pumped her wings.

The Skia lay on the ground in a sliver of sun. She could hear him gasping.

She circled once, but he didn't move.

She dove in for her backpack, and the shadow monster rolled. As she clasped the strap of her bag, he grabbed her wing and yanked.

A searing pain tore through her back. Panic and self-preservation drove her to kick out with her haunches, again and again. He released her, and gritting her teeth, she flew off the mountain.

The last rays of sun were slipping over the horizon as she tumbled from the sky.

She fell to the ground naked, just outside the abandoned barn, and crawled through the doors.

MERCER ISLAND SAT in the middle of Lake Washington, just east of Seattle. The island allegedly boasted beautiful views and prime real estate. Not that Hope cared about that.

Hope's attorney, Charlie Davenport, had an office in one of the yellow buildings in the hub of the financial district. Her grandfather, Jamie Treadwell, had the attorney draw up trust paperwork to make sure Hope's mom would always have sufficient money. Priska had worked for Mr. Davenport ever since he'd agreed to do the trust. He was almost like family. Almost.

Hope parked her conspicuous Civic among the more luxurious BMWs, Porsches, and Mercedes in the parking lot.

She'd barely slept at the small hotel outside of Cle Elum, but the bright rays of sun made the darkness of the Skia seem distant.

Hope walked into the office at eight forty-five.

The faintest hint of lavender reminded Hope of Priska, and she felt a pang of loneliness. Shrugging it off, she glanced around the waiting room. The empty leather chairs looked more comfortable than they were, and the thick area rug would be a better place to sit. The design of everything was subdued, as was the abstract art on the walls. It was very much a Priska way to decorate. And Hope felt some satisfaction that nothing had changed since Priska left.

However, the brunette woman arranging the refreshment area was not Priska. Judging from the number of baked goods she was heaping onto a tray, Hope was one of many clients this morning.

The woman turned as the door clicked shut, and with a look of polite deference she asked, "May I help you?"

"I'm Hope Treadwell. I have an appointment with Mr. Davenport."

The woman's smile was one of relief. "You're early."

Hope's mom ran early, too. "Is that okay? Is he running late?'

"No. He should be with you shortly. Can I get you anything?" She pointed at the tray of pastries and muffins.

"Just a water, please." Hope accepted the bottle gratefully and drank deeply. "Thank you."

"I'll let him know you're here." The woman finished stacking the tray, then walked down the hall. She returned a couple of minutes later. "He'll be with you momentarily."

Seconds later, Mr. Davenport appeared in the waiting room.

Charles Davenport was in his early fifties. Tall and fit, he kept his head shaved, but the outline of a receding hairline was faintly visible. He wore a dark, tailored suit, and the smell of expensive cologne wafted in with him. But something in the way he moved made it look like he carried a weight of worry squarely on his shoulders.

"Hope Nicholas, so nice to see you." His deep bass communicated the words with feeling, and he extended his hand. She took it, and he covered hers with both of his. His gaze held hers while he spoke, "I'm glad you're running early."

They walked back into his office, and he closed the door.

"Without Priska, I seem to make more of a mess of my schedule, and Melanie can't seem to work the same magic." He sighed.

"I thought her name was Melody?"

He frowned and looked off into space for a moment.

"No, I think that was the last one." He shook his head. "Honestly, I can't keep them straight. Gods, I wish she'd come back."

Hope's heart fell. She'd been hoping he'd have some news. "I'm sorry."

He met her gaze with a sad smile. "There is nothing for you to be sorry about. I know you miss her, too."

All she could do was nod. If she opened her mouth she'd start bawling. And she didn't know Mr. Davenport that well.

He exhaled a big breath and extended his arm. "Let's sign you into your inheritance."

Mr. Davenport grabbed a folder from his desk and pulled a chair up next to her. He shuffled quickly through the paperwork, and she signed where he indicated as he explained the purpose of each document. When they finished, Hope stood to leave.

But, after he put the paperwork away, Mr. Davenport remained seated.

He glanced up at her, his lips pursed. "There is something else we need to talk about. I think it might be better if you sit."

He pointed at a chair then clasped his hands together and paced the room.

With a growing sense of dread, she sat and waited.

After several uncomfortable seconds, he stopped in front of her and cleared his throat. "I hope you understand that I always try to act in your best interest." He paused, as if calculating what to say next. "Yesterday afternoon, Mr. Jeffers called. He was trying to confirm the date and time of our appointment."

Her heart stopped, and anxiety danced through her body.

"Melanie took the call, and of course refused to confirm that you were even a client here, but passed the message to me. I called the school back and spoke with him."

She nodded.

"Normally, I would have stayed on the side of the law and refused all information, but since we'd discussed this, I explained the law to Mr. Jeffers, and confirmed that you are a client. I did not confirm or deny any appointments, and reminded him that I work for you, and if frivolous action were taken, I would represent you and ensure he became unemployed."

Hope's mouth dropped open, but the words were slow in coming. "Um, I . . . I can't believe you did that."

He waved away her words. "I'm not sure I did you any favors. The man was livid. Perhaps my threat was a bit much. Are you struggling in school? He called you . . . an 'at risk' student."

She shook her head. "No, I'm getting straight *A*s."

"Then this is ridiculous. Would you like me to call him back?"

It would be nice to let Mr. Davenport handle it, but the battle wasn't his. "Let me see what happens when I get back. There are only a couple more weeks of school, so it shouldn't even matter. Maybe . . ." She shrugged. "I could try and smooth things over."

"Of course, my dear. And if I might make a suggestion, since your absences seem to be an issue in Goldendale, you might consider moving before the next school year. Something to think about."

It was a reasonable suggestion. But she didn't want to move.

Mr. Davenport stood. "Your aunt loved you very much. And I want you to know, if you ever need anything, you can call me."

Hope stood, but words eluded her. Emotion she'd held in check threatened to burst. She closed her eyes, willing herself to hold it together.

Warm hands cupped her shoulders.

"I miss her, too," he said.

Hope looked up and saw in Mr. Davenport's face pain that mirrored her own.

She swallowed and nodded. "Thank you."

He walked her to the office door, and she went down the
hall toward the waiting room by herself.

THIRTY

SHE DROVE PAST the diner, past the motel, arriving in windy Goldendale with an hour of school remaining.

Plenty of time to turn in her completed assignments. It might help. It certainly couldn't hurt.

One by one, she stopped into each class. Each of her teachers thanked her for the work and wished her a good weekend. The last bell rang as she walked down the hall. Students poured out, and Hope swam upstream through the crowd.

Students' voices filled the halls, and the smell of the numberless bodies tickled her nose. With a sigh, she looked for Athan but couldn't see his tall figure anywhere. Tristan stood by his locker with Lee, and she walked over to them.

"Hey, you're back!" Tristan greeted her. His smile was a direct contrast to the cold one from Krista standing just behind him.

If she were more vindictive, Hope might've felt some satisfaction that the nasty girl was sporting matching black eyes. Instead, guilt tugged at Hope's heart, and she avoided making eye contact with Krista, instead zeroing in on Tristan.

"Yeah, I just got back," Hope responded. "Is Athan here today?" She glanced around as if he might materialize.

"No," he said, his shoulders sagging. "He's been gone since Tuesday. With his dad, I think."

"I thought his dad was dead," said Lee.

"Nah," Tristan responded. "He travels a lot, so Athan couldn't stay with him."

Obviously she wasn't the only one he'd shared with.

He turned back to Hope. "They were going hunting, maybe?" His face scrunched.

"Really?"

"Yeah. He's been gone, same as you." He tilted his head. "Someone said you two were skipping together, but obviously not."

That again? She drew back. "No."

Lee raised his eyebrows. "Yeah. Obviously."

"Huh." Tristan frowned. "Maybe he really went hunting."

"I didn't know he hunted."

"He's never talked about it before." He shrugged. "Maybe I misunderstood."

"Okay. Well, have a good weekend." She turned to leave, and Tristan called her back.

"Hey, Hope! We're going to go down to Maryhill Park tomorrow for the day. BBQ and all that. You're welcome to come if you'd like. I know Haley would love to have you there."

"Thanks. I'll try." She forced a smile and waved goodbye.

BETWEEN THE SKIA, the hours in the car, the stress of school, and Athan being unavailable, Hope felt like she would explode. All she wanted was to go for a run. The late afternoon sun lolled on the horizon, keeping the night chill at bay. The smell of summer played on the wind. Hope decided she would not let fear rule her actions. With resolve, she strapped her golden dagger at her hip and left the house.

Hope took a deep breath and started at a jog.

She would not worry about Mr. Jeffers.

She would not worry about Skia.

She would not worry about Athan.

She would not worry about Priska.

She would not worry . . .

The tension in her shoulders and back drained as she pounded the pavement. Sweat dripped from her hairline, leaving tracks down her face and neck. Her tank top was saturated.

It was good to be home. Everything was going to be okay.

She'd looped through the town twice and was halfway through a third loop when she saw Athan's truck at the school, in the back lot. Had it been there this afternoon?

Hope walked to it and put her hand on the hood. Wasn't that supposed to tell you if it had been driven recently? Gods, she'd make a terrible spy. She looked around but didn't see him. She went to the school, on the pretense of getting a drink, but the doors were locked.

She crossed the empty bus lot as the sun continued its descent. Cerulean blended into lavender, and orange tinged the horizon.

Athan's truck still sat unoccupied.

She turned to go home and crossed the street, passing by the abandoned factory.

This time, she felt his presence even before she saw him.

Nausea roiled through her, and the smell of decay travelled on the breeze.

The Skia stepped out from the shadows; the tall figure's sallow appearance bordered on emaciated. He walked with a limp, as if the bone had not been set right after their fight last night.

Her fear turned to anger. How dare he come back?

Her training dictated her actions unconsciously. She stepped back, coiled to run.

"It won't do any good," he rasped. "I can follow you, monster. Through the shadows, I can see you."

Her muscles tensed.

"What do you want?" She gritted her teeth. He was well out of striking distance, and despite her anger, she'd rather not fight him. "Why did you attack me?"

"You are wanted by my master."

"Hades?" She clasped her clammy hands to her hips. She could throw the immortal dagger, but she wasn't trained to work with blades. Her fingers itched to reach for the weapon, or to close the gap and beat him. But . . . She reined her emotions in. Fight smart, not angry.

He stepped toward her. "You are very ignorant."

Even if it was true, she didn't want to hear it. She stepped away. "Did you kill that man? In the Dalles?"

He chuckled. "You mean the spawn of Dionysus? Why would you care? If he had found you alone, he would have killed you . . . or worse."

With his eyes just all-black orbs, it was impossible to see exactly what he was looking at.

"I would have been fine," Hope spit out.

"Perhaps." He pulled out a black blade. "But you are not invincible."

"Neither are you." Her anger pulsed in waves, and all her training flashed through her mind. The first lesson in self-defense is to use your voice as a weapon.

"Stop!" Hope issued the command as loud as she could yell. She gripped the gold dagger with the blade pointing down and held it close to her chest. She took another step back. "Go back to your master and tell him there is nothing here for him.

I am not dead. I will not come with you. Leave. Me. Alone. Or I will kill you."

The Skia chuckled, and he dissolved into a shadow.

That was almost too easy.

Hope let out a sigh of relief, but her shoulders stopped mid-slump as cold metal rested at her throat.

His cold breath was like sleet against her skin, and he whispered in her ear, "You do not command me."

He grabbed her shoulder; his icy grip chilled her from skin to bone.

Her pulse jumped a staccato arrhythmia as fear pulsed through her.

"Not now, not ever." He pulled the icy blade across her skin. "I will take you, and you can't stop me."

A tingling sensation gave way to shards of ice bludgeoning down her neck and into her chest. The pain was unreal, and she gasped. Blood welled at the cut and then dripped down her chest, staining the collar of her tank black in the twilight. He pulled her back, dragging her, but she couldn't find any strength to fight.

"Sphinx," he hissed.

She glanced behind her and saw him step into the shadows. Oh. Gods.

He dragged her closer to the darkness, and she watched in terror. He'd completely disappeared into the blackness of Hades except for his arms. It was a portal to the Underworld.

She wanted to scream. She wanted to cry.

This was not how she was supposed to die.

He yanked her toward the blackness, and it felt as if she'd hit a brick wall.

Pain blossomed and flowed from her scalp to her chest. Icy tendrils stabbed in pin-like projections, and the Skia pulled at her again and again, slamming her into an invisible barrier.

He swore, and then the tension was gone. Hope fell to the ground, dropping the gold knife into the dirt. She lowered her head, and on her hands and knees she vomited. Wave after wave of glacial pain stabbed her. She screamed and sobbed, begging for mercy as her tears turned the dirt to mud.

But the pain would not stop.

Her cries grew weak, and when she collapsed, it was with a plea for death.

But death refused her.

The night sky was dotted with silver when Hope rolled over. She blinked again and again, the pain waning ever so slowly, and Hope shivered with the cold. The pain in her chest persisted, it's throbbing, an unremitting thump-thump. With a deep breath, she pulled herself up.

The ground spun and then settled, then spun again as she reached for her knife. If she ever met that Skia again, she wouldn't hesitate.

The sour smell of vomit clung to her hair, and her shirt was sticky with her own blood. Hope tried to suppress the shuddering cold as she crawled to the sidewalk. Using a street sign, she dragged herself upright. When the world stopped spinning, she staggered home in the shadows.

By the time she got through the door, she didn't care that she smelled of vomit and blood and sweat. She didn't care about anything. She pushed the door closed and fell to the floor exhausted.

THE SUN STREAMED through the open curtains. Hope turned to get out of the light and groaned. The stabbing pain had been replaced by a dull throbbing, and the shaking chills had left her sore and achy. But she was alive. And glad for it.

She rolled onto her back and stared at the image of Hecate. She never really believed it before, that the little statue kept the Skia from her house, kept them from crossing through her doorways. She wanted to carry the effigy everywhere, and at the same time she was bitter that the gods had that much power. With a grunt of disgust, she stood.

The shower was pure heaven. Clean clothes like nirvana. And her bed . . .

Elysium.

It felt like minutes later that the noise forced her to peel her eyes open. There was an insistent pounding on her front door. Not even seconds later, the knocking was accompanied by her phone chiming.

"Just a minute," she shouted toward the door as she glanced at her phone. Haley.

"Hello?" Hope answered the phone as she pulled an over-sized sweatshirt from her floor.

"Where have you been?" Haley's question sounded like an accusation.

Hope pulled the hoodie on over her tank top then held the phone back to her ear. "Home."

"All weekend? I came by, Hope. You weren't there."

Hope crossed through the house while she talked. "Yes, all weekend. I . . . I was sick. I must have picked up something while I was in Seattle."

She peeked through the peephole.

Athan.

"Listen, Haley, Athan just got here. Call you back a little later?"

Haley laughed. "No. I'll just see you in school tomorrow. You're well enough to come, right?"

"Yep. See you tomorrow." Hope pressed End and opened the door for Athan.

THIRTY-ONE

ATHAN STOOD BEFORE her in jeans and a pale-olive sweater. His scent tickled her senses, and she drank him in. There were dark circles under his eyes that told of too little sleep, but the jade jewels sparkled with emotion. A hint of joy played at the corners of his mouth.

"Hey." She tried for a casual smile, but her grin broke through, and she reached for him.

"Hey, yourself." His voice was low and soft, and his hands felt rough when he touched her cheek. He pressed his lips to hers. "Can I come in?"

Emotion ignited between them, and she couldn't look away. "Of course."

She backed away from the door, allowing him passage.

"How was your weekend?" she asked, noting his sallow appearance. His hands were scraped, and there was a fresh scab on his neck that was long and thin.

"Loads of fun." His smile was wry and his voice heavy with sarcasm. He moved to the couch and patted the cushion next to him. "What about you? Did you do anything fun?"

"No." She waved her hand around the house as she continued. "I cleaned house and finished my mythology essay. And then I got sick."

She collapsed on the couch and snuggled close to him.

"Finished your mythology essay? The final?" Athan pursed his lips. "The one that isn't due for another week?"

She nodded. "I know I'm a nerd." Her laugh was tinged with embarrassment. "I heard you went hunting?"

He sat up. "Who told you that?"

"Tristan."

"Oh." He sat back. "He must have misunderstood."

"Well, you look like you've been in boot camp or survival training." She reached out and traced the scab on his neck.

"You're not far off," he replied with a snort. "It felt like boot camp. I was working for my dad."

"Working for your dad? I thought you said your dad owned a courier business?" She frowned, pulling away to look at him.

"Yeah, and a guide service." He shrugged.

"So were you delivering a package or giving a tour?" She worried the tassels of a pillow.

"I was searching for something that got lost."

307

"A package got lost?" She swallowed. "Or a person?" What kind of business *was* this? And why did he look like he'd been in a war zone?

Athan laughed. "Don't worry."

He took her hand away from the pillow fringe.

"Did you find what you were looking for?" It shouldn't matter, but it did.

"No," he replied, staring down at their entwined hands. "But I'm close. I know it," he whispered to himself. He traced circles on the back of her hand. "What about you? What did you get sick with?"

Hope relayed the same lie she'd told Haley only minutes before.

"Ugh, that's awful." His gaze travelled over her face and stopped at her neck a moment. "All better now, though?"

She nodded.

"Well, that's lucky." He touched the base of her throat. "Are you feeling up to going to the observatory? We could go look at the stars."

She flinched at his touch as much as the suggestion. "I think I'd rather stay in, if you don't mind."

"Not at all. Do you want to watch a movie?"

"Sure. What do you want to watch?"

He shrugged. "You choose."

He released her hand, and she stood to put something in the DVD player. She grabbed the case sitting on top of the rest of the stack: *What's Up, Doc?* Her mom's favorite. She put it in and pushed Play.

Athan stretched out the length of the sofa. "Here, come lay down in front of me."

She shook her head. "No. You look like you need it. I'll sit right here." She grabbed a couple of pillows and made a make-shift chair up against the couch. She took his hand and draped it over her shoulder.

He leaned forward, and she twisted to meet his lips. The kiss was tender and soft, and Athan pulled away with a smile.

"Do you want to watch the movie . . . or something else?" He waggled his eyebrows.

"No, let's watch the movie. I think you'll like it, and I could use a laugh."

They both chuckled and hooted throughout the movie; the slapstick humor was ridiculous, charming, and . . . distracting. It was just what she wanted—really, what she needed. When it was over, he grabbed a pillow from the couch and stretched out on the floor next to her.

"That was hysterical."

"I'm glad you liked it. My mom said you could always judge a person's sense of humor by watching that movie with them."

"Oh, so it was a test?" He arched his brow.

"Yeah," she countered, "and you failed. Miserably." She reached out and touched his nose.

"Do you think your mother would have liked me?"

She sighed. "Yeah."

But she wouldn't let me be with you. We would've moved as soon as you showed interest in me, or me in you. I would have been gone before you knew it. The thoughts came unbidden and unwanted, and she fought for control.

"Hope." He touched his finger to her lips. "I'm crazy about you."

Thoughts scattered into a swirl of colors, and her breath caught. "Really?"

He pulled back. "Haven't I made it obvious?"

She reached out and stroked the tired shadows, traced his nose and then his lips. She closed her eyes. She couldn't lie, and there was no way to down play her feelings.

"I'm pretty crazy about you, too." The truth tore at her heart.

"Is that a problem?" His brows pinched together.

"No, it's just . . ."

"You know you can trust me, right?"

"I do trust you." But even as she said the words, she knew they were a lie.

"Come here." He stood and pulled her up to him. His fingers traced her lips, and he drew closer. "You have turned my world upside down, and I don't think it will ever be the same."

Their breath mingled, and his scent was overwhelming.

It was too much. She took a step back.

"Do I make you uncomfortable?" He dropped his hands to his side as he studied her.

She closed her eyes, unable to even look at him while she spoke.

"Yes." She sighed. "It's just . . . I've never had a boyfriend before." That wasn't the whole of it.

He chuckled and stepped up to her, tracing her face with his forefinger. "I promise I'll take it slow, and you can always say no. To anything. I want you to be comfortable. I want you to be happy. I want you to feel safe."

And then he was kissing her. His lips were soft, barely brushing hers, again and again. Her breathing became shallow as he kissed her jawbone, her neck, and pulled her hoodie to kiss the base of her throat. His hands slid down her back to her hips, and he pulled her into him.

Hope let go of her worry. Let go of her fear. There was a stirring, and she yearned to be closer. She gripped at his arms, drawing the embrace tighter. His lips parted, and her world exploded. Emotions of vibrant colors pulsed through her body, heat and light, sweetness and desire.

He backed her against the door, his hands at her neck and then in her hair. His body pushed up against hers.

"Hope," he breathed her name, and then he kissed her again. He tugged at her sweatshirt, and she pulled it off.

Her fingers splayed across his back, clinging to him. She could not get close enough, and it felt like she was drowning in happiness.

Athan kissed her neck and then pulled back with a ragged breath. "Hope, please stop."

Her eyes drew down in confusion.

"What's the matter? Did I do something?" Her hands fell to her sides. Hurt and doubt crowded in and pushed at the passion she'd felt only seconds before.

He traced over her collarbone, leaving the warmth of his fingers. "*You* are perfect." He bent, kissed her softly on the mouth, but pulled away before it could go any further. His features battling in a mixture of desire and restraint, he glanced down at her neck, and his countenance shifted. His eyes widened. "I . . . I need to go. I'll see you at school tomorrow. Don't forget to lock up."

And he was gone.

Hope grabbed her sweatshirt off the floor and threw it over the couch. What in the name of Hades?

As she stood in front of the mirror, brushing her teeth, she saw it.

She leaned forward and touched the scab from where the Skia blade had cut her. What the Kracken was *that*? Not only was the scab black, but the surrounding skin was dusky with streaks of pitch.

Oh gods.

No wonder Athan took off. He probably thought she had some disease—

No.

He'd said she was perfect *after* he'd seen it. And he'd touched it.

What did he know?

THIRTY-TWO

"NICE FACE, KRISTA." Tristan chuckled.

"Shove off, D-bag."

Hope turned to see Krista, the skin around her eyes still mottled yellow and purple. Their eyes met, and Krista glared.

"What are you looking at, harpy? Gloating because you broke my nose?"

Hope cringed at the thought. She leaned forward to apologize and then stopped herself.

"I didn't attack you, Krista. All I did was block." She straightened her shoulders. "It's not my fault you don't know how to fight." She went to her locker, leaving Krista sputtering among their friends.

"What the Kracken, Hope?" Seconds later, Haley pushed Hope's locker closed. "You never called me back."

Hope frowned at her friend. "I thought we agreed that we'd just see each other at school."

Haley raised her eyebrows as she gave Hope a once over.

"Was Athan over late? Is that why you're wearing that?" She plucked at the high collar on Hope's shirt.

Hope batted her hand away. "Eww. No. I mean yes . . . and no." She turned and dialed her combination. "He was over late, but we just kissed." The blush spread from head to toes.

"Oh. Well, too bad for you, I guess."

Hope grabbed her mythology book. "No, I think we did all right."

Her eyes widened.

Athan strode down the hall, his glowering expression sending underclassmen scattering.

Haley turned around, took one look at Athan, and faced Hope. "Ah, I've got to go. I'll see you at lunch?"

She didn't even wait for Hope to answer.

"I want to talk with you," he growled.

"Okay." What was his problem? "Uh, if it's going to take longer than five minutes—"

"It won't." He grabbed her arm and pulled her toward a stairwell.

"Athan . . . my locker . . ." Hope turned as if she could still reach and close it.

"It'll be fine. It's not like there's anything of value in there."

She disagreed. Her books. Her work . . .

"Get out," he snarled, and the couple kissing on the stairs ran past them.

"What's up with you?" She wrenched her arm free.

"With me? *Ouia*, what's up with you?"

"What are you talking about? Not much has changed since last night *when you were over*."

He took a deep breath and released a slow exhale.

"Do you want to tell me where you got that . . . cut on your neck?" His fists clenched and unclenched.

She narrowed her eyes. "Why?"

"Why? Because I think I should know."

"*You* think you should know? Um, last time I checked, it was my body. My life."

"Are you serious? You get injured, and you don't think I *deserve* to know?" he yelled.

It was like someone had thrown a switch. The young man she *thought* she knew was gone. And this person was a complete stranger.

"What's going on with you?" She couldn't reconcile the difference in her mind.

"What's going on with *me*? Gods, Hope. I said you could trust me. You said you did. And now . . . You won't even tell me how you got hurt?"

"Why does it matter? I'm fine." Well, mostly she was fine. The pain was gone this morning, and aside from a small ache

. . .

"How can you even be standing here?" He reached out and grabbed the top of her collar, pulled it down so the blackened skin was exposed. "How does something like that happen?"

She grabbed his wrist and threw his arm back. "How dare you. Don't—"

"If you can't be honest with me . . ."

She drew herself up and clenched her fists. "Are you kidding me? What about you? Where did you go with your dad? And how did you get all beat up? How about you tell me what you're hiding?"

He exhaled. "I already told you. I wasn't in a fight. I've been helping my father."

"Right. With his courier service."

"He's my father. And I would do anything for him. It's called loyalty. And this isn't about me." He ran his hand through his hair.

Right. Well then. "I'm sorry. I can't tell you."

He stared at her as if waiting for something. But if he thought she was going to change her mind, he was crazy. This was her secret, and maybe he was right. She didn't trust him. Not with that.

"If you can't be honest with me, maybe we shouldn't be together." Without waiting for her reply, he turned and left.

Her heart fell into her stomach, and she gaped after him. That was it? Just like that. Hope collapsed on the bottom step.

The bell rang.

She felt like there was a flashing sign in her mind . . . *Does not compute*.

With her world upside down, Hope went to close her locker.

Six hours later, she slammed the door to her home, shutting out the pity that had followed her all day. She saw it in Haley's eyes. Felt it in the conversation. And by the end of school, *everyone* knew.

The ache in her chest had nothing to do with the Skia blade, but she wished it did. Perhaps, if he had cut just a little deeper, she would be in the Underworld?

She shook her head. What in the name of Hades was she thinking? Good gods! She was not going to let Athan breaking up with her turn her into a moping child.

Hope reviewed the last several days with sudden clarity.

Skia were watching her. Her principal had all but threatened to expel her. Her boyfriend—She got tingles when she thought about him and then wanted to slap herself. If she was anyone else, she would slap herself. Because her *ex-boyfriend* was a liar. She didn't know exactly what about, but did it matter? Well, maybe he wasn't lying, per se, but . . . He was being deceitful. And it didn't even matter because they weren't together.

Yes, she had friends, but the smart thing to do would be to leave. She should leave Goldendale.

Start over.

It's what her mom would have recommended weeks ago. No, it's what she would've demanded they do.

Hope took a quick trip to DT Moving Supplies on Main Street. The sun was just setting when Hope started packing. One by one, she pushed the boxes into the living room. Linens. Toiletries. Dishes.

Even while her heart was breaking, she knew it was for the best.

She liked Haley. She liked Athan. Hades, she *like* liked Athan. But he'd ended it. And really it was probably for the best. She'd been crazy to think she could get close to anyone. And what kind of a jerk broke up with you for lying when he was lying, too?

There was nothing safe about staying in Goldendale.

THIRTY-THREE

SIMILAR TO HER first day at Goldendale High, Hope arrived early. The pine disinfectant hung in the air, and coupled with the silent halls, she felt a shiver of déjà vu. However, today she knew her way to the office, she expected the bell announcing her arrival, and she addressed the assistant without having to glance at the nameplate.

"Good morning, Ms. Slate. Is Mr. Jeffers in yet?"

Ms. Slate stopped her typing and picked up the phone.

She waited while the plump woman called into his office. Seconds later, Ms. Slate waved her through without a word.

Hope took a deep breath, forcing the butterflies and caterpillars to the depths of her soul. This was for the best; despite what her heart said, her mind was made up.

She knocked.

"Come in," a deep voice instructed from behind the door.

Hope opened the door and walked into his practical office. He looked up from his computer screen and met her eyes. "Hope Treadwell, what can I do for you this morning? Not planning on missing more school are you?"

He extended his hand.

Clenching her teeth, she swallowed a snide remark, and grasped his hand briefly. "No, sir. But I do need to talk with you about that."

"I can appreciate your concern. You seem to have an issue with attendance." He pointed at the chair across from his desk.

Hope pulled the chair far away from the glare of the sun, offered a tight smile, and sat. "Yes. Mr. Davenport spoke of your concerns. Though, I think it's interesting, this concern you have."

He clenched his jaw. "Interesting? How so?"

She took a deep breath, as if contemplating the words. "One would assume that your interest is in your students learning and their progress. However, if that were your focus, you would've noticed that I have straight *A*s. I make up all my work. *All* of it. If you were attentive to the needs of the students, you would see their suffering and struggles, not just their attendance. If *learning*— actual knowledge and education—were actually your concern, you would make your students, not attendance numbers, your focus."

His eyes grew wide.

"And don't even get me started on your choice of counselor, and her serious lack of confidentiality. Not only does her daughter seem to know everything that happens, but she shares it with the entire school. If you decide to report me"—she glared at him—"I will let them know every single violation that goes on here. Besides, I don't think that the absences of a straight *A* student who, incidentally, has lost her mom and her aunt both in the last six months, would really meet criteria for an at-risk situation, or whatever it is you call it."

He sat back in his chair and exhaled. Then with a wave of his hand he dismissed her concerns. "No. No need. We'll just . . . move forward. In the event of future absences, please just provide a letter stating the necessity of said absence."

She swallowed, but her anxiety didn't disappear. "I understand, Mr. Jeffers. But I came in to let you know I will be withdrawing from school."

He set the papers down and narrowed his eyes. "When?"

"Today."

He frowned. "I hope this choice to move is not in response to any . . . misunderstanding."

"Why would you think that?" Not waiting for an answer, she stood. "I've been advised to move closer to Seattle so I have easier access to the services I'm using. I'm sure you've had other students coping with loss, so you understand." She extended her hand. "Thank you for your time."

Mr. Jeffers wheeled around the desk. "Of course. My door is always open to the students."

He clasped her hand; it was clammy with sweat.

"I'm sure it is, sir."

As she shut the door, she could hear the clicking of his keyboard.

Students filed in as Hope walked to her locker. Might as well get her stuff while she was here. Bitter anger surged. It was so unfair. She turned the dial quickly, missing number after number. A growl of frustration escaped, and she hit the metal door.

"Hope."

She turned, her heart flipped, and her mouth went dry.

"I think we should . . ." Athan's brow creased. "You don't look so well. Are you ill?"

For the first time in her life, she was grateful that her emotions played so obviously on her face. "Why would it matter to you? Go away, Athan."

She turned back to the locker and spun through the combination.

"No. I want to talk to you about yesterday."

She shoved notebooks into her bag and pulled out the textbooks, putting them into her locker. "I'm not feeling up to it right now. I'm just here to grab my stuff, then I'm heading home."

"What? You're going home?"

She offered him a tight smile. "If you have something to say, say it. Otherwise . . ."

Athan's brow creased. "I . . . I'm sorry I lost my temper yesterday. I . . . I want us to still be friends."

Was he *kidding*? "Okay. Fine."

"Okay? Oh, great. Good. So maybe—"

She slammed the locker shut. "See you later, Athan."

He sighed. "I hope you feel better. Will I see you tomorrow?"

He reached out as if to touch her, but she pulled back. "Yep. See ya."

It was so much easier to hide behind her anger than acknowledge her hurt. *Friends? Whatever*. She just needed to finish packing, and then she could leave.

BY EARLY EVENING, the house was packed. She'd moved her mother's box, the boxes of books from the study, and the duffle bags into the front room. She'd call a moving company in the morning, but she wanted to get on the road tonight. She grabbed the two duffle bags and went out to her car.

The air had cooled with the sunset, and her feet dragged as she walked back to the house. She needed to move a few more boxes into the living room, finish packing her car, and then she'd be ready.

She opened the front door to the ringing of her phone. It had been ringing all afternoon. All evening, too. The lit screen showed ten missed calls. All Athan, and no messages.

Looking through her house with boxes stacked all around, she felt the walls closing in. Hot emotion roiled through her body, and her head ached with the tension. She wanted to hit something, or someone. She ran through her breathing exercises, trying to calm down, but the energy needed an outlet. With a dare to the universe, and the Skia from Hades, she grabbed her running clothes and went to change.

Night had fallen by the time she stepped outside, and she closed her eyes to the veil of darkness. With a deep breath, she turned the key, and someone coughed behind her. Her heart thudded, and she turned.

Athan stood under the streetlight.

"What is it with you today?" he said, unhitching himself from the post. He wore long baggy athletic shorts, a T-shirt, and running shoes.

"What?" she squeaked.

"You don't answer my calls, you ran off in school . . ."

The urge to tell him off was almost as strong as the urge to cry. She mentally pounded it into oblivion and fixed her eyes on the ground. If she glanced his way, she knew her will would crumble.

"I have a lot going on, and you're not helping. Besides, I thought you didn't care."

"Why would you say that?" He stepped closer, his gaze darting to her neck.

"Um, you *broke up* with me." She itched to hit him.

"You think I broke up with you because I don't like you?" He sounded incredulous.

She laughed. "I may not be well versed in the whole boy-friend-girlfriend thing, but usually you don't break up with someone you like."

He shook his head. "You don't know what you're talking about."

"Look, I need a run . . . to clear my head." She looked up at him. "Do you ever do that?" She started walking briskly and wasn't at all surprised when he kept stride.

"All the time." He trailed his hand down her arm.

Despite yanking her arm away, she had an almost over-whelming compulsion to share her plans with him. Keeping her focus on the road, and her mouth clamped shut, she picked up the pace. It wasn't until she was running that her desire to bare her fears, her plans, and her secrets passed.

She lost herself in the release.

After lapping the town twice, she slowed their pace to a jog and then a brisk walk. On Broadway, still three blocks from her house, Athan broke the silence.

"You can't avoid talking to me forever. You can't just ig-nore something and have it go away."

"Are you *kidding* me?" How dare he? He knew nothing about why she did what she did. "You want me to be all open and honest, when you're clearly not forthcoming with informa-tion, either, Athan. So don't you dare lecture me."

She sprinted up the stairs to her house and shoved the key in the lock. She couldn't get away fast enough.

"Wait!" he called, following her up the stairs. "I really like you, Hope. I'll . . . I'll tell you everything."

She paused with her hand on the doorknob and waited.

"Everything I told you is true. My dad runs a courier service. A few months ago, a package went missing." He took a deep breath and continued, "Why didn't you tell me about the Skia?"

She couldn't process his shift in topic. "What do you mean?"

He pointed at her neck. "When did you get attacked?"

How could he tell? Oh gods. She wanted to run right then. Panic thrummed through her, and her gaze darted to the car.

"I just want to talk to you, Hope. I promise, that's all. And, maybe, I can help."

Was he serious? There was no way he could know and be offering help. She swallowed her fear and waved him forward. "We'd better go inside."

It was just safer there.

As soon as she turned on the light, he gasped, and she knew it had been a mistake to have him come in.

THIRTY-FOUR

BEFORE SHE COULD say anything, he grabbed her arm. "Hope?" The intensity of his voice was cutting. "What is all of this? You're leaving?"

His glare seared her.

She swallowed, almost afraid to answer. "Yes."

"You're moving? Where?"

"Why does it matter?"

"It matters. To me." His voice was steel and then dropped to a whisper. "You were going to leave and not tell me."

"Athan. You broke up with me. We're finished." What was the point in trying to explain something that made no sense to her?

"You planned this . . ." His voice trembled with the raw emotion. "Why?"

"You. Broke. Up. With. Me—"

"To keep you safe." He pulled her collar down, exposing the still-mottled flesh. "You think I don't know what this is? There's only one type of blade that leaves a mark like this. And if you were mortal, it would have killed you." He dropped his arm. "I wanted you to tell me. I wanted you to trust me. But you wouldn't."

"So you dumped me? How exactly was dumping me going to keep me safe?"

He shook his head. "I'm sorry. I said I was sorry. I let my emotions get in the way, but—"

"Well, I decided it would be better to move closer to the city. Regardless of your emotions."

"Don't lie to me." The intensity in his voice was mirrored in his eyes. "I know you care—"

"Don't *lie* to you?" She yanked her arm from his grasp, and glared at him. "All you've done is lie to me."

"That's not true," he yelled, throwing his arms up in frustration. "Why didn't you tell me that you were immortal?" His eyes bore into her, tension etched in every feature of his face. "All of this could have been so much easier if you'd just told me. It's not like I couldn't tell."

Her heart stopped. "You can tell?"

He bit the side of his mouth and regarded her. "You hide it better than most. You definitely have some characteristics, but it's not as clear as say, Chelli and Brand." He sighed. "I just wish you would've told me."

"You didn't tell me." Did he not get how hypocritical he was being?

His ember of anger flared into flame. "Well, it's not like I tell—"

"You *lied*!" Her anger overwhelmed the fear, the fatigue, and her worry.

Closing his eyes, he rubbed the back of his neck. With a slow exhale he met her gaze, his eyes boring into her again. "Point taken. I just . . ." He shook his head. "*Skata!*" His voice was tight, and he rocked back on his heels. "How much do you know?"

"Know about what? Immortals?" When he nodded, she continued, "I know the academics—demigods have an immortal parent. Skia kill demigods. My mom always kept us on the move; she said it was the best way to keep hidden from Skia." *And you.*

He nodded in response as if he were listening but still thinking. "How old are you?"

"Seventeen."

He looked at her, questioning. "Really?"

He was asking her age? What in the name of Hades? "Really. I turned seventeen just over a month ago, April 5th."

He shook his head. "Who is your mom?"

The truth slipped out before she could contemplate the repercussions. "My mom's dead, Athan."

"We don't have time for this." He folded his arms across his chest, his lips flattening into a thin line. "I'm done playing games. At this point, I just need the truth."

Her veins thrummed with adrenaline. "Why don't you answer some of my questions?"

His brows pulled down. "I can answer your questions later. I need to get—"

"*What?*"

"There are Skia after you. I'm trying to assess what I'm dealing with, so I need to know: Who. Is. Your. Mother?"

"*She's. Gone!*"

He took a deep breath. "Fine! I'll *pretend* that's true. What's her name?"

She collapsed in the chair. Her chest heaved. Tears ran rivers down her cheeks, and her nose clogged with mucus.

"I'm still waiting. What's your mother's name?"

Hope wiped her face with the hem of her tank and answered in a voice as small as her shriveling feelings for him. "Leto."

"Leto?" He moved so quickly he was just a blur. In his face, his alarm was sharp and pungent. "Are you lying to me?"

She was momentarily dumbfounded. She sucked in air and tried to steady her thoughts.

"Are you lying to me?"

"Stop it!" she screamed. "Just stop!" She shoved him away, and he stumbled back a step. "What about you? Who are you?"

He sighed. "Hermes's son."

"Hermes? As in god of thieves?" She shook her head as things fell into place. His ability to persuade. The running. His talent with music and languages. "Of course. What are you doing here?"

"What? I'm trying to figure out—"

"No. What are you doing here in Goldendale?"

"Oh." He ran his hand through his hair. "I'm *psachno*. Usually, I don't know who I'm searching for. Sometimes, the gods report their offspring, then it's easy. Otherwise, I go to areas where either a demigod or another immortal reports someone with potential immortal characteristics, and I check it out. Like what happened with Brand and Chelli. Sometimes I get lucky and stumble across someone . . . like you." He sucked in a deep breath. "Leto? The Titan goddess?"

He pointed to the boxes with her mother's name on them. "*Skata*. I'm pretty sure she didn't report you. Gods, what a mess."

Her heart skipped a beat. He'd misunderstood.

Leto was a Titan goddess, one of the few that weren't bound in the Underworld when the Olympian gods took over. She was goddess of motherhood and modesty, consort to Zeus, mother to Apollo and Artemis. Athan thought her mom was *that* Leto. He didn't know.

So what did he know? Something was missing from his story. "What about the hunting with your dad? The whole lost package thing?"

Athan drew a deep breath and let it out slowly. "Okay. Total honesty as a gesture of good faith, okay?"

She nodded and waited.

"About forty years ago, my dad led the Sphinx to the underworld. We thought she was dead, hundreds of years ago." He paused momentarily. "No, *thousands* of years ago. But it turns out the Sphinx had a daughter, and she was also a Sphinx. Not even a year ago, she died, the daughter of the first . . ." Athan drew in another deep breath. "Recently, someone reported the monster near Goldendale. I've been tracking her ever since." He cleared his throat, looked around the room, then pulled a chair over and sat across from her, knee to knee.

Her heart stopped, and she wondered if he could hear it. Panic struck, its lashes quick and brutal. He was hunting her.

"Finding you was a fabulous surprise." His words were gentle, and he moved closer to her, his arms up in surrender. "You saw that *Skia* at the bonfire, didn't you? That's when I first knew—"

"Wait a minute." She held up her hand as she spoke. "You asked me out *after* you were suspicious about my mortality. Is that . . . Is that why you asked me out?"

She put it out there, knowing the answer, knowing she would hate hearing the truth.

"Maybe initially, but—"

"And then you broke up with me because I wouldn't tell you?"

"I wanted you to trust me. And as *psachno* . . . I need to take you somewhere safe." He spoke quickly, as if knowing she would cut him off again.

"What is it with you?" All of her feelings for him turned to ice. "Was everything you did calculated?"

"Of course." He ran his fingers through his hair, making it stick up where it was wet with sweat. "But not the way you're implying. At first, I was trying to figure out if you were a demigod. There were things about you that are . . . different. And when I started to suspect that you were . . . It's my job to make sure you're safe. But along the way, something . . . something changed."

His hesitation put her in physical pain.

"Really?"

He reached his hand out as if to touch her but dropped it when she pulled back. "This . . . this is different. I've . . . I've fallen in love—"

"Don't!" Her voice broke. "Just . . . Stop. Don't say it." She was pleading. Tears filled her eyes, and she was fighting to stay in control.

"Come on. You knew that. It's obvious."

"I don't. I thought I did, but . . ." She moved toward the door, but he moved with her. The hair on her neck stood up with his proximity.

"Please. Let me help you. Even if you don't believe me on anything else, I can help you. That Skia, whoever he is, he'll be back. They always come back. You don't know what you're dealing with."

"You think *you* can help me?" she yelled. "*You* are at the root of every one of my problems in Goldendale. Since I met you, I've seen more Skia than in the rest of my life combined, I've had to leave school, and—"

"Those things are not all my fault, and you know it," he cut her off. He took a deep breath, and then, more calmly, continued, "Skia can be anywhere, and once they know who you are—"

"That's why I have to leave!"

"No. Please listen. I can help." His eyes were pools of pleading.

She wrenched her hands away as if his touch burned. Unable to stand in front of him any longer, she paced the room. "I was doing fine until you got here."

"Until I got here?" The spark roared to life. "You weren't even alive when I got here." His finger rested on her chest. A vein in his neck pulsed. "I'll tell you what I see; I see a scared girl pushing away the best help she has because of pride and fear."

The words stung, as if physical blows. She needed him to stop. "I want you out. I want you to leave me alone. Let me go, and—"

"You are so naïve. You don't even know what you're suggesting. The Skia will hunt you. Like a dog."

How dare he? "I'm not asking, Athan. This is my home. I'm telling you to get out."

She pointed at the door to reinforce her point.

"No." He closed the distance until he stood before her. "I know you're mad at me. And you have every right to be. I screwed up. I hurt you, and I'm sorry. But don't ask me to leave you unprotected."

She shook her head while he spoke. "Do you not get it? I don't want you here. You saying sorry doesn't make anything better—"

He grabbed her arm as pain flashed across his face. "Hope—"

"Get. Out!" she screamed. She yanked her arm from his grasp and shoved him toward the door.

The boxes were everywhere, and Athan stumbled, tripping over a stack in his path. He fell, just as the boxes spilled their contents on the floor.

Oh, gods. No.

THIRTY-FIVE

ON THE SHAGGY beige carpet, the *Book of the Fates* lay on the floor face up. The deep-maroon leather was worn at the corners, and in gold lettering was the inscription *Curse of the Sphinx*. The black velvet lay in a heap, the silver dagger with the ruby hilt fully exposed.

Athan stared at the book and the weapon. His gaze went to the golden hilt at her side, then back to the book. Then finally, he looked up at her with wide eyes. "Why do you have that?"

With a few steps forward, Hope bent to grab the book. But he was faster.

He snatched it up, then backed away from her. His hurt at her refusal of him morphed to shock and then horror.

He snapped the book shut and stared at the cover, and then he flipped it open.

Hope stood still, her hand going to the dagger at her waist.

"Why do you have this? Hope! Why do you . . ." He shook his head. "Oh, gods, you . . . You're the Sphinx?" He took a step forward.

Hope yanked the book from him, then scooted out of his reach.

"Don't come near me." Adrenaline still ran through her veins, and her heart beat a rhythm of fight or flight. She stepped back again and brought the weapon out in front of her. She didn't want to fight him, but she would, if he took one step forward.

"It's you," he whispered.

"Please just leave," she pled. She didn't know if she'd be safe if he left, but she couldn't fathom killing him. Her hand trembled, and she clutched the blade tight in an attempt to make her shaking stop.

"You're the Sphinx. Oh, gods." He reached for something at his belt, hesitated and then brought his empty hands up in a gesture of surrender. "You're the Sphinx."

He knew. Hope's mind raced. He was a demigod. Demigods killed monsters. Gods, was he one of them?

The surprise on his face disappeared, and he shored up his obvious emotions. He clenched his jaw, and his eyes hardened with a look of resolve. "I'm so sorry, Hope. I'm going to need you to come with me."

He grabbed at her arm, and she pulled away. She brought the blade in front of her and waved it at him. "I told you to stay away."

Athan shook his head. "I didn't want it this way."

He grabbed her wrist, his hand slid up her forearm, and then his thumb became a nail driving blinding pain up her arm as he pressed on a nerve.

Hope dropped her blade, and his grip became a steel trap, so different than his touch only seconds before. With his other hand, he yanked the Book of the Fates from her. "Where did you get this? These have been bound—"

"It's mine." She reached for it, but he held it away. She tugged and pulled to try and get away, but Athan was not letting go.

The pressure turned to pain as he tightened his grip. "I'm not letting you go, Sphinx. My father has been looking for you. He needs you."

"So you're just going to take me to him?" Her shock made her stupid. How could he do this? How could he . . .

"You tricked me—"

"I never lied!" she screamed at him.

But his face was all closed off with no feeling. The son of Hermes pulled her out the door, and she stumbled down the steps.

She couldn't believe this was happening. Why would Hermes want her? How could Athan do this? The questions ran through her mind as he led her to his truck. As he pulled the door open, she realized there was nothing but death if she went with him.

And death was not an option.

"No!" Her panic exploded, and she kicked and hit, lashing out with everything in her. She heard Athan grunt as a strike landed, and the pressure on her arm lessened. She took the opportunity to wrench her arm free, and without looking behind, she took off running.

Maybe if she could get far enough ahead, she'd be able to find a hiding—

The force that collided with her threw them both to the ground. Hope bucked and threw everything she could at the weight that sat on her.

"Hope!"

She had no idea how long he'd been yelling her name, and she didn't care. If Athan meant death, she would fight him for the rest of her life.

"Hope!"

"Let me go!" she screamed.

Athan dropped his entire body on her. Chest to chest, his breath caressed her face. His gaze dropped to her lips, and then back to her eyes.

She could see the conflict, but he was not even her friend anymore. He was the enemy. Tears pricked her eyes. She'd really liked him, and his betrayal was a knife in her heart. She turned her face to the side and shut her eyes, refusing to let him see how much he'd hurt her.

He sighed. "I'm going to help you up. Please stop fighting me."

The pressure lessened and then disappeared except the grip on her wrists. He pulled her up until she was standing. "We're going to get in my truck and then go talk with my dad."

Was that code for kill you?

Hope opened her eyes, searching for a way out, and saw her potential salvation in the man strolling toward them.

His gait was oily and fluid, and there was something strangely familiar about how he moved. The man passed under a streetlight, and Hope gasped.

Skia. The one that had attacked her. She could make out the blackness of his eyes and the sharp angles of his features. The leer made her stomach clench in fear. He was not salvation. She was dead either way.

"Darren." Athan's voice seethed. Releasing his grip on her arm, he pushed Hope behind him.

She pulled back in shock, her heart skipping a beat. "You *know* him?"

"You've seen him before?"

"He was the other guy in the Dalles. The one that gave me this." She pointed at her neck as if Athan could see it.

"*Skata.*" Without looking back, he pulled a small silver blade from each hip. "Hold it, Darren."

"You two immortals. . ." Darren's voice rubbed like sandpaper. "Together. Who would have thought?" He laughed. "It's like two for one."

Not only could Athan see the Skia, he actually knew him. Gods!

"What makes you think we're coming with you?" Athan questioned, and, with supernatural speed, he flicked his wrist, sending the dagger flying.

Quick as lightning, the Skia dropped, rolled, and came up with a black blade in each hand.

At the sight of the dark daggers, Hope shuddered. She knew the pain that would come. But she refused to let the monster from the Underworld decide her fate.

"I will kill you, Darren," Athan swore, as he advanced on the demon from Hades.

The rasp from Darren could've been a laugh, but it was menacing and full of hate. "You are not capable, demigod."

Athan dodged a blade, then punched the Skia in the gut.

Hope stood frozen as Darren's elbow stuck Athan's side. With only a small wince to acknowledge the hit, Athan pulled back and circled the shadow demon.

The two figures squared off, and it became a brawl.

Instead of fleeing, Hope inched forward, stopping to pick up Athan's blade on the sidewalk. It was lighter than her gold one, and the blade appeared to be the staff of the caduceus that Hermes was known for. The snakes wound around the hilt, and Hope guessed it was an emerald the snakes had for eyes.

She looked up, transfixed, while the two enemies traded punches, kicks, and elbows. Athan had great technique, but he hesitated as if the moves were unfamiliar, or he was trying to

341

recall them. Nevertheless, he moved quickly, and his blocks and intuition were solid.

The Skia was a force to be reckoned with. What he lacked in technique, he made up for in speed, force, and sheer prowess. Grunts and curses singed the air.

It was the perfect time to leave. Both were so occupied she could disappear before either even knew she'd left.

She backed away, slowly so she wouldn't draw their attention.

She'd barely gotten a few feet when there was a crack of bone, and Athan screamed, falling to his knees. The Skia held a fistful of his hair, forcing his head back, exposing his neck.

Time stopped.

The Skia was going to kill him.

She told herself that it was the best thing that could happen. With the demigod's death, her secret would be safe. She could kill the Skia with the weapon in her hand and then disappear. It was for the best.

But something in her heart screamed in protest. She would live to regret it she was sure, but if she let Athan die, she would be the monster he claimed she was.

And she refused to let him be right about that.

Hope looked down at the silver dagger, and she *knew* she was not going to be an accomplice to Athan's death. She would not be a monster.

"Stop!" she screamed, running toward them as fast as she could. "Stop!"

The two immortals froze.

It was all the time she needed.

She leaped forward and dragged the blade across the Skia's chest, slicing through his clothing, the blade biting into his pasty flesh.

The Skia's blade clattered to the ground, then disappeared.

"Agghhh!" Darren hissed. Something dark oozed from the wound, staining his shirt with dark shadows. He opened his mouth, vomiting light. The cut pulsed a bright beam, and the Skia flickered, his very body seeming to fade.

Athan swore.

Hope dropped the knife, and the clang made her jump. She stared at the weapon, then glanced up at the Skia, but he was gone. She stooped to pick up the blade, but it was covered with a sticky pitch. Athan jumped up and grabbed the blade, wiping the darkness on the hem of his shirt.

His skin was pale and clammy, and his hands shook.

She stared at her hands and wasn't surprised to see them trembling. She wanted to throw up.

She wanted to run away.

And she couldn't move.

Athan walked toward her, his voice gentle and slightly awed. "Hope?"

He tucked the silver blade somewhere at his hip. And then he stood before her, his hands out with an empty offering. "You saved my life."

"Please leave me alone," she whispered, and then she ran to her car.

THIRTY-SIX

HER EYES BURNED, but the tears had long since dried by the time Hope pulled into the well-lit lot with the blinking vacancy sign.

After paying for her room, she drove through the parking lot until she located 217 and parked just below the door. She wasn't sure a second-story room was best, but she had been just as uncertain of a first-story room.

Housekeeping must have left the air conditioning on, and the bite made her shiver as she turned the deadbolt on the door. She surveyed the dark shadows.

Furnishings, she told herself. Wanting to turn on the lights, she battled her fright and closed her eyes. Afraid of what might be in the room, afraid of who—or what—might see the glow of lights from outside. If someone had followed her . . .

It didn't matter that she was being unreasonable. She was terrified.

She focused on her breathing. In, two, three, four, five, six. Out, two, three, four. After nine slow breaths, she opened her eyes. Nothing in the room had moved. What was initially lost in shadows was now clearly visible to her adjusted eyes. The bed, armoire, desk, and chairs. A small table sat against the window.

She leaned over, pulled the curtains closed, and secured them to the wall with the table. No one would be able to see through the window. She turned off the air conditioner, turned on the light, and climbed onto the bed.

The filtered light of the sunrise didn't wake her. In fact, she hadn't noticed the sunrise at all. She lay on the bed, staring at the black screen of the television as the room lightened around her. She'd spent the night fretting. What if? What if? What if?

But by the time the sun was up, Hope decided fretting wouldn't do. She probably hadn't been fair to Athan, but it didn't matter. Life wasn't fair.

As she saw it now, she had two choices: She could run, or she could stay.

With a sigh, she acknowledged the truth: There was nothing to run to, and there was little to stay for. Would running away solve anything? She wasn't sure. She wasn't sure about much.

But besides the two bags in her car, she'd left everything of value back at her house in Goldendale. And by everything of value, she meant her immortal blades, the statue of Hecate, and the *Book of the Fates*.

She squared her shoulders. She would face whatever was there. And she would deal with it.

AS SHE APPROACHED the house, she saw Athan's monstrous truck. Of course he was still there. Of course.

Her heart beat furiously, trying to leap from her chest. Mixed emotions warred momentarily before hurt settled hard in her gut.

This was her house. Her stuff. Her space.

How dare he? And yet, she'd expected it, hadn't she?

And what if Hermes was there? What then?

Maybe it was suicidal, but with fierce determination, she decided she'd deal with him, too.

She parked the car and stormed into her home.

Athan was lying on the couch but sat up as soon as she opened the door. The thick, heavy *Book of the Fates* fell to his lap, lying open somewhere in the middle. With lithe grace, he closed the red leather cover and stood in one movement. He held it out to her.

She crossed the room, pausing to grab her golden dagger that still lay on the floor, before snatching the treasured tome from him. Holding it close to her chest, she glared at him. "How dare you?"

He'd been reading her history! The history of the curse. From the divine birth of her great-grandmother and her refusal of Apollo leading to the cursing of her grandmother, the first Sphinx. It was all in there.

He inclined his head, and his eyes closed just too long to be a blink. "I'm sorry."

"Sorry?" Like that would make it better? How much had he read? How much did he know?

She didn't know what to say. Her eyes bulged, and the lump in her throat wouldn't go away.

"I was there." He swallowed as if the words were painful to speak. "I was there when your mom died."

Her heart stopped. "Oh, gods. Did . . . Did you kill her?"

He shook his head. "NO! *Skata*. No. I was there when Apollo showed up."

That couldn't be. Skia had killed her mother. "You're lying."

"Gods. I have no reason to lie, Hope. Apollo came, yelled at your mom about fulfillment of the curse, and Thanatos ripped her soul from her body. I saw it happen."

"Apollo would have no reason to kill her."

"If she was married, it would fulfill the curse, right?"

"Get out." Every fiber wanted to lash out at him, but fear held her in place. He was a liar, a thief, and a demigod.

"Hope—"

"GET OUT!" Desperate to make him leave, she flung the red leather volume through the air, the pages fluttering.

Athan caught the book, slamming the cover shut. "No. Not yet. You need to hear me. Then if you want me to leave, I will. Please . . ."

She said nothing, but, clenching her teeth, she pulled out the golden dagger. "If you even try—"

"I won't hurt you, Hope. Not ever." He blew out a long breath and set the book on the couch. "I'm sorry. So, so sorry. I was surprised yesterday, and I wasn't thinking clearly. I won't take you to my father." He pointed at the book. "I didn't know all of that."

He then told her how he was there when Apollo had Thanatos kill her mom, how his father, Hermes, wanted to find the Sphinx, to get back at Apollo. He told her how he'd come to do a job, find the Sphinx, but that he'd found the demigods Brand and Chelli, and how he'd tried to get them to go to a conservatory. Chelli only went after Brand was killed. Athan told Hope how she'd attracted his attention, and then he had to investigate her, too.

"But remember the night we kissed? It was the first time in forever that I actually cared about something other than my job, or pleasing my dad. I tried to tell you . . ."

She did remember. She'd been so confused by his words. She took a deep breath. "How do I know you're not playing me now? How do I know you're not going to leave and call your father?"

He rolled his eyes. "Really, Hope? If I was going to turn you over, don't you think I would have already? I mean, why be here now talking to you?"

Good point. "What about the Skia, Darren? Will he be back?"

Athan chuckled. "The wound was superficial, but it still came from an immortal blade. He won't be back in this realm for a while. You made nice work of him."

Hope felt a stirring of pride.

"Please. Don't run. Don't leave Goldendale. Stay here. You have people who care about you. Please."

"I don't trust you."

He nodded. "I know. And I deserve that. But I'm hoping you'll let me earn that trust back."

Was it wrong that she wanted to? "What about your dad?"

It was the last of her protests.

"Let all of this settle down, and I'll talk to him. He'll understand. You'll see."

Her exhaustion pulled her to the ground, the walls around her heart crumbling, and she sat in a heap. "How do I know I can trust you?"

He sat next to her on the beige carpet and put his arm around her. Leaning over, he kissed her temple.

"Trust me," he whispered.

She leaned into him; the swelling in her heart told her she already did.

THIRTY-SEVEN

"I **THOUGHT YOU** guys broke up?" Haley frowned. "Not that I wanted you broke up, but Krista's been telling everyone—"

Hope rolled her eyes. "You think Krista would know?"

"I guess not. Did you guys skip together yesterday?"

Hope blushed. "We just had to figure some things out. Athan's a little . . ."

She searched for the right word.

"Dramatic?" Haley asked, grinning from ear to ear.

"Sensitive," Athan finished as he wrapped his arms around Hope. "Miss me?" He kissed her.

Her blush felt like the sun scorching her skin. "I . . . uh . . . yes."

"Ugh. I'm going to go find Tristan. You two . . ." Haley waved her hand. "Carry on. I'll see you at lunch."

Athan laughed, his gaze soaking her in. "Did you talk with Mr. Jeffers?"

Hope nodded. "He was very understanding."

She didn't bother to say how the principal had stuttered over his "welcome back" speech, and praised her "exemplary study habits."

"I'm still going to have to figure out something for next year." She sighed.

"Always planning ahead, aren't you?" He turned her so they were facing each other. "We'll figure it out. Maybe Myrine could adopt you." He leaned forward.

"Eww." Hope pulled back. "That would be sick."

"Shhh. Stop worrying, and let me kiss you."

And she did.

HOPE SAT IN chemistry, watching Mr. Burgess write his name in alcohol and then set it on fire. There was seriously something wrong with him.

She closed her eyes, and Angela's excitement burned her ears.

"No, his name is Tre. And he has two older brothers," Angela said.

Hope shook her head and opened her eyes.

Krista was practically glowing.

Tre. The new kid. Of course. Hope had only seen the young man from the back. He was tall and blond, and his neck was tan. Very tan.

"He is, by far, the sexiest thing I've *ever* seen. Like, so much hotter than Athan." Krista turned to Hope and offered a smirk. "No offense."

Hope shrugged. "None taken."

Most of the venom from the little cheerleader had dissipated over the last couple of weeks. To have someone else absorb all of Krista's attention? Hope couldn't be happier.

"So, why isn't he in school? I saw him yesterday in the hall, and he said he was registering." Krista pushed her lips out in a pout.

"Oh, no. He's not starting school till next year. They moved here from Tennessee, and the school year there gets out in May. He's already finished."

Of course Angela would know.

"Really? Dang it. I could really use the eye candy. I'm so over this already."

"There's only three days left," Angela said in a conciliatory tone.

Hope smiled to herself, thinking of summer plans with Athan, Haley, and Tristan.

Hope stared out the window at the blue sky while Mr. Burgess continued to ramble about how chemistry made the world go round.

The bell rang, and Hope caught the end of Angela and Krista's conversation.

"Well, get your mom to get his address so we can invite them to do stuff. I don't want to wait till next year."

Hope shook her head.

Poor guys.

"MR. STANLEY!" HOPE smiled at the butcher as she walked up to the meat counter. "Why didn't you tell me Haley was your daughter?"

The balding man laughed as if she'd cracked a joke. "I knew you'd figure it out. Done with school, eh?"

She nodded. "I need something to help me celebrate."

"I have just the thing." He turned and grabbed a pair of gloves. "Do you have a riddle for me today?"

"Actually, I do. What's more powerful than Zeus, more evil than Hades, the rich want it, the poor have it, and if you eat it, you'll die?"

He laughed again. "I'm not sure I agree with your assessment of the gods, but I know this one: Nothing." He started packaging up her meat. "Are you and Haley going into Portland to . . ." His eyes narrowed.

Hope turned to see what he was looking at.

Three boys—two of them looked more like men—stood at the deli. The tallest one was talking with the man behind the counter, and the other two pushed each other in some testosterone-laden contest. Hope shook her head. She'd seen them a couple of times around town. The three blonds were equally tall, with broad shoulders. These were the guys Krista wanted to get to know; the youngest one would be in their class next year.

Mr. Stanley muttered something under his breath and then turned back to Hope. His normally jovial face was set in a hard line.

"I hope they don't knock something over," Hope said in an attempt to lighten the mood.

Mr. Stanley came around the counter and handed Hope the package of meat.

"Don't hang out with them, okay?" His gray eyes were hard as stone. "Those guys . . . those kinds of guys are nothing but trouble." But it sounded like he meant those guys in particular.

Hope took the steaks, a little freaked out by the butcher's intensity. He'd never given her advice before. Strange that he thought she needed it now.

"I wasn't going to." She had no interest in the brash trio. "Thanks Mr. Stanley."

He nodded, but his eyes stayed on the three young men.

HOPE WALKED THROUGH her door and then kicked it closed behind her.

Arms full of groceries, she walked through her living room, pausing to look at the pictures on the mantel—one of Hope and

Athan soaking wet and laughing after a water fight a week ago, and another of Hope and Haley down at the river. There was another of Hope, Athan, Haley, and Tristan outside Stonehenge in Maryhill. The pictures of Hope's mom and Priska were harder to look at. No, not harder, just more bittersweet.

There were still a few boxes scattered throughout the house. Items she hadn't needed yet sat neglected in half-empty boxes. She'd finish unpacking when she got back this weekend.

Hope set the groceries down and started putting things away.

In the morning, she would change into the Sphinx. There was no dread in her anticipation of the change. It was amazing to think that tomorrow morning she'd be flying through the mountains. And when she got back, Athan would be waiting.

Her phone rang.

She glanced at the screen before answering it.

"Hello. Yes, I will wait for Mr. Davenport." Hope thought she was being cheeky. She was feeling cheeky. Her smile fell when the woman spoke.

"Hope is that you?"

Hades in hell.

"Aunt . . . Priska?" Her mind spun.

Priska sobbed into the phone, her words incoherent.

Hope slumped to the floor. How . . . How could this be? Her heart thundered.

Priska was back! Un-freaking-believable.

"Where have you been?" she whispered.

Hope said nothing while Priska unfolded the impossible.

She'd gone to Nashville. There was an Athenian temple downtown and a conservatory in the suburbs. Priska had convinced a group of demigods that she was one of them. Hades, she *was* one of them. She moved in and then fished for information.

"I thought . . . ." Priska hiccuped. "I got careless. I must've gotten careless. I thought I was covering my tracks."

Silence.

"What happened?"

"There were three. Sons of Apollo." Priska's voice was little more than a whisper. "They . . . kidnapped me."

Hope had no idea what to say. Kidnapped? Thoughts of torture, beatings, and hateful words pulsed in her mind. She wanted to know, and yet . . . She dreaded the information. "What did they do?"

Priska sucked in a deep breath. "It was Apollo, Hope. Apollo killed your mom. Oh, gods Hope. Your mom . . . She married Paul . . . the day she died. The wedding certificate was here in the mail. She fulfilled the curse."

It wasn't the question Hope had asked. Somehow she knew it was horrible. Or Priska would've told her.

But she'd confirmed what Athan had said. He'd been right. Hope had accepted his explanation, but to hear it . . . to *know* it.

Apollo! She hated him! Hate wasn't even a strong enough word. How dare he?

She knew the answer, and it was bitter.

Hopelessness flooded her heart. Her breathing hitched, and Hope brought her hand to her mouth. Tears leaked in a slow stream, and she scrubbed at her eyes, trying to dam them. Fulfillment of the curse, and Apollo had killed her mother. There was nothing she could do.

"Where are you?"

The question brought Hope back to the present. "In a small town in Eastern Washington, Goldendale."

"Are you safe?"

Hope thought about the question. Safe? What did that even mean? Safe from what? Safe from whom? She had friends who cared. A demigod boyfriend who would fight Skia for her. "I think so." Hope told Priska everything. About Mr. Jeffers, the Skia, Brand, Chelli . . . and Athan. "I haven't seen a Skia since that attack almost a month ago. I think it's good. Athan and I—"

"Aphrodite and Eros. You fell in *love*." The words were quiet, but they exploded over the phone. "You've got to be kidding me," Priska seethed.

The anger burned, and Hope felt raw hurt. "I—"

"Don't lie to me. I can hear it in your love-sick voice. How could you be so . . ."

She didn't finish, but Hope could fill in the blank.

"I didn't mean to, but—"

"You didn't mean to?" Priska sounded on the edge of hysteria. "Do you remember what I just told you? I'm sure your mother didn't mean to fall in love, either."

The words were physical blows.

"How . . . how could you say that? Athan is—" Who was this woman? Her aunt was never so cruel.

"I'm trying to protect you." Priska fumed. "Did you sleep with him?"

"What? No!" Mortification heated her cheeks. What a nightmare! She could barely listen while Priska lectured on.

"Well, that's a mercy. Don't let infatuation with a cute boy be mistaken for love. And don't be stupid. Or maybe it's already too late."

Hope wished she'd never answered the phone, and then guilt poked her in the chest.

Priska sighed. "I want you to come live with me."

"In Seattle?" Was she kidding?

"I'll move to the Eastside if you like, or even up north, although the commute will kill me. But I can't have you over there at the whim of Hermes's son."

"No. I'm happy here." There was no way that was happening. No way.

"You can even bring your demigod boyfriend if he wants to come. I want you close to me." She sounded exhausted. "Hope, those sons of Apollo are after you. If they find you . . . I don't even want to think about what would happen."

"I'm in the middle of nowhere. They're not going to find me." It wasn't just Athan. She had friends. People who cared about her . . . Haley, Tristan, Mr. Stanley . . .

"Hope!"

"No." She let out a slow breath. "I'll come for a visit, but I'm not moving."

"Then maybe I'll move over there."

Hope wasn't sure if it was meant as a threat, a gesture of love, or a sign of fear. "If that's what you want."

Priska could make her own decisions, and so would Hope.

"Will you come for a visit? Maybe stay the weekend?"

Hope nodded. "Of course. I'll come . . . tonight. I have to change into the Sphinx, but I can just stay with you. I've missed you."

Priska started sobbing again. "I would love that. I've missed you, too." She coughed, then cleared her throat. "For what it's worth, I'm so grateful you found friends who helped you."

A mixture of love and pain crashed through Hope's heart. "Of course. I'm so glad . . . I'm so happy you're back."

They said their goodbyes, then Hope looked at her watch.

Athan would be home now. She could just take the steaks over there and tell him what happened. Because really, it was a miracle.

She texted him, then took a few minutes to gather up the food before she raced out the door.

Life wasn't meant to be lived in perfect safety. Living was all about risks, love, loss, joy, pain, sorrow, and triumph. Hiding was a shallow existence; it wasn't living. And now that she knew it, Hope wasn't going to stop living.

EPILOGUE

"**DAD, YOU'RE ASKING** the impossible." Athan shifted from foot to foot. "You wanted me to find one person out of millions."

Hermes lifted his eyebrows. "It's your specialty. Finding *people*." He frowned. "And, if you haven't found the Sphinx, then why are you still in this little town?"

Athan blushed, and, for the first time in his life, he was at a loss for words.

"Well, well. What *did* you find? Are you in love, my son?" Hermes laughed and clapped him on the back. "Love is a grand thing, to be celebrated for sure." He draped his coat over the back of the upholstered chair and faced his son. "You must tell me all about her, but first let's talk about the Sphinx. There is word on Olympus that Apollo's sons are hunting the monster."

Apollo's sons? Could he never catch a break? "What will you do with her? When I find her?"

"If Apollo wants his monster, surely he will bargain for it."

"You would hold her for ransom? Dangle her like bait?" Athan clenched his jaw. Was his dad always this calloused?

"It almost sounds like you care about this beast." Hermes sat and put his head in his hands. "Athan. I need to you to find the monster. Your love . . . she'll understand."

Athan faced his father. "I can't do what you're asking me. I . . . I don't want to hunt down the Sphinx."

Hermes looked up and frowned. "You are the best, and I need this." He stared at Athan, probing. "Have you already found it?"

Athan willed his face blank and shook his head.

Hermes sucked in his breath. "You would *lie* . . . to *me*?"

His father's gaze seemed to pierce Athan's mind, but he couldn't look away.

The god's jaw dropped then he whispered, "You fell in love with her?"

Silence descended.

There was nothing Athan could say.

Hermes sat back in the chair and exhaled long and slow. "How long?"

Athan collapsed into the other chair. "A month."

Hermes shook his head. "You do not know . . . Apollo will never let you have her."

Just his name set Athan on edge. "Why would he get to decide? Has he not done enough?"

It was bad enough that Hope was cursed to be a monster. But to not let her love who she wanted?

Hermes narrowed his gaze. "I will not allow this."

Something deep within Athan snapped. "You will not allow it? I love her, Dad. You can't change that. Whatever you had planned will have to change. I won't let you use Hope to bargain or barter."

Hermes straightened. "You will not allow?"

The door slammed, and Athan jumped. The sound of footsteps grew distant as Myrine ran down the hall then closer again.

"Athan?" Myrine's muffled voice came from somewhere deep in the house. She was probably in the kitchen. Or maybe her study.

"Be there in a minute," he called back. He had to get his father out of here before Hope arrived. He looked at his watch.

The floorboards creaked, and both men stood as footsteps approached the door.

Hermes leaned forward and hissed at his son. "The Sphinx is a monster. An abomination. If Apollo thinks you are toying with what is his, he will kill you."

Athan opened his mouth to protest, but Hermes continued his tirade.

"This false charity is beneath you. Get the monster, and bring her to me. That is your job. Now get it done." Hermes stood and grabbed his coat.

"Dad—"

Both men heard the gasp on the other side of the door, and then the rapid retreat of footsteps.

Hermes frowned.

The front door slammed again, and fear roiled through Athan. He stood and looked out the window hoping he was wrong. But it wasn't Myrine's car in the driveway. Myrine hadn't come home. Athan's fear solidified into dread in the pit of his stomach.

Hope's green Civic was pulling out of the driveway like a bat out of Hades.

Skata.

NOTE TO THE READER

Thanks for reading Cursed by the Gods! I hope you enjoyed it!

As an indie author, reviews mean so much. Not only do they let other readers know whether a book is worth investing in, reviews also give the author insight into what a reader loved (or didn't) about a story. If you have a minute, please take the time to leave a review. It doesn't need to be fancy-schmancy, just say how you felt about the Cursed by the Gods, the writing, the story, the characters, or whatever.

Please go to the website where you purchased the book to review. Heaps of thanks if you do!!

Turn the Page for an exciting preview of

DEMIGODS AND MONSTERS

RAYE WAGNER

PROLOGUE

GLASS SHATTERED, FOLLOWED by a *thud*. In one fluid movement, Athan slid his hands under the pillow, grabbed the matching silver blades, and sat up. The thin sheet fell from his shoulders, and he shifted to the edge of the bed.

The night was dark and thick with humidity. The ceiling fan continued to whir despite the escalating tension in the small motel room. Through the broken window, the sour stench of rotten humanity wafted from the street. Athan waited to hear what, if anything, else was coming.

He'd been following a lead, a mere rumor from an acquaintance of a friend. The message came via text a week ago and spoke of a golden girl at Athena High in Seattle. Thought to be a demigod, the girl didn't blend in with the rest of the senior class and made no attempt to. By the time he'd arrived, the mysterious girl had disappeared. Vanished.

No forwarding address. No next of kin listed on the records, no emergency contact. Just gone. The apartment was vacant despite the rent being paid through the end of the six-month lease. Even more frustrating, the girl had withdrawn from school weeks ago. Any trail she'd left was now cold. Bitterly so.

Desperation made a foolish companion, and he wore his recklessness like a heavy cord, tangling his intuition and instinct into a messy knot. Regardless, he'd spent the next several days talking to students, searching popular hangouts, even going so far as to call the conservatory. Unfortunately, he'd gotten voicemail. Not too surprising. Most demigods carried their own cell phones. It was rare to use the conservatory's line, and even more rare for someone to call it. Perhaps it would be worth a brief visit to see if there was any news of Hope, or rather the Sphinx. The thought of a visit to the demigod residence made his stomach roll. But if it led to finding Hope, it would be worth it.

No sound came from the small sitting room on the other side of the bedroom door. If there were visitors, they weren't human. He stood and crossed the room.

As he reached for the handle, the door crashed open, and a thick, pale hand grabbed his wrist in a crushing grip.

Athan ducked as black steel swept over his head. He tilted away from the hulking figure and kicked his heel into the Skia's stomach. The soft give told him he'd missed the ribs. Not that the dead needed to breathe, but a punctured lung might've slowed the monster down.

2

Crouching low, he swung his leg close to the ground in a smooth arc. The minion from Hades anticipated the move and closed the gap with a knee to Athan's face. The taste of copper filled his mouth, and warm blood ran down his chin. He spit a mixture of saliva and blood and then swung his jeweled dagger at the Skia restraining him.

Before he could connect, his wrist was released and he received an upper cut to his solar plexus. The air rushed from his lungs as he fell backward into the coffee table. The cheap furniture splintered to the ground.

He rolled to the side, onto his hands and knees, allowing one gasping breath before forcing himself to his feet. The small amount of light coming in through the window was enough to confirm what he'd suspected. Pallid skin, onyx eyes, the telltale leer. Minion of Hades. Zeus Almighty! Would he never catch a break?

He wiped the blood from his chin and faced the Skia. "You know I'm going to send you right back to Hell."

The only response was a wheezing crackle.

They circled the debris, measuring each other, anticipating the first move that would begin the dance of death.

Athan kicked a piece of the broken table at the Skia, but the monster skirted away. He kicked another and another, and the creature slapped each down before it made contact with his body.

This was not going to be easy. The man was tall, taller than Athan, which would affect his reach, and judging from the two blows he'd taken, the demon knew how to fight and he was strong.

He weighed his daggers, wishing for a distraction.

A heavy thumping sounded through the thin ceiling.

"Hey! Keep it down!" The deep male voice from above was loud and angry.

The Skia's head tilted up.

Athan threw the dagger in his left hand. Anticipating that the Skia would move left, he spun that way and hooked his leg hard, catching the moving figure in the crook of his knee. Both of them crashed to the ground. The Skia swung his black knife, and Athan felt the pressure of the deadly blade on his leg. Gasping, he lurched up, drove his blade deep into the Skia's chest, and rolled away. Bright light pulsed from the wound. Then the Skia began to hiss and fade.

"*Skata.*" Athan pulled his leg close. His pajama bottoms were ripped where the Skia had tried to slice him, but the skin was unbroken. He exhaled his relief and tension all in one breath. That had been close. Too close.

He staggered to his feet and picked up the knife from the carpet where the Skia's body had dissolved. A few more steps and he retrieved the second blade from the kitchen where it was lodged in the wall. The adrenaline coursing throughout the fight began to wane, and his body shook.

No time for a meltdown. He had to leave. He grabbed his duffle bag and threw his clothes and toiletries inside it. He slipped his shoes on, not bothering to tie them. No time.

Opening the door into the dingy hall, he spotted a heavyset man with a red face headed his way. Athan backed into his room and locked the door, hoping to delay the man long enough to get away. Crossing the room to the broken window, he acknowledged his luck at being on the ground floor. Using the curtain, he pushed the broken glass away from the sill.

A heavy pounding came from the front of the motel room. He yanked the window open and pushed out the screen. The angry beating urged him to hurry. The splintering of wood announced his human visitor right as Athan dropped the duffle to the dirt. Another second later, he pulled his body through the cramped opening. As soon as his feet hit solid ground, he ran toward his car on the other side of the lot, pushing the key fob to unlock and start the car. He needed to be gone.

He slid into the driver's seat and put the car in gear. As Athan merged onto the street, the sounds of sirens drew closer. He cursed his own stupidity. So focused on looking for Hope, he'd left a trail a mile long and a mile wide. It was a wonder Skia hadn't attacked sooner.

The ringing from the console pulled him from his morbid thoughts.

"Athan Michael."

"It's Peter Stanley." The butcher Hope had befriended in Goldendale, the one that just happened to be a demigod son of Hephaestus.

5

"Peter. Nice of you to call." Athan couldn't help the sarcasm leaking into his voice. "And at three in the morning. What's got you up at this fine hour?"

"Oh, did I wake you?" He knew he hadn't. It was clear in the mocking tone of his voice.

Athan sighed. His frustration wasn't with the butcher. No sense in taking it out on him. "No. Sorry, rough night." He released a long breath. "What's up? Everything okay there in Goldendale? Have you heard from our friend?"

"I'm not calling just to chat. You're not that charming."

Athan snorted. "I'm well aware."

"She and Haley just talked. She's still in Seattle."

It was something. "Did she mention where? I've been in Seattle for a couple months, and the closest thread I've picked up was a week old."

"Sorry, no. But she did say she'd met someone that knew me." A heavy pause. "And you. Do you think she could be at the conservatory? They have someone new. Thenia called and asked for a phone chip a couple weeks ago," Hephaestus's son whispered.

It better not be Hope. The demigods would crucify her if they discovered her true nature. Priska would know better. She wouldn't let her. Hope couldn't be so stupid. "No."

"If the other demigods found her, wouldn't they take her? It makes sense. And it would be safe for her there."

Of course it made sense. *Until you knew what she really was!* "Um, yeah. Right. I'll check it out in the morning."

"You could go now and find out."

Athan glanced at himself in the rearview mirror. His lip was busted, and his eye was puffy and purple. His chest was covered in his own sticky blood, and his plaid flannel pajama pants were ripped and stained. There was no way he was going right now.

"I need to clean up first and maybe grab a few hours of sleep." He paused but couldn't think of a reason not to tell the other demigod. "Skia attacked, and I'm a bloody mess."

Peter laughed as if Athan had shared a joke. "Well, you'd best get yourself all spiffed up then. After all, you never get a second chance to make a first impression, or, in this case, a first *second* impression." He chuckled again. "Good luck, son of Hermes"

Without a goodbye, the line went dead.

Athan thought about his options, but this was the best lead he had. And hopefully, *hopefully*, Xan wouldn't be there.

ONE

"**WHEN WE GET THERE**, let me do the talking, okay?" Priska's gaze darted to Hope and then back to the road. "You're only going to get one shot at this here—"

"I know." Hope blew out her breath, trying to expel some of the anxiety coursing through her. The plan had seemed like such a good idea last night. Now she wasn't sure. No. She *was* sure. She was just scared. Did Priska really believe they could summon a god? Hope wanted to believe it. Because she didn't know what else to do.

Apollo's curse made it impossible to love anyone without putting them at risk, *and* her. She thought of her mom's death and Paul's fear. Hermes's words to Athan, warning him. Didn't that speak volumes? And on top of that, there was the whole morphing into a monster, and demigods and Skia hunting her. She was ready to do whatever it took to get rid of the curse. Ready to take whatever chances were necessary. She wanted her life back.

Hope had left Goldendale three weeks ago, after overhearing Athan and his father, Hermes, talking about capturing her to use against Apollo. Hermes had given his son an ultimatum, and Hope wasn't going to stick around and see where Athan's loyalties lay. It was a risk she couldn't afford. Two days as a Sphinx had given her time to think, and when she'd morphed back into human, she drove into Seattle to stay with Priska. Hope wasn't going to be a pawn for the gods. But she wasn't above asking for a little help either.

"Do you have the puppy?"

Hope rolled her eyes. Where would it have gone?

They'd spent hours searching through breeders' ads online until they found a purebred Labrador retriever at the right age. When Priska had said they needed an offering, Hope balked at the thought. The idea of sacrificing a puppy was abhorrent, but Priska explained, with an exasperated shake of her head, that they weren't going to kill it. The dog would be a token gift for the goddess, something that would show she'd done thoughtful preparation before seeking a petition. Yesterday, Priska flew to Colorado to pick up the eight-week-old pup.

"Angel's right here." Hope held up the sleeping fur ball. The puppy cracked open an eyelid and licked her hand.

"Don't get attached. We're giving it away in thirty minutes. Maybe sooner."

They exited the freeway and followed the off-ramp back around. Five minutes later, they pulled up to a white stone temple. The grounds surrounding the structure were lush and green with statues of minor gods scattered throughout. The concrete bases of the statues were littered with tokens: food, coins, an envelope, a brush. A brush?

Hope stepped forward to get a better view of an offering to a young male holding a bow and arrow, and the puppy scampered on her heels. There was a plate with a cinnamon roll on it, the frosting dripping down its sides. It smelled good; the spicy sweetness perfumed the air and made her stomach growl. Eros better hurry up and get that, if he wanted it. And if he didn't, would it be offensive to take a nibble?

"Don't get too close, or you might offend by not leaving a gift," Priska pointed out.

Hope drew back from the marble statue of the god of love. Angel yipped, and Hope scooped up the floppy dog as it bee-lined for the food.

"Not for you."

Priska disappeared between two of the columns of the large temple, and Hope rushed to catch up.

Hope had never been inside a temple before. She'd been sheltered from so much of the world while she and her mom hid. Seeking a divine audience went against everything she'd ever been taught.

She felt like a tourist as she absorbed the surroundings. Humans had left offerings in hopes that the gods would take notice of them. If only the gods had never taken notice of her or her family. Life would have been much simpler if Apollo had never butted in when he wasn't wanted. Her great-grandmother had refused the god's advances, and he'd killed her and cursed her offspring. The root of all her problems came back to Apollo's curse.

She crossed the threshold and stopped. Twelve giant-sized marble statues, one of each of the major Olympians, lined the walls. Offerings littered the steps leading up to the daises of each god. These offerings were more than mere tokens. In front of Athena was a large planting container, and in it an eight-foot tree. Several cases of what she guessed was wine sat in front of the statue of Dionysus.

Circling through the open room were several men and women dressed in traditional chitons. The flowing robes were of different colors, and the priests and priestesses only talked with those who wore their same color.

Priska spoke to a young woman wearing midnight-blue trimmed in silver. Of course. Hope went and stood behind her aunt.

"Artemis hasn't responded to anyone this year." The priestess appeared older close-up, maybe in her twenties. Her dark hair was pulled into a simple braid, and she wore no makeup.

"I understand. But it's important for us to make our own plea, and it needs to be in private. Is there anyone in the inner sanctuary?" Priska stood with her shoulders back, chin held high, and gave the priestess a direct look.

The woman's posture stiffened. "The inner sanctuary is sacred. I'm sorry. I'm happy to take your gift there, but you are far too old to be allowed to make an offering to the Virgin goddess."

She was implying there was no way Priska was still a virgin and, therefore, unworthy to go into the inner sanctuary. Hope wondered if there were such rules for each of the gods, and were they all so hypocritical?

Priska raised her eyebrows. "What is your age limit here?"

"Sixteen. Unless you are an *Arktoi*." She bowed her head. "If your companion would like to act as your surrogate . . ."

Hope suppressed the urge to roll her eyes. She was *seventeen*.

"That won't be necessary. Is there a restroom nearby?"

The holy woman pointed to a doorway behind several hallowed icons.

"I'll be right back." Priska's posture softened as she addressed Hope. "Stay here, please. And keep Angel on a short leash."

Hope nodded at her aunt, then turned back to the woman in blue. The silence stretched into awkwardness.

"How long have you been here?" Hope asked, more for something to say than actual interest.

"Five years in May." The priestess tilted her head to the side and examined Hope. "Are you thinking of becoming an *Arktoi*?"

Hope's mouth dried up. "I . . . haven't—"

"She wouldn't be able to serve," Priska said.

Both Hope and the priestess stared slack jawed. Priska no longer appeared to be in her thirties. Now, she seemed no more than sixteen. Her dark, straight hair now hung well below the shoulders, and her face was fuller. She still wore the fitted skirt and tailored jacket, or Hope might not have recognized her.

"Is this young enough? I can drop a few more years if I need to." Priska sniffed.

The priestess's jaw moved up and down, but no sound came out.

Hope had never seen her aunt shift either, but she knew it could happen. Demigods could recapture the ages they'd lived. Priska had allegedly allowed her body to age until she was quite elderly, but for as long as Hope had known her she'd always been in her early thirties. This Priska, teen Priska, had more softness in her appearance, but her personality was still sharp.

"The inner sanctuary, please." Priska held out her hand and deposited several coins into the priestess's.

The priestess closed her hand, but her eyes remained wide, and she swallowed several times.

"We really don't have all day."

As if someone had pinched her, the priestess jumped and led them between two pillars into a narrow hallway. She repeatedly glanced from Priska to Hope, and while her eyes were filled with questions, her lips pursed until the edges were blanched.

Hope felt the same way.

The hallway was lined with intricately carved doors, and they stopped in front of one with a forest scene. Deer lapped from a river that wound through a copse of evergreens. The length of the door was carved into a long bow on one side and several arrows on the other.

"Your worship will be uninterrupted here," the *Arktoi* said. "Please be sure to close the door on your way out." The woman pulled a key from her belt and unlocked the door. "May the Goddess grant your petition." She bowed and left.

Priska eyed Hope. "Are you ready?"

With a deep breath, Hope opened the door.

The smell of fresh rain and dirt wafted out from the room.

Hope stepped through the door and held her hand up to feel along the wall for a light switch. Only there was no wall. Her eyes adjusted quickly to the dark, and what she saw took her breath away.

A crescent moon hung in the night sky. Patches of gray still covered the stars, and the air was thick with moisture. The ground was spongy, and Hope knelt to run her hand over the mossy covering.

"This is impossible." She glanced up at Priska. "How?"

"This sanctuary is dedicated." Priska's face radiated reverence and love. "If Artemis is willing to visit, it is always on her terms and in a setting to her liking."

"Priska!" An exuberant young girl ran from between the trees and launched herself at Priska. "I'm glad you're safe."

The two young women embraced. "It has been far too long since you've visited."

"I've been busy with my charge." Priska rested her hand on Hope's shoulder.

Hope gaped at the goddess of night. Artemis's dark umber skin contrasted with her pale, almost silver hair. Her slight figure was clad in black, fitted garments, and as she pulled the silver bow and quiver of arrows from off her back, her midnight eyes settled on Hope.

"You are very young." She set her weapons on the spongy moss and stepped up to Hope. "Very young, but not too naïve, I think." Her gaze held Hope captive for a moment, and then the goddess contemplated the puppy struggling in Hope's arms. "Who is this?" Artemis giggled as Angel licked her face.

"She's . . . she's for you." Hope held the pale Labrador out.

Artemis peered from Hope to Priska and back to Hope again.

"You are giving me an offering?" She raised her brows but did not take the dog.

Hope shifted her gaze to Priska for help. Hadn't she said she would do the talking? Priska was studiously examining the night sky.

"No . . . I mean, yes. Yes." Hope shook her head. "We got her for you." She extended her arms again, the dog's back paws dangling in the air.

"Hope wants to break the curse," Priska said, taking the puppy from Hope. "The Lab was my idea. She comes from a long line of hunters. She will be loyal and easy to train."

Artemis extended her hands. "Loyalty is difficult to come by. I will accept this with gratitude." She took the puppy and set her on the ground. The pale fur glowed in the moonlight, and the puppy scampered about. "What do you need my help with, Hope? It was my brother that cursed you, not I."

Hope shifted her weight. "Yes, but do you know anything that could help me? Has he said anything to you?"

Artemis drew in a slow breath and closed her eyes.

Hope again looked to Priska, but she'd chased after the puppy, leaving Hope alone with the goddess.

"She's scared," Artemis said, breaking the silence. "She feels responsible for what happened to your mother. And she feels bad about what could've happened to you." She grabbed Hope's chin and forced her head side to side. "You want to break the curse?"

Hope nodded.

"It won't solve your problem," the goddess warned, dropping her hand.

"It won't solve *all* my problems." Hope took a deep breath. "But it will give me freedom to love who I want, and no one will hunt me."

"Perhaps." Artemis grabbed an arrow and strung her bow. A faint *twang*, and the arrow lodged in a tree at least a hundred feet away. "Do you believe you are more deserving of this freedom than your mother or grandmother?" She released another arrow, which embedded in the trunk next to the first.

"No. No more deserving than they. But no one deserves to be cursed by a god."

Artemis dropped the bow and arrow to her side and faced Hope. "Who are you to decide that?"

Anger fueled her courage. "Really? Your brother got dumped, and he killed the girl who dumped him, *and* her husband. In the mortal realm, that's murder, and in some states it will get you the death penalty." She took a deep breath and continued, "But he didn't stop there. In his infinite *wisdom*, he cursed their baby and changed her into a monster. Along with that, he made it so if she didn't choose to sleep with him and have his babies, her posterity would continue to carry the curse. How exactly is there any shred of *fairness* or even a modicum of rationality to that?"

Artemis did the last thing Hope expected.

The goddess of night broke into peals of laughter. She dropped her weapons and held her sides as she chortled.

"Dear gods, what did you do?" Priska walked back to Hope with Angel in her arms.

Hope shrugged.

"She is . . . very much . . . like you . . ." Artemis took lungfuls of air, her smile bright like the moonlight. "When you were younger, you had a very strong sense of justice."

"Most youth do." Priska grimaced. "It doesn't make them right."

"But their naivety doesn't make them wrong, either." Artemis sobered. "You are becoming cynical, Priska."

"No, Mother, just pragmatic."

Artemis's focus shifted to Hope. "I can't take away the curse. No one can. Even the Graeae have said as much."

Hope stomach dropped. "Can you help me?"

"No."

Her heart stopped. Then why had they gone through all the—?

"I can't help you directly. There would be . . . problems on Olympus, if I did." Artemis scanned the night sky before facing Hope. "You need to start with all the facts. Which means you need to go to the *Olympian* library and do some research on my brother. Then, if you have time, read up on divine law. Do you understand what I'm telling you?"

"Yes." *No.*

Artemis rolled her eyes. "Priska will help. After you get your information, you'll need to see an oracle. Be careful who you choose." She bit her lip. "The rest will be up to you."

Research Apollo and divine law. Go see an oracle.

"Got it." Sort of.

Artemis turned to Priska. "I am proud of you. No matter what, I love you. You have become far greater than I ever could've imagined." The two hugged again. Artemis pointed at Hope but kept her gaze on her daughter. "Keep her safe. I will talk to my mother. You'll be able to get her in, but the others will be very angry if they figure it out, so be careful."

"Thank you. I love you." The women embraced again.

"Work hard and be smart, young Hope." Artemis clicked her tongue, and Angel bounded over to the goddess and wagged her tail. "Come, young pup. We have much training to do." The two walked into the forest and disappeared into the darkness.

The trees shimmered, and the surrounding forest's colors blurred with a soft breeze, like watercolors running down a page. The moon waxed full, then waned to a sliver of pale light. Hope's eyes adjusted, and they stood in a plain concrete room with a statue of Artemis with her bow drawn. The air was stale, and at the base of the statue lay a sundry of offerings, forlorn in their abandonment.

Priska sighed. "Let's go home."

Hope's shoulders sagged as the weight of the encounter settled. "How do we get into an Olympian library?"

The young Priska gritted her teeth and pulled the ornate wooden door open. "There's only one."

TWO

"HOW DO WE GET INTO the Olympian library? And where is it?" Hope asked when Priska walked in the door. She wasn't willing to remain silent forever. In the almost week since their visit to the temple, Priska had talked of her work, getting Hope enrolled in school, and how to spend the rest of summer. Not once had they discussed the subject of the library or the curse. But not for lack of Hope trying.

Priska had morphed back into her older self and was back to work at Mr. Davenport's office. "Good evening to you, too." She set her bag on the counter. "Are we eating out again tonight? What sounds good?"

Hope stared blankly at her aunt. She didn't care if they ate in or out. She didn't care if they had Italian, Chinese, Mexican, or Indian. What she wanted was answers.

"My choice? Excellent. Let's have Italian."

"It's not going to go away because you won't talk to me about it. I know that's what you want, but I'm not going to do nothing. If you won't help me, I'll—"

"Stop." Priska closed her eyes. "You don't know what you're talking about. You don't know—"

"I would know if you talked to me. You used to talk to me, tell me stuff. Now it's like you don't even care." Hope flopped down on the couch. "If my mom were alive—"

"I said stop!" Priska glared at Hope. "You want to know? The Olympian library has two ways to access it. Two." She held up a finger. "The first is from Olympus, where the gods live. The only way to get to Olympus is by invitation. Not going to happen." She held up a second finger. "The only other entrance is through a conservatory. A home for demigods. Which you are not."

Olympus was definitely out, so a conservatory was the only way in. "But—"

"To refresh your memory, I escaped from a conservatory about a month ago. Barely alive, I might add. And I feel the need to point out that the sons of Apollo are probably still hunting you. And did I mention that they were the ones that almost killed me?" Priska dropped her head into her hands.

What had happened to her fearless aunt? Where was the woman who hunted Skia and laughed about it? "Tell me what I need to do to be safe?"

"You need to not go."

This wasn't a whim. It was her life! "But Artemis said you would be able to get me in."

"She did, and I can. But before you decide—"

"You want to tell me all the risks?" Hope sucked in a deep breath, preparing for rebuttal.

"No. It wouldn't do any good anyway." Priska's shoulders dropped, and she studied Hope. "Your chin juts out when you get stubborn. Just like your mother. I can see it all over your face that you won't let it go." She picked up her phone. "Let's order dinner. Then we'll come up with a plan."

"I AM SICK OF THIS," Hope muttered to herself as she trudged up the sidewalk on her way home from school. She kicked at a pebble on the ground and listened to it skip up the street.

After all that planning with Priska, nothing was happening. Seriously, nothing.

Demigods used the conservatory as a safe haven, and young demigods stayed there to get training and education. They'd moved close to the one in Seattle, and the goal was to have the demigods "stumble across" them, invite them in, and then, somehow in the course of her studies, Hope would sneak into the library and do her research. Priska had made it sound easy, and of course Hope trusted her. But seriously? Were all demigods on holiday?

The overcast sky hung heavily with moisture, and rain oozed from the clouds, unable to be contained. Nothing like cold, damp weather to explicitly state that the extended summer was over.

Not that she even cared about the weather. Or school. Or that Priska was likely already at their new apartment, baking cookies. Well, actually, that sounded kind of nice, but the rest of it was all-around sucky.

All Hope wanted was for the stupid demigods to find her so she could get to the conservatory, find out how to break her curse, and maybe apologize to Athan. Maybe.

She still wasn't sure about that last one. In hindsight, she'd jumped to conclusions. He'd told her he'd been sent to hunt her. He'd also said he'd keep her safe. But when she overheard him talking to his dad, Hermes . . . No, it didn't matter. A relationship between Hope and Athan wouldn't work. Hermes had even said as much. And if Apollo found out, he'd kill Athan.

But she couldn't help the guilt that gnawed on her, especially late at night. Especially when she thought of how stupid she'd been. She shouldn't have let Priska talk her into another new phone and number. She shouldn't have put off calling him. Because when she *finally* had, he'd changed numbers too. And even though Haley still kept in contact with Hope, her best friend had no forwarding number for him.

She wanted it to be over already.

If patience was a virtue, Hope was a serious detriment to the moral fiber of society. Actually, the fact that she was a cursed monster would probably be considered worse than her impatience.

But really, what was taking so long?

Priska's brilliant plan was to get Hope "discovered." Like Athan's initial misunderstanding, they were banking on the demigods assuming she was one of their own, and then *hopefully* she'd be invited into the conservatory. At that point she'd have to figure out how to get into the Olympian library.

The Olympian library, where she could peruse every book ever written, every story ever told. It was going to be like finding a needle in a haystack. She'd need to figure out how it was sorted so she could focus on Apollo and her curse.

The whole thing would be overwhelming, except for the little hang-up of not being able to even get to the haystack. She couldn't do anything until she was found by some stupid demigods.

Stupid demigods.

She pushed through the glass doors into the sparse lobby of the high-rise apartments and strode toward the elevators. The doors were starting to close, and she cursed as she ran, sliding her arm into the shrinking gap at the last second. The doors slid back open, and Hope stared at the male occupant.

He was young, certainly less than twenty. He exuded a strength and power that made her want to back away. It wasn't just that he was well built, although he was. His shirt hugged his body, and the tattoos on his arms accentuated where his muscles dipped and curved. His hair was dark, almost black, cropped short, and although disheveled, it appeared to have been spiked up in the front earlier in the day. His eyes were a striking ice blue. Everything about him seemed hard.

She hesitated, debating if she should back out, and then he smiled. Not in a friendly way to put her at ease. His smile mocked her, like he knew the effect he was having on her, and she was somehow beneath him because of it.

"Are you coming in?" His accent was Irish or British . . . or maybe Australian.

She frowned.

"Or did you want to wait for your own lift, princess?"

Definitely not American.

"Hello?" He waved his hand at her.

Yikes. She was still standing with her arm blocking the elevator doors. She shook off the shiver of fear.

"Excuse me." She stepped onto the elevator and gave him her most withering glare. "Would you push twenty-one, please?" While her words were polite, there was no warmth behind them.

"Oh, but of course." He inclined his head, pushed the button, and then leaned back as the elevator doors slid shut.

Hope watched the numbers light up, one by one. A spicy smell, both strong and masculine, filled the small area. Hera and Zeus, he smelled good. Seven . . . eight . . . Trying to be discreet, she glanced at the young man.

He met her eyes with appraising ones of his own, and he lifted his brows. "See something you like, sweetheart?"

"*You* were staring at *me*." It felt imperative that she correct his blatant misrepresentation. "Didn't your mother ever tell you not to stare? It's rude." There was something arrogant and irritating about the stranger.

He laughed, a short guffaw, and a dimple appeared. "I'm certain she did, probably right afore she boxed my ears." He straightened up and held out his hand. "I'm Xan."

Hope refused to act intimidated, regardless of the butterflies in her stomach. Taking his hand, she replied, "I'm Hope."

"It's a pleasure to meet you, Hope."

"It's nice to meet you, too."

His hands were rough and calloused, and the handshake was brief. She took a step back as soon as her hand was released.

After a brief silence, the elevator doors slid open with a ding, and Hope moved toward the exit. A firm grasp pulled her back from the door. The contact was brief, but a whirlwind of anxiety coursed through her.

"I was thinking you don't want to get off here."

She looked at him again and couldn't help but feel like he was laughing *at* her. Even his dimple mocked her. Disgusted, she eyed the monitor. They were on the seventeenth floor. Someone must have pushed the call button and gone back to their apartment.

She backed into the elevator. "Umm, thanks."

"Right." He smirked.

The door slid shut, and they started climbing again.

An unsettling feeling gnawed at her stomach. Hope fixed her gaze on the climbing numbers. It was only another moment before the elevator stopped on the twenty-first floor.

"Um, thanks for uh . . . you know, making sure I didn't get off on the wrong floor, and uh . . . yeah." She forced her lips into something she hoped resembled gratitude and glanced at the keypad, making sure she was on the twenty-first floor. She also saw that Xan was staying on the top floor. Penthouse.

"You're quite welcome." He met her gaze, and his lip curled. "Have a nice day, Hope."

"Um, yeah. You too." The doors slid shut and she stood frozen, seeing only her reflection in the polished metal. Could she have sounded any more stupid? What in the name of Hermes . . . Her train of thought skidded to a halt.

Hermes, god of linguistics. Athan's dad.

Athan. She shook her head.

She needed to get over him. Because it was over. She'd probably never see him again. And even if she did, it wouldn't matter. She'd never put him at risk.

What Hermes had said about Apollo was true. He'd killed her mom because she'd married someone else. Apollo would never let her be with anyone but him. Ugh. And he was like a million years old.

No. She needed to focus on breaking the curse. Because that was the only way for her to be free. Free to make her own decisions about life and love. She swallowed her emotions and locked her memories of Athan away in the darkest corner of her mind.

She opened the door to the scent of chocolate chip cookies.

Index of Mythological Figures

Aphrodite: Goddess of love, beauty, desire, and pleasure

Apollo: God of light, music, arts, knowledge, healing, plague, darkness, prophecy, poetry, purity, athleticism, manly beauty, and enlightenment

Ares: God of war, bloodshed, and violence

Artemis: Virgin goddess of the hunt, wilderness, animals, young girls, childbirth, night, and plague

Athena: Goddess of intelligence and skill, warfare, battle strategy, handicrafts, and wisdom

Boreas: God of winter and the north wind

Demeter: Goddess of grain, agriculture and the harvest, growth, and nourishment

Dionysus: God of wine, parties and festivals, madness, chaos, drunkenness, drugs, and ecstasy

Eros: God of love and desire

Hades: King of the underworld and the dead, and god of the earth's hidden wealth, both agricultural produce and precious metals

Hephaestus: God of fire, metalworking, and crafts

Hera: Queen of the heavens and goddess of marriage, women, childbirth, heirs, kings, and empires

Hermes: God of boundaries, travel, communication, trade, thievery, trickery, language, writing, diplomacy, athletics, and animal husbandry

Hestia: Goddess of the hearth, home, and chastity

Hypnos: God of sleep

Leto: Titan goddess of Motherhood

Moirai: The Fates, the incarnation of destiny, namely: Clotho (spinner), Lachesis (allotter), and Atropos (unturnable)

Persephone: Queen of the underworld, wife of Hades, and goddess of spring growth

Poseidon: God of the sea, rivers, floods, droughts, earthquakes, and the creator of horses

Thanatos: God of death

Zeus: King of the gods, the ruler of Mount Olympus, and the god of the sky, weather, thunder, lightning, law, order, and fate

The Graeae: Three ancient sea spirits who personified the white foam of the sea; they shared one eye and one tooth between them. By name: Deino, Enyo, and Pemphredo

Acknowledgements

My favorite painting is *Sleeper, Lost in Dreams* by James Christensen. The artwork is both breathtaking and inspiring. There is a quote with the piece that sums up exactly how I feel.

We are, each of us, angels with only one wing.

And we can only fly embracing each other.– Luciano De Crescenzo

I'm so grateful to my family: Jason, Jacob, Seth, and Anna. Each of you have made sacrifices and offered heaps of support. Words are inadequate for how much I love you.

Pete, Ashlyn, and Nathan. Fabulous art skills. Danke for making everything so pretty!

And more family: Mom, Dad, Nate, La, Abby, Liv, Veronica, Clark, Max, Jared, Hilary, Carter, Avery, Maia, Colby, Jayne, Sully, Luke, Kirs, EmJ, Joshua, Benjamin, Samantha, Reillee, Kayde, Matthew, Sam, Emily, Kincaid, Henry, Miles, Charlie, D.J., Angie, Amelia, Bryson, Eli, Mari, Bobby, Mabel, Hazel, Margo, Peter, Ashlyn, Piper, Janice, Elisa, Shawn, Devon, Dorian, Taylor, Sara, Curtis, Karen, Cindy, Marcus, Rachel, Ethan, Sophie, Bella, June, Mike, Maddie, Matthew, Ryan, Jilene, Tristin, Donelle, Wes, Jared, Mason, Emma, Rob, Chandra, Lydia, Gabriel, Maria, Dan, Savannah, Xander, Dave, and Rita. Family is the bestest thing, and I appreciate all of your support.

To my bestie pals: Alli, Cassy, and Katie. I'm not sure how you ever finished the original tome, but thank you. It made me believe that the story was worth working for.

And my critique partners: April, Angela, and Chris. Your words of encouragement and constructive criticism helped me find what was good, and what needed to be better. And Ethan, you were right about the first line!

To the KidLit group: It is amazing what you learn about yourself, and your writing, one chapter at a time. Thanks Jamie, Janet, Angela, Sue, April, Jess, Chris, Lindsey, Kelly, Deena, Amanda, and Bev. Each of you have helped my writing become a craft.

To Lindsey Alexander: You helped me polish up the story. Thank you!

To Jen McConnell, Heidi Johnson, and Ashley Bodette: Thanks for finding the hidden holes and filling them up!

To Krystal Wade: You are an editing and proofing goddess. I have mad love for you!

To Jo Michaels: Thanks for making the reading experience fabulous. You're a formatting Queen!

And to you, my readers: Thank you for helping my story to fly!

ABOUT RAYE

Raye Wagner grew up in Seattle, the second of eight children, and learned to escape chaos through the pages of fiction. As a youth, she read the likes of David Eddings, Leon Uris, and Jane Austen. Inspired by a fictional character, Raye pursued a career in nursing, and still practices part-time. She enjoys baking, puzzles, Tae Kwon Do, and the sound of waves lapping at the sand. She lives with her husband and three children in Middle Tennessee.

Facebook:
https://www.facebook.com/Raye-Wagner-173068689524889
Twitter: @RayeWagner
Instagram: rayewagnerauthor
Website: RayeWagner.com

Made in the USA
Coppell, TX
24 September 2021

62874227R00239